Praise for Peter David and
Star Trek: New Frontier®

"Peter David mixes wry humor . . . with tense drama. . . . [His] narrative is populated by a vast array of previously minor characters from the screen incarnations of *Star Trek,* all vividly fleshed out into well-rounded personalities."

—Sci-Fi Online

"Peter David is the best *Star Trek* novelist around."

—*Starburst*

"A new *Star Trek* novel by Peter David is always a good bet."

—SF Site

Star Trek: New Frontier novels by Peter David
in chronological order

STAR TREK
NEW FRONTIER®

BLIND MAN'S BLUFF

PETER DAVID

**Based upon
STAR TREK® and
STAR TREK: THE NEXT GENERATION®
created by Gene Roddenberry**

POCKET BOOKS
New York   London   Toronto   Sydney   New Delhi

Pocket Books
A Division of Simon & Schuster, Inc.
1230 Avenue of the Americas
New York, NY 10020

This book is a work of fiction. Names, characters, places, and incidents either are products of the author's imagination or are used fictitiously. Any resemblance to actual events or locales or persons, living or dead, is entirely coincidental.

First Pocket Books paperback edition January 2012

POCKET and colophon are registered trademarks of Simon & Schuster, Inc.

For information about special discounts for bulk purchases, please contact Simon & Schuster Special Sales at 1-866-506-1949 or business@simonandschuster.com.

The Simon & Schuster Speakers Bureau can bring authors to your live event. For more information or to book an event, contact the Simon & Schuster Speakers Bureau at 1-866-248-3049 or visit our website at www.simonspeakers.com.

Cover design by Alan Dingman

Manufactured in the United States of America

10 9 8 7 6 5 4 3 2 1

ISBN 978-1-4516-1169-4
ISBN 978-0-7434-2965-8 (ebook)

STAR TREK
NEW FRONTIER®

BLIND MAN'S BLUFF

Xenex

Now

M'k'n'zy of Calhoun was alone, which prompted him
to wonder, *Where the hell are they?*

M'k'n'zy kept his back against the rocky wall of the
mountain behind him. His breathing was light and
shallow, and anyone listening in—and he was certain
there was no one around—would have been hard-
pressed to hear any manner of stress or strain in it.
Furthermore, if any observers had happened to have
biological sensors with them and been monitoring his
heartbeat from a distance, they would have discovered
that his pulse was slow and steady. Had he been lying
out on a towel at some comfortable beach resort, he
would have displayed about the same level of readings.

In short, anyone who was studying M'k'n'zy's current situation would never have guessed that he was
fighting for his life.

One might have surmised it was because M'k'n'zy
had been fighting for his life for as long as he could
remember, and had simply grown beyond both the
fear and the adrenaline rush that others had when
they were in similar situations. This, however, would

have been an underestimation of the man. It had nothing to do with repetition. Instead it stemmed entirely from the way he had trained himself since the beginning of his career as the warlord of Xenex.

It hadn't been that way in the beginning. When, at the tender age of fourteen, he had killed his first enemy, his breath had come in ragged gasps, and excitement had pounded through his body. It had taken long minutes for him to calm down as he stared at the corpse of his enemy and both savored and feared the fact that it had been his hand that had struck the lethal blow.

But he had learned in short order that such unfocused concepts as fright or excitement reduced his efficiency as a killer. That's what a warlord was, after all: A killer who was very, very good at his job. So good, in fact, that others were willing to follow him through the gates of hell if it meant conquering an enemy.

So M'k'n'zy had ruthlessly trained himself to get a solid grip on his own biology. To him, his reactions (or lack thereof) were simply another tool or skill set to be honed, along with aim and swordsmanship. He would observe the men he led into battle, and he would see the fire in their eyes and the fury in their movements, and he wished he could impart some of his own cold-bloodedness to them. But he knew that ultimately everyone had their limits and they did the best they could with whatever the gods had given them. It was simply one of M'k'n'zy's gifts—along with an ability to sense danger that bordered on the supernatural—that he was able to go into battle with such dispassion that he might as well have been a passive witness instead of a participant.

As a result, some who watched M'k'n'zy in action came to the conclusion that he was indifferent to the outcome of his battles. Some even whispered to each other, when they were sure he wasn't around, that he had some manner of death wish.

Nothing could have been further from the truth. M'k'n'zy had no desire to die. This was the reason he had developed the technique of disconnect that had served him so well. Too many people perished in skirmishes because they allowed the heat of the battle to overwhelm them, and thus either made mistakes or got themselves in so deep that they froze in fear, suddenly believing that they would not get out of the situation alive. To allow for the possibility of your own death was to see it in your mind's eye, and mental visualizations could lead to real-world consequences. Imagining what would happen if an opponent succeeded in splitting your skull open with an axe or blowing it off with a blaster was exactly the thing that could lead to your decapitation.

He who hesitates is lost. A worthwhile and salient human saying, and one with which M'k'n'zy readily agreed.

So removing oneself emotionally from the fray was the best way to survive it. This was the philosophy under which M'k'n'zy had lived his life and, as a result, he had continued to live.

It was uncertain, however, just how much longer he was going to be able to claim that status.

Where the hell are they? M'k'n'zy wondered yet again. He did not allow fear for his followers to cloud his concerns. It was more irritation that they were not where they were supposed to be. He had waited long enough to realize they were not going to meet with him as intended. That meant one of two things: They had been wiped out to the man, which of course he hoped was not the case; or, the enemy had managed to cut off their route to the rendezvous point. Naturally M'k'n'zy had anticipated that possibility, and so he had arranged a backup meeting place.

The only remaining question was whether M'k'n'zy would be able to make it there.

He reached out with his finely honed senses, endeavoring to determine if he was truly alone. The rocky pass in which he was secreted was an excellent place for an ambush. He was under a stone overhang that shielded him from the view of anyone who might be above him, while offering a clear sight line into a passageway below. Anyone trying to make their way through the crevasse running through the mountain would be a perfect target for him.

He had to work on the assumption, though, that the enemy would not be that stupid. If they were, well, then it was a gift and he would take full advantage of it. But there was no point in sitting around and waiting to see if anyone showed up that he could try to pick off from hiding, particularly if it delayed his meeting up with his troops.

It wasn't as if the enemy was especially stealthy;

their armor made a distinctive clanking when they approached. Then there was the fact that his sixth sense for danger, which had never let him down before, wasn't alerting him to any immediate threat. He was safe, or at least as safe as the current situation permitted.

M'k'n'zy knew his way around the mountains of Xenex better than any other man alive. He knew that, from where he was positioned, there was an angled, sheltered pathway that would get him to the ground without exposing him to attack. It would be an easy matter to make it to that path unobserved.

The ideal course of action would have been to wait for night, but he had no desire to remain separated from his troops for that long. They needed him. They were up against a devastating, even overwhelming enemy, and his leadership and skill were an absolute necessity. He cursed his inability to communicate with them over long distances, and resolved that—once this business was done— he would make certain that the Xenexian army was properly outfitted with the sort of equipment necessary to fight a war. Certainly he had to assume that their enemies possessed the ability to stay in touch with each other, as if the Xenexians didn't already have enough disadvantages.

The sun was not quite at its zenith, and M'k'n'zy decided not to wait any longer. Keeping to the wall as closely as possible, he started making his way toward the path that would take him to the ground. From there he would head due east, trying to stick to areas of cover as much as possible. There would be a few points along the way where he would be vulnerable to observers, but it couldn't be helped. He would just have to trust his reflexes and experiences to see him through.

Frequently the planet itself was the single greatest defense against intruders, because off-worlders typically found the brutal Xenexian climate to be nearly overwhelming. Unfortunately that was not the case now. The enemy that M'k'n'zy was facing was as indifferent to the heat as was M'k'n'zy himself. He could not count on the environment to wear them down or make them think that departing Xenex in exasperation was the best option. If he and his men were going to get rid of them, it was going to have to be done by outthinking and outmaneuvering them.

The long minutes crawled past. The entire way down, M'k'n'zy kept waiting for some sort of attack. He was holding a sword in his hand, keeping it firm and steady.

Ten feet shy of reaching the ground, he stopped dead.

Something was wrong up ahead. He wasn't sure what it was, but that alone was enough to bring him to full alert. He strained, trying to see what could possibly be waiting for him that presented a threat, but there didn't appear to be anything. Nevertheless the hairs on the back of his neck were prickling, and that was enough to keep him rooted to the spot.

He glanced down and picked up a rock at his feet. It had some decent heft to it. He cradled it for a moment and then lobbed it down the stony, uneven path before him. It clacked and clattered its way down, and for a few moments, M'k'n'zy was sure that his sixth sense had betrayed him. He wasn't quite sure how to react to that: Was it better that someone wasn't trying to kill him, or that the instincts upon which he had depended for so long had somehow gone awry?

The ground exploded in front of him.

Landmine screamed through his head even as the blast knocked him backward. He cursed himself for his sloppiness; he should have braced his back against the rock wall again rather than standing there like an idiot, waiting to see what would happen. He fell back heavily, scraping his elbows, pain shooting through his arms. In a strange way, he welcomed it. It was a harsh reminder that he could take nothing for granted and had to allow for every possible eventuality.

He heard a familiar clanking from below. His sharp ears told him that it was only one person approaching him. A lookout must have been left behind to monitor the booby trap. And that sentinel, M'k'n'zy realized, would likely think that he was going to come upon the remains of a badly shredded body instead of an enemy who was ready for battle.

With the thought came instant action; hesitation simply was not part of M'k'n'zy's genetic code. He was still about ten feet above the pathway below, and without pausing, M'k'n'zy scrambled to his feet and vaulted off the uneven path. For an instant he hung in the air, and it felt free and liberating, and then he landed noiselessly on the ground below. He had kept his arm extended and away from him so that he didn't chance landing on his own sword, since that would certainly be an ignominious way to end a storied career.

He sprinted forward, silent, and within seconds saw exactly what he knew he was going to see.

An armored figure, with a helmet that completely encased its head so that no hint of features was visible, stood at the base of the path that twisted upward into the hills. It was scanning the area, using the thermal imaging that M'k'n'zy knew provided it with the ability to see its surroundings. He also knew that he had scant seconds before the armored figure became aware of him, and he raced toward his enemy.

He was not quick enough.

The armored figure turned and looked right at him, and then brought its palm level with M'k'n'zy. It was frustrating to M'k'n'zy that his enemies did not carry sidearms. Blasters or disruptors or phasers could be knocked out of their hands, rendering them weaponless and giving him an advantage. These bastards had all their weaponry built right into their armor, and that made disarming them impossible. The only option left was killing them. Not that M'k'n'zy would hesitate to do so, but it seemed a waste, making it impossible to take one of them down and grill him for information. They had two modes: attack and dead.

The one thing that M'k'n'zy had going for him was that, when his enemy did fire, the weapon required a few moments to recharge. By contrast, M'k'n'zy's sword didn't need any time at all.

Energy crackled in the palm of the armored figure's

metal gauntlet and M'k'n'zy knew he was going to have to time his movement perfectly. He also needed to get his attacker to commit to the assault. He charged with all of his body weight leaning forward, howling a defiant battle cry, conveying in every way the image of someone totally committed to this particular path and trajectory, either unaware or uncaring of whatever offensive strategy the enemy might employ.

The armored figure unleashed a blast of energy when M'k'n'zy was still ten feet away.

M'k'n'zy never slowed his attack. Instead he leaped to the side, rebounding directly off the mountainous wall to his right. He felt the air sizzling just to his left, and some of his hair crispened slightly. If the blast had struck home, or even provided a glancing blow, he would have been finished.

As it was, the angle of his attack brought him within range of his assailant. He saw the target that he needed: the small vent on the side of the helmet, the one that permitted the creatures to keep their inner temperature balanced. It was incredibly narrow, seemingly impregnable. A flaw in their armor that should not have put them at risk in any way.

M'k'n'zy drove the point of his sword forward, trying to stab deep into the vent.

He almost made it.

The armored being moved with a speed that belied its appearance. It brought up its hand and brushed aside M'k'n'zy's blade just before the sword could strike home. The enemy's weaponry had not recharged yet, but it didn't matter. The soldier swung his fist around in a pile driver move that struck M'k'n'zy in the temple, knocking him to the ground. Scalding heat radiated along the glove and seared M'k'n'zy's skin. M'k'n'zy cried out as he hit the ground and the sword was jolted out of his grasp.

M'k'n'zy twisted around and saw the bottom of his enemy's boot driving straight toward his head. He rolled to the side, barely evading the attack, and instead the foot came down on his sword, shattering it.

Quickly M'k'n'zy got to his feet and tried to find a new direction from which he could come at his opponent, but the armored figure wasn't giving him the opportunity. Instead it brought its hand up again, its weapon fully charged, and from this distance it seemed there was simply no way that it could miss him.

The armored figure fired.

And missed.

M'k'n'zy had dropped to the ground faster than would have seemed possible, and the air again fried over his head. The cliffside behind him exploded, rock fragments flying. Pieces rebounded around him, and he brought up his arms to shield his head. There was a series of rapid *pok* sounds as the debris ricocheted off his opponent's armor.

Then M'k'n'zy saw several shards of rock within his reach. He grabbed them up, lunged to his feet, and collided with the armored figure even as he brought his hand up and around and shoved as hard as he could. The prolonged contact with the superheated armor was even worse this time, and M'k'n'zy wanted to scream in agony as he clutched on like a bat, pounding the rock fragments into the vent. But he refused to give his opponent the satisfaction of hearing his weakness.

Instead he punched his fist once, twice more against the vent, which was all he could do before his mind nearly went into sensory overload from the pain of being against the armor. Then he fell backward and hit the ground, rolling into a crouch. His battle-trained mind was already coming up with a new plan of attack.

As it turned out, it wasn't necessary. The armored figure was staggering, clutching at the area of the vent access. M'k'n'zy was thrilled to see that there were fragments of rock wedged in, and they weren't coming out anytime soon. The thick fingers of the figure's gloves were unable to get any sort of grip on them.

The armored figure twisted and spun bizarrely, as if it were some sort of stringed puppet whose operator was completely inebriated. The legs began shaking, the knees buckling, and it was clawing at its helmet. For a moment, M'k'n'zy thought he might actually see the unprotected head of one of the damned things. He wasn't entirely sure if they could survive without the helmet since he wasn't certain of the environment that had spawned them. For that matter, he wasn't altogether positive that—if one of them exposed its head—he wouldn't be able to restrain himself from grabbing the nearest blunt object and using it to reduce the bastard's skull to a bloody pulp.

The armored figure was shuddering even more

violently, and then M'k'n'zy was sure that he heard
a muffled explosion from within the armor. The
soldier's arms flew out to either side and his body
trembled one final time. Then, like a newly chopped
tree, he fell slowly forward and hit the ground with a
resounding thud. He lay there, flat and unmoving, and
it was obvious to M'k'n'zy that his opponent would
not be trying to kill anyone else in this life.

He stood over his downed foe, knowing and
regretting the fact that he didn't have any tools that
would have enabled him to crack open the armor.
Then, before he even knew he was going to do it, he
drew back a leg and drove a furious kick straight into
the side of the armored figure. It tilted slightly from
the impact but otherwise didn't move.

It was a rare indulgence for M'k'n'zy, allowing
anger to seize him in such a way that he would waste
the energy on physically assaulting someone who
posed no threat.

He was surprised by the result as yet another
explosion, this one even louder, sounded from within
the armor. He jumped back, alert to whatever danger
might be posed by the discharge, but he needn't have
concerned himself. The armor contained the detona-
tion. It bent outward slightly, bulges appearing all
over it. Other than that, aside from the muffled noise,
no one would have known that anything untoward
was transpiring. Indeed M'k'n'zy, standing a short
distance away and looking on in confusion, wasn't
entirely certain what had just happened. He couldn't

tell whether the second explosion had been some biological follow-up—perhaps a cataclysmic release of internal gasses—or if it had been some sort of fail-safe within the armor itself, determining that the warrior within was no longer capable of functioning and self-detonating to prevent enemy capture. Either way, it was the final movement that the downed combatant made.

M'k'n'zy allowed himself only the briefest moment of relief, a quick exhalation in a situation where others might have needed to take a few minutes to compose themselves. It wasn't as if near-death experiences were uncommon for those who walked the same path that M'k'n'zy did. But it was a somber fact that M'k'n'zy seemed to have far more close scrapes with death than the average individual.

He briefly considered the idea of trying to drag his fallen opponent with him. Perhaps someone else might have some thoughts as to how to crack open the armor. He then dismissed the idea in short order, for two reasons: First, the surface of the armor was still hot to the touch, and waiting around for it to cool down—presuming it ever did—simply was not an option. And second, the armored figure was just too damned heavy. If he had an antigravity sled or maybe about a dozen extra hands, it might have been feasible. But he possessed none of those things, and so dismissed the idea.

Leaving the body behind, he continued to the backup rendezvous point. It was a network of caves at the base of the Tower Rim, a mountain range that had often served him in the past as a refuge where he could elude pursuit.

As he ran, doing his best to stick to concealment, he was already developing new strategies to use against the enemy, new ambushes that might be planned, and new ways to marshal his forces as effectively as possible. There was never a moment where M'k'n'zy considered the notion that his people might be defeated and that he himself would fall before the weaponry of the enemy. He was prepared for setbacks. Everyone had them. But there was no question in his mind that he would eventually triumph.

He encountered none of the enemy as he made his way to the Tower Rim. He wondered if this was simple happenstance or if it was indicative of something bigger. Was there a possibility that they had withdrawn from Xenex entirely? If that was the case, then how had he happened to encounter and kill one of them? Perhaps he was the last one remaining on the planet's surface, separated from the rest of his squadron, and they'd had the poor luck to run into each other. *At least the other guy's luck wound up being poorer than mine,* M'k'n'zy thought grimly.

It seemed to M'k'n'zy that the sun had not moved in its path across the sky, as if time itself had come to a halt.

He made it to the base of the Tower Rim, so named for the unusually tall peaks that dotted the area. It was one of his favorite hiding places, since the height of the rocky spires that surrounded them made aerial attack problematic. The spires provided some degree of protection. Even if enemies got it in their heads to carpet bomb the entire area, the network of caves that threaded through the Rim afforded considerable protection.

He arrived at the mouth of the cave entrance where he was expecting to see his people. The stench of death wafted through the air.

"No," he whispered, as he froze there in a rare instance of uncertainty as to what to do next. He wanted to believe that his senses were wrong. Or it could have been that he was detecting the remains of some random animal rather than what he was afraid that he perceived.

It only took moments for his olfactory senses to confirm for him, however, that his first impressions were exactly correct. The contents of the cave were precisely what he feared them to be.

His feet growing heavier with each step, he entered the cave. He knew that he was potentially heading into danger, but he trusted his instinct to alert him to any such hazards. Furthermore, on some level, he simply didn't care. If something was lurking within, then he was essentially inviting it to take its best shot. He would either kill it or he would be killed, and at that moment he wasn't sure which outcome was preferable.

He moved slowly through the dark, his eyes adjusting immediately to the dimness as they typically did. To some degree it didn't matter; his nose would have been able to guide him even if he'd been stumbling around sightless.

Bastards. Bastards, kept going through his mind, stoking the fire in his chest that was helping to propel him forward when so much of him simply wanted to give up.

M'k'n'zy stopped just short of the first body, his foot nearly bumping up against it. He knelt next to the corpse and discovered it to be one of his lieutenants, a young woman who had possessed a steely gaze and a projected sense of invincibility. In that regard, she had reminded M'k'n'zy of himself. The reality, however, had proven to be other than that which she had believed, as evidenced by her corpse. The right side of her face and much of the right side of her body had been burned away. It might have been from the superheating of the enemy's armor or perhaps an unleashed blast of power that had broiled her flesh. M'k'n'zy supposed that it didn't make much difference either way. Dead was dead.

So were a number of the others.

Bodies were scattered all over the cave. There was blood everywhere, on the ground and spattered against the interior wall, mixed in with scorch marks indicating that considerable power had been unleashed. It was painfully obvious what had happened: The enemy had tracked them there somehow, found them, and attacked. M'k'n'zy's people had put up a valiant defense; that much M'k'n'zy was able to discern by looking at the scuff marks on the ground. From those he could determine how many people had been engaged in battle and exactly how the fight had gone, even if the bodies hadn't been lying there to inform him of what he already knew.

He sagged to his knees, momentarily overwhelmed. How long had they been waiting for him? Did they die thinking that M'k'n'zy was already dead and their situation hopeless? Did they hold out hope for a rescue right up until the last moment when the life had fled their bodies?

"I'm sorry I let you down," he whispered.

Then he began counting.

Within sixty seconds, he determined that several people were missing. That meant one of two things: They had managed to escape, or else they had been taken prisoner. The former was far more likely, because this particular enemy wasn't big on taking prisoners.

Either way, it meant that M'k'n'zy could still save some lives.

He had not noticed anything on the ground at the entrance to the cave, but that was because he hadn't been looking. His awareness of what was awaiting him in the cave had distracted him. Now, though, he scrutinized the ground, looking for a hint of where the survivors had gone, and—even more important—if there was some way that he could follow them.

Any other eye would have been stymied in the attempt, but M'k'n'zy was quickly able to discern small fragments of dirt, broken stone, and marks that served to tell him with clarity which way his people were and what their condition was.

He set off after them.

And as he did so, he couldn't help but ponder the fact that mere decades earlier, he had been a youthful warlord, his clothes little more than tatters, his shaggy mane of hair hanging askew around his shoulders, leading his Xenexian comrades against a foe determined to crush them. It was during that time that he had made a name for himself, a name that had united the Xenexians and made them a formidable race that would never again allow itself to be conquered. It was also a name that had attracted the attention of one Jean-Luc Picard, a Starfleet officer who had taken an interest in the young M'k'n'zy and had suggested to him that a career in Starfleet was a path worth pursuing. M'k'n'zy had taken him up on his offer after much consideration, and eventually he had become better known as Mackenzie Calhoun.

Now his two worlds had collided. Calhoun was using all the knowledge, all the cunning and savvy that he had learned under fire in his youth, combined with all the tactics and wisdom he had accrued over the years as a Starfleet captain, to aid his people in battling a fearsome enemy that he had encountered during his tenure as captain of the *Excalibur.*

The Brethren—the fearsome armored race that had slaughtered so many aboard the *Excalibur*'s sister ship, the *Trident*; the race that Doctor Selar had died battling—were pursing him and his people across the face of Xenex.

And there was no way of knowing when, or if, help would ever arrive.

Starfleet Headquarters, San Francisco

Sometime Earlier

Admiral Alynna Nechayev remembered nearly every word of the conversation she'd had with Mackenzie Calhoun weeks earlier. They had been filled with consequences to which Calhoun was utterly oblivious.

Calhoun had been dutifully reporting back to her about the events on the remote world of AF1963, which had resulted in the death of Selar and the discovery of mindless bodies being "grown" in a subterranean lair. Most of the bodies, according to Calhoun, his image flickering on the communications screen, had been destroyed in the massive explosion that Selar had touched off . . . the explosion that had enabled Soleta and the infant Cwansi to escape, even though it was at the cost of Selar's life.

"Do you have any idea what intentions these D'myurj might have had for them?" she had asked Calhoun. She had labored to keep her voice flat and even and not betray, in the slightest, the concerns that were hammering through her brain.

"I've been thinking about that," Calhoun had said, *"and consulting with my people. We have a theory . . ."*

"I'm all ears."

"Well," Calhoun had said, leaning in slightly toward the screen, *"our initial question, of course, was why they would have all these bodies being grown with what were essentially blank slates for minds. But if you walked into a large warehouse and saw uniforms hanging there with no one in them, you wouldn't wonder what the purpose of them would be, correct? Wouldn't wonder what they were designed for?"*

"Not especially. I would assume that they were designed to be . . ." Her voice had trailed off. "Truly? You think they were designed—"

"To be worn. Yes. Something in the genetic makeup of half-breeds enables either the D'myurj or their associates the Brethren to transfer themselves into these bodies, once grown."

"But, good lord, why?"

"Any number of reasons. Infiltration. Manipulation. Passing themselves off as members of the Federation, in an undetectable disguise. They might be creating wars in the hopes of 'testing' us to see if we rise to the occasion. According to anyone who has had contact with them, they keep claiming that they want to advance us. Soleta told me about something that happened some months ago, during the Paradox *incident,"* he said, referring to a time ship that had gone missing temporarily. *"She encountered an alien vessel that appeared to be upgrading the* Paradox. *Advancing it. Outfitting it with improvements."*

"Are you saying that might have been the D'myurj?"

"It fits the pattern. A race dedicated to evolution of what they see as lower species, no matter what the cost. Individuals purporting to be beneficent when they're really destructive. Who knows how far it goes back? There was an incident I studied involving a probe—I think it was called Nomad—that was upgraded and advanced when it encountered another, more advanced entity."

"I know of that incident, yes. We had theorized it was the Borg."

"But why would the Borg upgrade something else? They just take. They don't give. That might well have been connected to the D'myurj as well. That means we're talking at least a century of their getting involved in Federation affairs."

"It sounds to me, Captain, as if you're treading on very thin ice here. Pulling together disparate strands and trying to weave together a whole that doesn't quite work. Still," and she had drummed her fingers on her desk, "this merits further investigation, at the very least. It would probably be wiser to keep this quiet, at least for the time being."

"I'm sure you're right, Admiral."

"All right. And, Mac . . . my condolences on the loss of Doctor Selar. A tragic story all around."

"Thank you, Admiral. Calhoun out."

The screen had gone blank, leaving her leaning back in her chair, her thoughts racing. *Calhoun knows. Something is going to have to be done . . .*

There had been much thinking on her part about that, and some discussions that she had not especially been looking forward to, nor did she enjoy them while she was having them. In doing so, however—in taking firm actions regarding Calhoun and what he did know, or didn't know but strongly suspected—Nechayev had set upon a course that she knew was ultimately going to cost her one of her most reliable and useful allies.

But it could not be helped. If Calhoun had to go, then he had to go. And she had to do whatever was necessary to make certain that happened. There was too much riding on it.

He was clever, though, and even though he trusted Nechayev implicitly, he would not blindly fall into line and obligingly march straight into a trap. He had survival instincts that made cockroaches look like lemmings.

So she had to lure him in, and the only way to do that was to play upon the trust that he already had in her. Trust was not something that Mackenzie Calhoun embraced easily. He was the most suspicious bastard in the galaxy. The flip side of that, fortunately enough, was that once that trust was given, it was a sacred thing with him. He was relentless with his enemies, but utterly dedicated to his friends. In some respects, it was arrogance on his part. Once he trusted someone, the trust became self-sustaining, a reason unto itself. The notion that someone could betray that trust never entered into his thinking because if he trusted someone, then they were permanently worthy of it. Circular reasoning. Q.E.D. It was the one vulnerability in Calhoun's intellectual makeup, and the only one that she was in a position to exploit.

She intended to do just that. And the first step in that process had already been put into motion.

Nechayev was sitting in her office, absolutely immobile. Anyone glancing in at her would have thought that she was either dead or a statue. Her gaze focused on thin air, as if she had selected a particular point at random and was now putting all her attention on it. She could have remained that way for an indefinite period. If an earthquake was shaking the building to pieces around her, it would not have jolted her from her meditative state. She had "preset" her mind so that only one thing would allow her to be roused from her contemplations.

The office intercom beeped and her aide said briskly, "Admiral. Captain Calhoun is here."

The admiral blinked once, twice, and then pulled herself back into the real world. "Admiral?" came the aide's voice a second time, but she was already clearing her throat and saying, "Send him in."

The doors hissed open and Mackenzie Calhoun strode in. Despite everything that he had been through and all that had happened recently, his back was as ramrod straight as ever, and there was a dangerous determination in his eyes that underscored his indefatigable personality. He was a cork in an ocean, capable of being pushed down by waves and storms but always bobbing back to the surface. He could never be kept down.

It was her job to find a way to do so.

You're his friend. He trusts you. You need nothing more than that to do what needs to be done.

She stood, none of the uncertainty or hesitation in her mind evinced in the slightest in either her face or her body language. "Mac," she said, extending a hand. "Good of you to come."

He shook it firmly. "Always happy to when you summon me, Admiral."

"I hate to think of it as a summoning," she said, gesturing for him to seat himself, "but instead simply a chance to catch up and confer with an old and valued ally."

"I appreciate that." Calhoun sat as she indicated he should do, smoothing the legs of his uniform trousers but never taking his purple eyes away from her. Yet despite the fact that his gaze was fixed upon her, she had no doubt that he was hyper-aware of the world around him. If someone came charging in through the door, hoping to get the drop on Calhoun, they would find themselves eating phaser before they had taken two steps into the office.

Nechayev took her seat as well. "I assume you know what this is in regards to."

"Well, I would imagine you didn't have the *Excali-bur* divert to Earth just because you felt a deep need to inquire after my health. I assume this has something to do with the Brethren and the D'myurj."

"Partly."

"Partly?" One eyebrow lifted slightly. "I would have thought entirely."

"I'm an admiral, Mac. It's my job to think about more than one thing at a time. I won't lie to you: This business that you discovered on AF1963 is incredibly disturbing." She made certain to paste an expression on her face that conveyed just how disturbed she was. "The notion that there are people in Starfleet who are not what they seem . . . that there may be some sort of alien intelligence insinuating itself into the highest ranks of command . . ."

"But this isn't the first time you've had to deal with this sort of threat."

Now she was the one who was cocking an eyebrow. "I'm not sure I follow your meaning, Captain."

Calhoun doubtlessly noticed the change in her voice to a more formal tone, but as was typical for him, he didn't allow it to affect the way he was conducting himself. "I'm fairly sure you do, Admiral. I know about the conspiracy some years back, when those parasitic creatures—offshoots of the Trill symbionts, from my understanding—were taking over the minds of Starfleet officers. I assume your office looked into that matter, but I don't believe there was ever a fully satisfying explanation as to all the detail until they resurfaced more than a decade later in the Bajoran Sector."

Nechayev rocked back in her seat, her jaw going slightly slack. "How in the hell did you find out about all of that? The information was sealed, in the deepest recesses of . . ." Her voice trailed off and then she answered her own question. "Morgan."

He tilted his head slightly in acknowledgment of her realization.

"Are you out of your mind?" she said.

"Admiral . . ."

"Are you *out of your mind?*"

"With worry, yes," Calhoun said, not backing down in the slightest from Nechayev's ire. Naturally, his assumption was that her concern stemmed from worry over confidential materials and Starfleet security. Her worries were actually more broadly based, in that the powerful computer entity in control of the *Excalibur* might somehow figure out her complicity in all of this.

"We stumbled upon a potentially massive threat to the very foundations of Starfleet," Calhoun went on, oblivious to the real concerns on Nechayev's mind. "A threat that goes so deep it's impossible to determine who to trust and who not to."

"You think that hasn't occurred to me, Captain? You think I don't know that I have to proceed with utmost caution because I can't be certain who I can talk to without playing into the enemy's hands? This race, this D'myurj . . . I'm not sure what to make of them. Their motivations are murky at best, contradictory at worst."

"I know," said Calhoun grimly. "There are the ones who claim that they're only interested in advancing the cause of humanity, except they don't care who they hurt while endeavoring to do so. And then there are the others who feel that their race should be running things since, from an evolutionary point of view, they're the best qualified."

"Based on all that, don't you think I have enough problems without having to worry about your ship's computer strolling through secure files in the Starfleet database? I could have you brought up on charges, Calhoun. I could have your ass thrown into solitary until you rot. You understand that, don't you?" She leaned back in her chair and tiredly rubbed the bridge of her nose. "Why do you do this to me? Why do you put me in these kinds of positions?"

"To be entirely candid, Admiral—"

"That would be greatly appreciated."

"—it was not something I instructed Morgan to do. She did it on her own because she knew that I was concerned about potential threats to Starfleet from within, and she decided to see if there were any similar cases that were being kept under wraps."

Nechayev lowered her hand. "So you're passing the blame onto her?"

"No, because she gave me the option of listening to what she had to say or not doing so," Calhoun said evenly. "I could have told her to forget it . . . literally. Instead, once I knew she had the information in her possession, I remonstrated her for the means by which she went about acquiring it, and then I told her to tell me everything. The buck stops with me, Admiral. It's my ship, and I take responsibility for everything that happens aboard her."

"Well, that's terrific, Mac. I'm thrilled you're that conscientious."

"You don't sound thrilled."

"Imagine that." She shrugged. "All right. Nothing to be done about it now. Not sure there's really any point to clapping you in irons, as much as it might give me a sense of satisfaction."

"I wasn't aware that Starfleet had irons anymore."

"We bring them out for special occasions, and I think this would most certainly qualify. But never mind that," she went on briskly. "I'm just going to have to trust you to keep this information to yourself."

"Have I ever given you reason not to trust me in the past?"

"No," she said softly. "No, you haven't. And I've no reason to think otherwise now."

"Your vote of confidence is greatly appreciated," said Calhoun, shifting in his chair. "You're sure that this new business with the D'myurj is unconnected to the parasites?"

"Reasonably so, yes. But that doesn't lessen the paranoia level. It's difficult to know exactly who to talk to about this entire business, so obviously I have to proceed carefully."

"I appreciate that you're talking to *me* about it."

"You're the one who brought it to my attention, so obviously . . ." Her voice trailed off and then she added, "And I'm honored that you trust me."

"We've been through far too much for me to stop trusting you at this point," said Calhoun easily. "And besides, I rely on my instincts enough that if there were something wrong with you—if you were duplicitous in some manner—I would know it."

Good. Good. His ego and overconfidence will be the end of him yet. None of those thoughts were conveyed in her expression. "I have no doubt that you would. However, Mac . . . and we've been a while coming to this point, for which I apologize . . . the reason I wanted you to come here really has nothing to do with the subject of what you discovered on AF1963."

Calhoun crossed his legs, tilting his head slightly in that way he had that made him look like an inquisitive dog. "What, then?"

"You touched on it already in the course of this meeting. It's Morgan."

"Ah," was all he said at first.

"I'm worried, Mac," she said. She had interlaced her fingers tightly and was now leaning forward on her desk. "Once upon a time, she was a living, breathing being with a soul and a conscience. But the being—the creature, if you will—that's taken up residence within the core of the *Excalibur* . . . that isn't Morgan."

"We're not entirely sure of that," said Calhoun guardedly. "She's not the woman she was, I'll give you that. And I freely admit that there have been some changes in her personality. But she's become cut off from humanity. It's impossible to say whether she's Morgan Primus having undergone behavior altera-tions due to an existence that neither you nor I can begin to comprehend . . . or if she's an incredibly sophisticated computer simulation that thinks she is Morgan Primus, when she's truly . . ."

"A ghost in the machine?"

He nodded. "A phrase coming from a philosophical work about mankind heading inevitably toward self-destruction."

"Exactly."

"Written centuries ago and yet," he gestured around them, "mankind is still here."

"True enough. But if Morgan Primus decided to shrug her shoulders and rid herself of us, I can't entirely say she wouldn't be successful." She started ticking off her concerns on her fingers. "She's astoundingly powerful. She has access to all manner of information, as you've just demonstrated in this very conversation. And as near as I can determine, she is more or less bereft of conscience. What if . . . ?" She hesitated, as if she were just coming to the realization instead of having thought it all out ahead of time. "What if she decided to send a self-destruct pulse into every shipboard computer all at once? She would have access to the prefix codes. She could override every attempt to manually stop the self-destruction. What if she decided she wanted to wipe out the entirety of Starfleet in one shot?"

"Why would she do that?"

"Would she need a reason?"

"Generally speaking, yes, she would."

"Because she feels threatened. Because she wants to issue a warning. Because you beat her at chess. Any one of a dozen reasons, and I don't accept your contention that she requires one, but even if she did, it certainly wouldn't have to be a good one. True?"

"True," Calhoun admitted. "All it would have to do is make sense to her, even if it made none to anyone else."

She paused, keeping her gaze fixed upon him, trying to get a read off him. None was forthcoming. She'd never played poker against him, but she couldn't imagine what his poker face was like, other than to think that he epitomized the concept of inscrutability. "Mac," she said finally, "you are one of the best strategic thinkers I've ever encountered. I can't be telling you anything that you haven't already considered. Am I right?"

"Yes," he said without hesitation.

"So I'm saying things you already know."

"More or less."

"So you've been . . . what? Fencing with me? Just automatically being defensive of someone you consider one of your crew?"

"More like letting you play devil's advocate in order to solidify things that are already in my mind."

She carefully projected an air of frustrated helplessness. "Then tell me how this ends, Captain. If you're as concerned about Morgan as I am—and I believe you are, if indeed not more so—tell me that you've got something up your sleeve. That you've analyzed the situation and are already making plans to address it."

"I have, and I am."

Nechayev immediately perked up. "Really."

"Really," and he nodded. "The truth is that I've

studied the situation, and I've been giving it a good deal of thought, and I've come to conclusions as to what can and should be done about it. I believe that Morgan poses a threat both to my ship and to the Federation. I can tolerate one, but not both."

She looked at him in confusion. "Do I even want to know which would be the sticking point for you?"

"Probably not."

"All right," she said agreeably. "I won't ask. What I do want to know is: What do you have planned to deal with it? I assume that you're going to try and find a way to disengage her or purge her from the *Excalibur*'s computer core. What methods do you plan to employ?"

His answer surprised her, although in retrospect she imagined that it really should not have: "I would rather not say at this time, Admiral."

She tried not to look taken aback. She couldn't recall a time when Calhoun had been less than fully forthcoming with her. "You'd rather not."

"No."

"Well then," and she folded her arms across her breast, "I am now ordering you to tell me."

"Then I'm afraid we're at an impasse, Admiral." Calhoun didn't seem particularly upset about it. No surprise there. Calhoun had faced any number of threats in his lifetime, many of them involving weapons aimed directly at assorted vital parts of his anatomy. So squaring off against a Starfleet officer, even a superior one, was hardly going to faze him.

Nevertheless, for form's sake if nothing else, she couldn't let it pass unchallenged. "You're disobeying a direct order?"

"I am taking an action that I feel is in the best interests of Starfleet."

"You're not the one who gets to make that decision, Captain."

"In this instance, Admiral, I believe I am."

She made an annoyed growl in her throat. "Why do you do things like this, huh? I'm going to say it again, Mac. Why do you put me in these sorts of positions?"

"I'm not trying to do anything to you, Admiral. I'm trying to do something *for* you. Whatever plans I have for Morgan, it is in the best interests of all concerned to have as few people as possible know about it."

"Are you saying you don't trust me, after everything you said before?"

"I'm saying I don't trust the world we're living in at the moment. Unless you can assure me, with absolutely one hundred percent certainty, that Morgan is completely unaware of the discussion we're having right now. Can you tell me, with complete conviction, that she wouldn't have found a way, via whatever monitors you have in here, to be spying on every single word that's passing between us?"

Nechayev was about to answer readily and quickly in the affirmative. But then she thought better of it, looking around herself in concern and realizing that Calhoun's point was well taken. Obviously she *thought* her office was secure, but wasn't the entire point of her worries about Morgan steeped in the possibility that nothing was safe from Morgan's prying "eyes"?

"No, I can't," which was an annoying thing for her to have to admit. "But if that's the case, and she is watching us even as we speak, then she just learned that you have something planned."

"She would already deduce that," said Calhoun. "She's a living computer. She knows the threat she represents, and she has to know that I know it. And knowing that, she would safely assume that I'm preparing for a time when her presence can no longer be tolerated. But . . ."

"But she doesn't know what you have in mind."

"No," and then he added ruefully, "at least I hope not. Let's be optimistic and say she doesn't. If that's the case, then it would be the height of foolishness to tip her off."

"You're playing a dangerous game, Mac. Who's to say that the next time you use the transporter, she doesn't just decide to scramble your molecules from one end of the galaxy to the other?"

"There's no fun in that."

"Fun?" She shook her head, once again not understanding.

"Admiral," said Calhoun, "she is quite possibly the smartest entity in the galaxy. If you're immortal and all-knowing, then more than anything else, you're someone who has a great deal of difficulty finding challenges."

"And you believe that's how she sees you? As a challenge?"

"I think so, yes."

"And because of that, she's going to keep you around, even if you wind up outthinking her and costing her her existence?"

"She probably believes that I don't have a hope in hell of outthinking her, making her utterly safe while she gets to amuse herself watching me go around like a rat in a maze."

"So you're like her pet?"

"That's probably how she sees it."

"I hope you're right, Captain," she said, "because there's just as real a possibility that—rather than see you as a challenge—she perceives you as a threat and she'll dispose of you with no more thought than you would give an insect on the bottom of your boot."

"Oh, believe me, that's occurred to me as well."

"And what do you intend to do about it?"

"Why, obviously, I'm going to attempt to be as much of a challenge as possible. Step up my game to her level."

"You sound almost excited about it."

He shrugged. "We brilliant strategic thinkers have to find our entertainment where we can."

"High-stakes entertainment, Captain, especially if the safety of the Federation—not to mention your crew—hinges upon it."

"Quite true."

"That being the case," she said, concern furrowing her brow, "may I make a suggestion, Captain?"

"By all means."

"You damned well better win."

"That," said Calhoun, "is an order I will most readily follow, Admiral."

Tendara Colony

During the Meeting at Starfleet Headquarters

i.

Seven of Nine, the former Annika Hansen, hadn't expected the smells to be what would trigger the tears. Indeed, she hadn't been expecting to cry at all.

She had thought that perhaps the mere act of setting foot upon Tendara Colony would be enough to prompt some sort of reaction. When she stepped off the shuttle, however, absolutely nothing happened. She looked around as any other stranger would, trying to feel some manner of connection to either the colony or the colonists around her.

Nothing presented itself.

She came through a small, albeit busy, spaceport, where everyone was attending to whatever their respective business was. No one gave her a second glance. This was unusual for her, and once again she had to take the time to remind herself that there was no reason why they should. It was natural for her to expect some sort of particular extra attention, considering that for the last few years she had lived her daily existence with implants attached to various parts of her, most noticeably her face. People—especially civilians— would glance at her, do a double take, and occasionally back away if they recognized the accoutrements that adorned her. She had become accustomed to being stared at and regarded with concern. *How odd that it is not being looked at that requires the adjustment,* she thought.

Not that she was entirely devoid of being paid attention to. She was still a tall, strikingly good-looking woman. Her blond hair shimmered and she moved with an easy grace and a confident sway of her shoulders and hips. Men cast sidelong, admiring glances at her, and plenty of women did as well. But it was always quick, fleeting, and then they were on to something else. Looks did not linger upon her. No one was assessing her potential as a threat.

She certainly couldn't say she missed that aspect of her life.

Once she had arrived planetside, she rented a grav car that would enable her to get around easily. The colony had certainly grown since she had spent the first few years of her life here, but it hadn't grown *that* much. It was still less than a day's journey by grav car from one end of the settlement to the other. In point of fact, she could have walked it. Seven was in no rush; however, she saw no reason to dawdle, either.

She climbed into the car, stowing her minimal belongings in the storage compartment. A few changes of clothes, some holos of the old crew that she liked to take with her wherever she journeyed. She had so little that passed for family anymore, and her old ship's crew had been the closest thing to it. It gave her some measure of comfort, having them with her, even if it was just images of them.

Seven steered the car out onto the main road. She hadn't done a lot of driving. She'd spent most of the last year in San Francisco at Starfleet Academy and had more or less walked everywhere she'd wanted to go or, for longer distances, had used convenient transporters. Before that, of course, had been the starship. Not much call for vehicles there. Nevertheless the grav car was easy enough to maneuver and within minutes she was heading down the road at a brisk clip. She slowed down where she needed to in order to let pedestrians pass in front of her, and she would nod to them in greeting while they tipped their hats to her. Most people wore hats on Tendara since the sun could be exceptionally bright and warm.

The buildings were unassuming. Simple curved one- and, at the most, two-story structures that were designed far more for function than style. She supposed that, were Tendara to remain around long enough, the spartan buildings would eventually give way to something more elaborate and festive. Seven placed little store in such things, but she knew plenty of other people did. She hoped that someday she would be one of those people. She desperately wanted to be. Wanted it so much, in fact, that it was more than a little embarrassing. Part of her remembered fondly when such overwhelming things as emotions were something that she observed from a comfortable distance. It was much easier to exist on a day-to-day basis that way. Yet now that they were available to her, she was eager to embrace them as well. Eager, but filled with trepidation. What was it called again?

Ah, yes. Mixed emotions. How appropriate.

She reached an intersection and knew that her true destination lay to the right. She had made certain of the address and was perfectly aware of which way to go, even if the onboard locator hadn't been already providing her guidance. Ultimately, however, she decided to keep going straight. Seven wasn't quite sure why she was doing so. After all, she'd come all the way out to this colony for a purpose, and there was no reason for delaying it.

Then again, wasn't the definition of being human doing something without any good reason?

She continued down the road, and soon the buildings began to thin out until they appeared only sporadically. It told her that she was getting farther into the farming community. There was a fairly obvious division in the colony between the scientists and the farmers, and both groups tended to regard each other with a sort of haughty disdain. The scientists saw the farmers as a necessary evil, using hydroponics and other techniques to make the colony self-sustaining so that they, the scientists, could tend to the truly important, even groundbreaking work that would ideally serve the overall betterment of mankind. The farmers, by contrast, saw the scientists as wholly unnecessary, not understanding why the farming couldn't simply be a means to its own end. They didn't need the scientists, whereas the scientists most definitely needed them. On the other hand, it was the presence of the scientists that had prompted the development of the colony in the first place, and so the two groups were stuck with each other whether they liked it or not.

None of it seemed familiar to her. She was reasonably sure that her parents had never brought her to this area of Tendara. Then again, she had only been a few years old when she last lived there, so it would be understandable if none of it . . .

She slowed the car and then stopped it. Seven sat atop the car as it bounced up and down slightly, responding to the shifts in her weight.

The smell of wheat wafted to her, tickled her nostrils and stroked parts of her memory that she had just assumed were long forgotten; memories she never even knew she had.

She disembarked from the car and simply stood there, taking it all in. Her nostrils flared, the aroma working its way into her, and suddenly she was four years old again. (It was shortly before the time that her parents became preoccupied with studying the Borg, an obsession that would put them on a small vessel called the *Raven*, which would become a second home to Seven.) Her mother had brought her out here (she could not believe she had not recalled that) to smell the fresh harvest. It had been so long ago, and Seven had literally been a different person back then, yet the recollections came hammering back to her with such force that they nearly knocked her off her feet. As it was, she was barely able to keep standing, and she leaned against the grav car in order to steady herself.

And Seven was a child once more, and she was looking up at her mother, who had the most magnificent smile in the world. Erin Hansen beamed at her child. In Seven's memory, Erin was a gigantic woman, although intellectually she understood that was not truly the case. Nevertheless that was how she remembered her: a woman of boundless energy and patience, well suited to her father, who was the epitome of strength and invincibility. They would always be there for Seven, of that there was no question. And on that particular day, brought back by the smell of wheat, her mother laughed and said, "Someday, Anni, all this will be yours."

She was being facetious, of course, but young Annika hadn't understood that at the time. "Oooooo," Annika had said, rather taken with the thought that someday all she could see would be hers. Instantly she started contemplating the things she could do with a vast field of wheat once it was permanently in her possession. An impressive number of possibilities crossed her mind, and the smell of the wheat simply added to it, making the field seem rife with opportunity.

Her mother was long gone, as was her father, but the wheat field was still here. She had no idea how many crops had been harvested in this place. The principles of crop rotation more or less guaranteed that wheat hadn't been growing there for an unbroken string of years. But it was here, now, and so was she, and she was overwhelmed with a sadness and longing for a time that could never, ever be again.

That was when the tears that she had not remotely expected began to flow. They streaked down her face, trickles at first, but then copiously. She wanted to cut off her nose so she didn't have to smell the wheat anymore, but it was too late. The memory was far too strong. It was entrenched now, and nothing short of finding a shovel and staving in the side of her skull would put an end to it. As each moment passed, the head-staving option seemed increasingly appealing.

"Damn them," she whispered, and she wasn't sure if she was referring to her parents or the Borg or both. She tried to wipe away the tears with the back of her hand, but there seemed to be plenty more where those came from. "Damn them," she said again.

"You shouldn't curse."

Seven jumped slightly and let out a startled gasp. Once upon a time, such a reaction would have been unthinkable. Nothing surprised her; she would simply stare at the new piece of data, whatever it might be, and then mentally catalogue it and go on about her business. Jumping, crying out—these were all extremely human reactions and thus unusual for her.

When she turned, her hands automatically went into a defensive position, as if she were concerned that whoever had just spoken was about to attack her. She remained like that, her hands frozen in a sideways chopping manner.

A child was looking up at her. It was a small, blond-haired girl with a quizzical expression and an utter lack of anything threatening about her. She didn't seem to be aware of the fact that Seven was in a defensive posture, probably because it never occurred to her that anyone could—under any circumstance—feel the least bit intimidated by her. "That's what my mother says, anyway. That you shouldn't curse."

For a moment she saw herself through the child's eyes, seeing the girl's bewilderment at Seven's unusual pose. Hesitantly the girl held up her own hand in something approximating an attempted handshake, clearly thinking that was Seven's intent. Seven had to force herself to relax and slowly she lowered her own right hand and shook the girl's tentatively. It felt gentle and loose in her own grasp; the child had not yet learned the technique of solidly and firmly gripping someone's hand. "I'm Seven. Your mother is very wise."

"Thank you," said the child politely. "And that's a very unusual name."

A simple "Yes, it is" seemed the best response, promptly followed with, "What's yours?"

"Caroline."

"Caroline." She rolled the name around in her mouth as if trying it out. She released the child's hand and said briskly, "How old are you, Caroline?"

"I'm six," and she proudly held up all five fingers on one hand and one on the other. Then she lowered the hands and scrutinized Seven's face. "Were you crying?"

"I was just remembering some things." She wiped the remainder of the tears from her face.

"Sad things?"

"No. But they were things that made me sad because they were from very long ago and I miss them. Actually, they were things I didn't even know I missed until just now."

"Okay," said Caroline, looking a bit uncertain.

Seven let out a sigh. "Six years old. When I was six years old, I was living most of the time on a ship."

"A spaceship?" When Seven nodded, the girl's face lit up. "I've always wanted to go on one. I want to travel far away. I don't like it here. It's boring. But my parents," and the expression turned dour, "they said I should stay here. They said space is dangerous. But I," her eyes glittered with excitement, "I bet it's amazing. Is it amazing?"

Very slowly, Seven knelt so that she was on eye level with the child. "Yes. It is amazing. But your parents are also very right. You should listen to them. There are areas of the galaxy that are filled with wonders you cannot imagine, and terrors to freeze your soul. It's not safe out there. It's wondrous, with treasures to satiate desires, both subtle and gross. But it's not for the timid."

"I didn't know a lot of those words, but I know 'timid.' I'm not timid."

"No, you're not. But you're not ready, either. You're not ready because you're incredibly young, and your life is an endless vista of possibilities." Her voice dropped, becoming grave. "You haven't considered that your parents can be snatched from you. You haven't worried about the notion that you could die, or that something even worse than death could happen to you. Before you set foot off your home, you should weigh all that and more, and fully realize what it is you're risking. Because it could well be your very soul, and you might not be lucky enough to hold on to it or ever get it back."

Caroline stepped away from her, her lower lip trembling, and instantly Seven was contrite, realizing that she had scared the child needlessly. "Listen to me," she began.

"No. I don't like you. You're scary."

"I didn't mean to be. I—"

"Caroline!"

Seven stood immediately upon the arrival of a woman she took to be the child's mother. The resemblance was remarkable. The old saying was that if you wanted to see what a girl would look like in twenty years, just study her mother. That certainly seemed to be the case here, although the mother had the slightly world-weary look of one who kept too long hours for too little reward. Caroline's mother was running at a steady trot up the road, and appeared both relieved to have found her daughter and concerned since she had no idea who it was that Caroline was talking to.

Before Seven could say a word, Caroline turned and ran to her mother, practically leaping into her arms even as she pointed accusingly at Seven. "She was telling me scary things!"

The woman's eyes narrowed, apparently sizing up

Seven to be a potential threat. Her voice frosty, she said, "What did you tell my daughter?"

"I said that space was a dangerous place, and that she should listen to your advice about staying safely at home."

"Is that what she said, Caroline?"

The child's head bobbed up and down, at which point her mother's expression softened a bit. "Oh. Okay, well . . . that's all you said?"

"That is all," Seven assured her.

"All right, well, I'm sure you didn't mean to upset her."

Yes, I did, by all means. I wanted to drive into her the notion that she should appreciate what she's got, because you never know when it's all going to be snatched away. There's no security in the void, and everything you know and love can be taken from you in a heartbeat, leaving you bereft and with a hole in your very being that's as vast as space itself.

"Of course I didn't," said Seven, considering with amusement the fact that once upon a time, lying would have been unthinkable for her. It took her becoming more human to be able to be duplicitous.

"Are you from around here?"

"I . . . used to be. Actually," and she cleared her throat, "I was hoping you could tell me if Annie Kalandra still lives here."

"Oh, absolutely. I know Annie. Sweet woman."

"Mommy!" Caroline said insistently. "Make her go away! Please!"

Caroline's mother looked mortified at what she

saw as her daughter's rudeness, but Seven simply could not blame the child for her attitude. The truth was that Seven was indeed a very scary person; a child could simply see it, whereas an adult could not.

Very quickly, Caroline's mother told Seven where she could find Annie Kalandra. Seven thanked her and headed off, casting one final glance toward Caroline, who was still holding tightly on to her mother with her arms around her mother's neck and her legs wrapped around the woman's waist. The child kept her face buried in the base of the woman's throat, not even wanting to chance catching Seven's eye.

What a relief that I'm a teacher at the Academy rather than working in the recruiting office. I'd single-handedly reduce the entire rank and file of the fleet to nonexistence.

ii.

Annie Kalandra—a teacher by trade, specializing in art—lived in a modest apartment in a small complex of buildings. She was a pleasant enough woman, generally displaying the sort of attitude that in a man would be described as avuncular, but didn't have a direct corresponding word for a female. She wasn't really anyone's aunt, but in one case, a very long time ago, the title had been bestowed upon her, like a knighthood. She had become "Aunt Annie" through the oddest of happenstance: coming upon a pregnant woman who'd been taking a nice, relaxing walk in wide-open fields and had unexpectedly gone into labor. The child had shown an unconscionable determination to rush into the world, and was not waiting for summoned help to arrive.

Annie Kalandra had been there to see the mother and child through the birth. It had been Annie who had carefully unwound the cord from around the child's neck, the cord that could have strangled her, and then eased her into the world. It had been Annie who had cleaned the wailing infant up and wrapped her in a shawl that she would never use again, and then laid her upon her mother's chest.

And it had been in honor of her that her first and surname had been combined into the child's name: Annika.

And she had remained a close family friend, introduced under odd circumstances but embraced and a part of their life for as long as they had lived on the colony world. She had thrilled at watching the infant's progress, and dandled her on her knee, and fantasized what her little namesake's life would be like.

She could never have imagined what it would actually be like.

For that little girl was now long gone. Instead, from what Annie had heard, she was now calling herself Seven of Nine, and was not remotely the joyous child that Annie had known for the first four years of Annika's life. Sometimes at night, she would envision her beloved little Annika being made into one of the Borg Collective (a threat now ended, but too late, far too late) and Annie would cringe under her blanket and pull the pillow tighter around her ears, trying to drown out her fears and push the darkness away. She knew it was, long term, a losing game. Someday the darkness would ensnare her and drag her away into it, and she would know what lay on the other side. It was not something she was looking forward to.

Her front door chimed. She was in the middle of carefully painting flowers on a newly crafted vase and didn't feel like getting up. Without giving the slightest consideration as to who might be at the door—one simply didn't worry about such things on Tendara Colony—she called out, "Enter, if you're so inclined."

The door slid open. The person filling the doorway did not enter. Instead she stood there, in the arch, as if afraid to come in because she wasn't certain as to what sort of reception she would receive.

Annie glanced up at her, most of her attention still focused on the vase. Then the brush suddenly slipped from her now nerveless fingers.

"Aunt Annie?" the newcomer said tentatively.

Annie got to her feet, her legs trembling. "Oh my God," she whispered. She had not seen her for so many years, but the woman looked so much like her mother, how could she be mistaken for anyone else? Unheeding of her surroundings, Annie started forward and banged into the table upon which the vase had been balanced. The vase tumbled off, struck the floor, and shattered. She walked right over it, the pieces crunching beneath her boots. "Oh my God," she said again. "Annika?"

She didn't notice the young woman flinch at the name, and bite back a response. Instead she said evenly, "I'm home," and then Annie was across the room and threw her arms around her. The pressure knocked the breath right out of her and she had to gasp to get it back.

Annie drew back for a moment and touched Seven's face where the implants had once adorned it. She could see where they had been; the skin around it was slightly browner.

As if reading her mind, Seven said, "I could go in for tanning treatments to even out the skin, but I decided to let the sun do it naturally."

"*Oh my God!*" she said a third time and hugged Seven once again, so fiercely this time that it seemed to Seven as if her ribs might snap. "Oh, my little girl! This is . . . it's a miracle!"

Tears began to run down Seven's face. They came so easily these days, but that didn't matter. All that mattered was this: this place, this person, this life. She said the first thing that came to mind: "I'm sorry about your vase."

"To hell with the vase," said Aunt Annie. "Let it be broken. At least my family is back together."

iii.

Seven had spent most of the week at Aunt Annie's doing one of two things: listening to stories of her youth, and sleeping. Fortunately at no point did she do both of those things simultaneously.

My name is Seven. I will not be Annika. Not for anyone. That had been the immediate response that had almost sprung from her lips. It had become reflex to her.

But this was the woman for whom she had been named. This was the woman who had saved her life in infancy. This was the one thing left from the life that she had once known, a life that she was feeling the need to connect with in order to become a truly whole person. And the first thing she was going to do to that end was to reject the name that was based on Annie Kalandra's own?

Not for anyone but her.

Annie regaled Seven with all the stories she'd had pent up all these years. Tales of little Annika: her first word ("light," as it turned out, and not the more predictable "mama" or "dada"), her first faltering steps. All the typical remembrances of a life long past. Plus she also had many other stories that, as a close friend of the family, she'd learned: tales of Seven's father when he was growing up, and how he had first met her mother (it was a long, protracted story having to do with an umbrella). These were the kinds of tales that one heard incessantly growing up so that, by the time someone was as old as Seven was, they would be common knowledge, part of the family history.

In this case, however, it was the equivalent of getting a protracted information dump in one extended sitting. It was rather odd for Seven in many respects.

She was hearing about her own life, and the lives of her parents and family, and yet it was like listening to a series of anecdotes about total strangers. But at least she was able to listen with empathy. When she was Seven of Nine, Tertiary Adjunct of Unimatrix Zero-One, the stories would have been meaningless. When she was the recovered Seven of Nine aboard *Voyager,* the stories would have had some mild interest to her in that they related to a past that she knew was hers, even if she did feel utterly disconnected from it. Now, as Annika Hansen—in actuality if not in regular practice—she was able to appreciate them for what they were, even as she was only partly able to . . . well, to assimilate them.

She realized that she was coming up against the limits of her new status. She was now fully human in most aspects, with no trace of her Borg identity manifest on her body. Yet—and it was difficult for her to admit, but it was true—inside she was still dealing with the learning curve of being a "normal" person.

She didn't allow any of her inner concerns to be on display for her "aunt," however. Annie was so overjoyed to see her, and was clearly enjoying the entire process of doting on her namesake, that there seemed no point in dropping any of her inner turmoil on Annie. It wasn't as if it was something with which Annie could help her. The feeling of disorientation was something that she needed to work out on her own, and she hoped that she would be able to do so, given enough time. For now, simply spending time with Annie was a good start to acclimating herself to the worlds around her. Aunt Annie was her point of entrance back into the life of Annika Hansen, and perhaps something that would enable her to leave behind the voices that still rattled around in her head.

Besides which, Aunt Annie was not only a great recounter of anecdotes, but she also made a formidable apple tart.

It was on the sixth day of her vacation with Aunt Annie, while she was in the middle of eating one of those apple tarts in the kitchen, that Annie came to her with a concerned look on her face. "There's someone at the door asking for you," she said.

"Really?" Seven cocked a curious eyebrow. "The only person who knows I'm here is my supervisor at Starfleet Academy. Who could it possibly be? Is it . . . ?" She suddenly perked up. "Is it someone from *Voyager*?"

"How would I know that?"

"Is the visitor in a Starfleet uniform?"

"No. It's a Vulcan, if that's of any use."

"Tuvok!" she said immediately, springing to her feet. "I wonder what he's—"

"It's not a he. It's a woman."

She remained where she was. "A woman?"

"I may not know if someone is from *Voyager*, but I'm reasonably sure I can tell male from female," Annie said drily.

"Very well," said Seven. She came around the table and started to head out into the living room.

Annie stopped her for a moment, picked up a napkin, and wiped some crumbs from the edges of

Seven's mouth. Seven wanted to tell her that she was perfectly capable of wiping her own face, but kept it to herself. Annie had married once, but it had not lasted, and she had never had children of her own. So she had a boatload of maternal instinct and was happy to utilize it anywhere the opportunity presented itself. Seven smiled inwardly and allowed Annie to finish cleaning her up before she went out to see who this mysterious Vulcan visitor was.

She walked into the living room and there, indeed, was a female Vulcan. She was dressed simply, in nondescript clothing . . . so nondescript, in fact, that it caught Seven's attention. Most Vulcans she knew were either ambassadors or members of Starfleet; that seemed to be the two professions that prompted Vulcans to leave their world. Otherwise they tended to be rather insular; certainly they didn't show up on random colony worlds. The fact that this particular Vulcan was attired in such a way that she more or less looked like a colonist prompted Seven to wonder just why she was dressed in that manner. It made her think that she might be hiding something.

"May I help you?" she asked politely.

"Annika Hansen," said the Vulcan. She was tilting her head slightly, like a canine trying to listen carefully for sounds that only she could hear.

Seven glanced in Annie's direction. She automatically wanted to correct the Vulcan, but the fact that Annie was right there . . . "Yes," Seven replied, trying not to grit her teeth.

The Vulcan paused and then said, as if to verify it, "Seven of Nine."

Seven actually felt more comfortable hearing that name, even as she heard her aunt draw in her breath sharply. "Who wants to know?"

"Well, I do, obviously. You're," and unusually for a Vulcan, a smile seemed to tug at the edges of her mouth, "not exactly what I was expecting for a former assimilated Borg."

"Please state your business or I am going to have to ask you to leave."

"All right," she said. "First of all, I wish to extend my condolences on the passing of Kathryn Janeway. I never had the pleasure of meeting her, but from what I understand, the two of you were very close."

"We were, yes," said Seven, "and I appreciate the sentiment. I think I'd appreciate it a little more if I knew what you were doing here."

"I'm here because of the nature in which Admiral Janeway passed away. It involved . . ."

"I know what it involved. I was there."

"You were?" It was Aunt Annie who had spoken. "You were there when Admiral Janeway passed away? During that whole awful business when the Borg ate Pluto? You didn't tell me that, dear."

There was a great deal that Seven had not told her. She hadn't wanted to give Annie the impression that the most recent years of her life had been a walk in the park, but neither did she feel the need to tell her in extraordinary detail every hazard that she had encountered.

The Vulcan's gaze darted from Seven to Annie, and then, before Seven could reply, she said, "She was there in an advisory capacity, watching from a distance. Without her . . . advice . . . the situation would not have been resolved in a manner favorable to the Federation's interests." She then regarded Seven with an upraised eyebrow as if to say, *Do you wish to contradict me?*

"Yes, that is precisely what happened," Seven told her without inflection.

There was a dead silence for a moment, and then Annie said, "You know what? I think it would probably be best if I went out for a walk. Let you two talk about . . . whatever you need to talk about . . . for a while."

"That would be most considerate," said the Vulcan.

Moments later, having picked up her hat and light jacket, Annie walked out, leaving the two of them in the living room, both standing and staring at each other, like sculpted bookends.

"Who are you?" said Seven the moment the door slid shut behind her aunt. "Why are you here? And why is the manner of Admiral Janeway's death of any importance to you?"

"My name is Soleta."

"Soleta." The name was familiar to Seven, but it took her a moment to recall it. Then she did, and her eyes widened. "You were the Vulcan science officer who turned out to be a Romulan. You were discharged from Starfleet as being a security risk."

"I didn't turn out to be a Romulan. My mother was Vulcan, my father Romulan."

"From my understanding of the antipathy between the races, I am surprised your mother took up with—"

"She didn't 'take up' with anyone. It was not remotely consensual."

That stopped Seven for a moment. When she ran the conversation back through her head, she realized that she had sounded rather stiff, even Borg-like. It was almost as if thinking and reacting like a normal human was something that required practice. "I am . . ." She cleared her throat. "I am sorry. About that."

"So was my mother, but she didn't let it affect the way she raised me, so . . ." And she shrugged. "In any event, I am here because I was sent by Captain Mackenzie Calhoun."

"Calhoun, your former commander." When Soleta nodded, Seven said, "I met him. Jean-Luc Picard introduced us at Kathryn Janeway's memorial service. He seemed very . . . interesting."

"He is that."

"But he is your former commander. Yet you are here on his behalf."

"I owe him more than a few debts that, in truth, can never be repaid. So he knew he could count on me to help him perform this service."

"And what service would that be? Does it pertain to the passing of Kathryn Janeway?"

"Only in that you have more experience with artificial life forms and computer intelligences than any other human."

"And you need me to apply that experience to a problem?"

"Yes."

"And what," said Seven, "would the nature of that problem be?"

"Captain Calhoun needs someone to help him terminate a once-human computer entity that could possibly destroy the entire Federation."

Seven stood there silently, taking that in. "Can I get you something to drink?" she said at last.

"Is it alcoholic?"

"It could be."

"Then yes, definitely."

iv.

Soleta had not known what to make of the note that had been left in her quarters on her ship, the *Spectre*. The vessel had been stolen by the D'myurj—technically by her former (and now deceased) lover, but the D'myurj had been pulling the strings—and recovered by the crew of the *Excalibur*. She had not expected to find a hand-written note from Calhoun, however, if for no other reason than that she couldn't remember the last time someone had handed her something written on paper. She couldn't imagine where Calhoun had managed to acquire it, although she supposed that she shouldn't have been surprised. There was very little Mackenzie Calhoun could not accomplish if he put his mind to it.

The fact that he left a note at all was enough to pique Soleta's interest, because she couldn't fathom the reason for it. She had picked it up and read it with curiosity. By the time she got to the end, it was all she could do—even with all of her training in suppressing her emotions—to prevent her hands from trembling.

She knew that there had been problems with Morgan. She knew that the being that had once been human, and was now the computer heart of the *Excalibur,* was becoming somewhat unpredictable. But the notion that Calhoun felt the need to embark on this secretive, even byzantine, course of action in order to remedy the situation was enough to drive home to her just how dire things had become.

She was a spy. She was a Romulan spy, or at least she had been. She was the absolute last individual that any reasonable person should trust with any sort of delicate mission, particularly when it involved something that could impact on the internal security of the Federation. Yet she was the one upon whom Calhoun was now depending, in the name of old loyalties that he couldn't possibly know for sure she would respect.

Except he did know. That was the damnedest thing about him. He knew and had every confidence that she would not let him down.

She knew that she wouldn't. As certainly as she knew anything else in this life, she knew that she would not let Mackenzie Calhoun down, especially when she was the only one upon whom he could count.

It made sense, after all. Morgan would monitor any normal form of communication that he might employ. He could hardly send a standard subspace communication to Soleta, even encoded, because it would lay bare his concerns and plans to the very entity that he was trying to undo.

But a simple piece of paper facedown on a table was out of reach for Morgan, unless she was in a holographic form. And since there was no holotechnology in Soleta's quarters, Calhoun was able to leave it there for her with relative impunity. In order to thwart something exceedingly high-tech, the best way to do so was something very low-tech.

Of course, it was possible that Morgan was going to be monitoring Soleta's comings and goings as well, seeing her as a potential threat. But she didn't think that was going to be the case. There was no reason for Morgan to regard her as a threat, particularly since she was a solo operative with no direct connection to the Federation. She was the absolute last person that Calhoun would turn to.

Which might make her think you'd be the first person he'd turn to . . .

Soleta, with impressive discipline, had forced herself to shut down that line of thinking. Incessant paranoia could wind up immobilizing her, make her second-guess her every move. Should that happen, she would be of no benefit to Calhoun or to anyone. She had to proceed as best she could, in as careful a manner as she could, and trust to both her instincts and Calhoun's chess-like ability to outthink an opponent by being five steps ahead.

She just hoped that five steps would be enough in this case.

Tracking down Annika Hansen had been simplicity itself, because Seven had made absolutely no effort to cover her tracks. Why should she? It wasn't as if she was on the run from anyone. She had formerly requested vacation from her Starfleet superior, and had filed a flight plan, itinerary, and emergency contact information with the proper authorities. Naturally all of that had been confidential, not remotely intended for public dissemination. It was available only for Starfleet and not meant for prying eyes.

As a consequence of these extended security procedures, Soleta had required a full six and a half minutes to crack into the Starfleet mainframe and extract the information she wanted as to Seven's whereabouts (as opposed to the three or so that it would ordinarily have required). In considering such worries as Starfleet security, she took some consolation in knowing that only a former science officer such as herself would have the know-how to commit such a detailed piece of investigation, and there was not an abundance of people like her around.

Once she had obtained the information she wanted, she had piloted the *Spectre* directly to Tendara Colony. She had to think that this was a remarkable stroke of luck. If Seven of Nine had still been at Starfleet Academy, obtaining access to her might have been slightly more problematic. First of all, Soleta was still considered persona non grata. Second, computers monitored the comings and goings of anyone at the Academy. No one thought anything of this; it was simple routine security procedures. Yet now that very security which they thought computers offered was in fact putting security at risk, and almost no one was aware of it. Nor was warning anyone an option. Morgan would doubtlessly learn of it, and besides, they wouldn't believe Soleta anyway.

She had traded out her normal clothes, evocative of the Romulan lifestyle that she had adopted, for something more neutral that she hoped would allow her to blend in, or at least blend in as much as possible when one was a Vulcan, which she hoped people would assume her to be. If they knew there was someone with Romulan blood walking around among them, they might not be quite so accommodating.

So here she was, having accomplished the first part of what Calhoun had required of her. Soleta could only think that this had been the easy part of her task. From here on in, she was walking on uncertain ground.

In quick, broad strokes she laid out for Seven of Nine the reason for her coming and the delicate nature of her mission. Seven listened silently to the entire history of Morgan, at least as much of it as Soleta knew. Of how Morgan had once been a human, or far more akin to human than she currently was. She had been an immortal being, traveling the Earth, and later the stars, for more years than anyone could be certain about. Soleta told her of the one-in-a-million fluke that had destroyed Morgan's body but had transferred her mind, her personality—some even speculated her soul—into the heart of the *Excalibur*'s computer core. But it was becoming more and more evident through recent events that her soul had not, in fact, made the transition. Hers was a human mind with seemingly absolute power, and Soleta did not have to remind Seven of what both power and absolute power tended to do, at least according to the long-deceased Lord Acton.

"Morgan Primus is no longer the living, breathing woman that Mackenzie Calhoun once knew," Soleta concluded. "She has instead become a copy of a copy. With her lack of conscience and her apparently limitless potential, it is a dangerous combination that can no longer be tolerated. It must be attended to, once and for all. And what with your expertise and your connection to the Borg . . ."

"I no longer have any connection to the Borg," Seven reminded her, tapping her face where the implants had once been. "My feelings toward them are . . . complicated at best. And here you come, a relative stranger, representing a captain I've met only in passing, telling me you need me to thrust my head right back into the jaws of it. I just want you to appreciate what it is you're asking of me."

"I do."

"How do I even know I can trust you?"

"What do you mean?" Soleta looked at her in confusion for a moment, but then understood. "Ah. You think I could be a Romulan spy, using you as a means of disabling or even destroying a formidable weapon that resides in the heart of the *Excalibur*."

"The thought did cross my mind," said Seven. She had been holding a glass of homegrown ale, but she had nearly emptied it and now put it on the table. "As plans go, it would be rather cunning."

"Albeit extremely involved."

"True, but still . . ."

"May I endeavor to convince you?"

"How," said Seven, "would you go about doing that?"

Soleta had been sitting, her back straight, one hand resting on her glass, the other on her lap. Now she stood and walked across the room toward Seven. Seven watched her suspiciously, and she flinched slightly when Soleta reached toward her. "What are you doing?" she said guardedly.

"Convincing you," she said, "in such a way that my motivations are completely open to you. Unless you're afraid?"

"I'm not afraid of you."

"Then may I proceed?"

Seven hesitated for more than just a few moments. There was clearly something going through her mind, something that she didn't want to articulate. Soleta could readily guess exactly what that was. She came to the conclusion that Seven was very likely not only going to forbid her from putting a mindmeld anywhere near her, but might well try to take Soleta's outstretched hand and shove it up the Vulcan's ass. So she was mildly surprised when Seven tilted her chin and looked at Soleta defiantly. "Do as you wish."

Soleta reached toward her temple and touched it. She closed her eyes and reflexively Seven did likewise. Slowly, carefully, Soleta eased her mind into Seven's. She had no desire to be intrusive, nor to give Seven the slightest reason to believe that she was trying to shove her own will into her mind and perhaps even take control of it. It was just enough of a brush against Seven's consciousness to convince her of the truth of what Soleta was telling her.

As was always the case in a mindmeld, the actual passage of time was a bit tricky to determine. In this instance, though, Soleta could tell that it hadn't been much at all. It was no more invasive than the brush of a butterfly's wing, and once she had made the contact that was required to convey her sincerity to Seven, Soleta withdrew just as quickly, fluttering away.

The world swiftly came into focus around Soleta. Seven was staring up at her, but there didn't seem to be anything going on behind her eyes, which momentarily concerned Soleta. But then Seven blinked several times, recovering from the Vulcan telepathic technique, and she stared up at Soleta with conviction. "All right," she said. "I believe you."

"Good."

"Or at least I believe that *you* believe you are acting in good faith."

"I'll take what I can get."

"So," and she leaned back in her chair and stroked her chin thoughtfully, "do you intend to kill her?"

"You can't kill something that isn't alive," said Soleta. "I'm talking about purging her from the heart of the *Excalibur* so that she's no longer a potential threat to the ship or to anyone."

"There's only one answer: You have to introduce a virus into her. Not dissimilar from the tactic we used in attempting to purge Kathryn Janeway from her position as Borg queen."

"Exactly," said Soleta. "And since you were at the center of that operation . . ."

"Yes, but there's obviously a few things you aren't considering." She started to tick off each point on her fingers. "First, for all our efforts, as a rescue mission it was a complete failure. We lost Admiral Janeway. Second, the Borg were able to erect a firewall to block the virus and it was only by extreme luck that we were able to accomplish our goal. Third, the virus involved the destruction of the Borg vessel into which it was introduced. If you wind up destroying the *Excalibur* and everyone aboard, that would be an extreme means of solving the problem. Fourth—and most important—I'm no longer remotely cybernetic. It's not as if you can load a virus onto me that I will then wind up transmitting into her."

Soleta folded her arms, her face a scowl. Seven

would never have dreamt how odd a scowl looked on a Vulcan face. She had to think that, by this point, she would have realized that Soleta was part, if not all, Romulan. However her mother had raised her, she had obviously shaken off some of that training. "Those are all valid points," Soleta finally said after a few moments of thought. "And they are among the reasons that I—"

"You?"

"That Captain Calhoun and I felt you would be the ideal person with whom to confer on this matter. So . . . Seven. What do we do? Do you have any means of concocting and introducing this virus that you're proposing?"

"Me? No."

"So it's hopeless?"

"I didn't say that," Seven informed her. "There is, in fact, one being in the galaxy who might be capable of doing what's required."

"One person."

"Yes." She uncrossed her legs and stood up. "So I suggest we go see him before Morgan Primus destroys the Federation."

Bravo Station

Not Too Long After the Meeting Between Seven and Soleta

i.

Kat Mueller studied herself in the mirror, turning her head this way and that, and didn't like what she saw from either angle. She had never been a particularly vain woman. If she had been, then she most certainly would have attended to the scar that she had carried on her face since her youth. Instead she had borne the Heidelberg fencing scar with a great deal of pride.

Yet now, in her guest quarters at Bravo Station, Mueller looked over her face with renewed scrutiny and wasn't wild about what she saw.

When did I start looking so old?

There were crow's feet that either hadn't been there before or she was just beginning to notice. There were strands of gray hair mixed in with the blond.

But it was more than that, more than just the cosmetic aspects, and she knew it. There was a general air of weariness that was reflected in her eyes. Her skin looked saggy, as if some of her life force had been sucked out of it. She appeared like someone who had been emotionally kicked in the teeth.

There was no question in her mind why she looked like this.

In her mind's eye, she relived the events of the past days. The assault by the ominous, unyielding creatures known as the Brethren, who had stampeded through the *Trident*, slaughtering her crewmen at will. Her crew had fought back valiantly, and even taken a few of the bastards with them. And thank whatever gods there were that Mackenzie Calhoun and the *Excalibur* had shown up to save their collective ass.

But the hits they had taken, the body count that had piled up . . .

She had not been present when Doctor Villers had died, but she was able to visualize it from the recountings; the Doc going down in full fury, not backing away from formidable opponents even though she must have known she was facing her death. But Mueller had been right in the middle of it when her bridge crew had been brutalized, when Mick Gold had been slaughtered. And yes, Mueller had fought back, but she had been helpless to aid her crew. . . .

She realized that was what she was seeing in her eyes: the air of someone who had been helpless. Mueller had been many things in her life and career, but a helpless victim had never been one of them. It was a soul-deadening prospect for her, and she wasn't sure it was one she wanted to live with.

So what are you supposed to do? Fall on your sword in shame? Leave a message behind that tells everyone you simply couldn't live with the dishonor of letting your crew down? How utterly weak would that be? Is that truly how you want to go out? On a note of weakness, as if you couldn't face the prospect of everyone knowing just how spectacularly you failed?

She saw that weakness, that failure, in her reflection, and with a screech of fury she drew back her fist and slammed it into the mirror.

There was a loud, explosive crack.

The mirror trembled slightly but otherwise remained intact. Mueller, however, jumped back, uttering a string of profanities in German while clutching her fist. She looked in dismay and irritation at the blood that was on her knuckles and the swelling that was already starting to occur.

"Son of a bitch," she muttered, and then winced as she tried flexing her fingers. "Brilliant, Kat. Just brilliant." Of course it wasn't glass. If the space station came under assault, the last thing anyone would need would be glass shattering and flying around in people's faces. The *Trident* had similar indestructible reflective surfaces.

Maybe she should indeed fall on her sword and take herself out of the game, because she was starting to think that it was entirely possible she was too damned stupid to live.

ii.

Admiral Elizabeth Paula Shelby studied Mueller's damaged hand as the medtech worked on it and said, with a look of skepticism on her face, "*How* did you do this again?"

Mueller was perched on the edge of one of the tables, her dangling legs crossed at the ankles. The medtech had cleaned away the blood, used a bone-knitter to mend the shattered knuckles beneath, and was now finishing the job with a dermal regenerator to regrow the abraded skin. She stared levelly at Shelby and said, "Cut myself shaving."

"You cut your *knuckles* shaving."

"You get older, you get hair growing everywhere you don't want it to."

The medtech rolled his eyes but, after a warning glance from Mueller, said nothing.

Shelby folded her arms and looked skeptically at her. "See, my guess would have been that you were punching something hard out of frustration. A wall or something like that. And the reason for that is it looks exactly like what I did to myself the last time *I* did that."

"You?"

"I'm married to Mackenzie Calhoun. It comes with the territory, as you well know, having been his lover before that."

The medtech cleared his throat to remind them that he was standing right there and probably wasn't anxious to hear about any of this. The women lapsed into silence, although Shelby was working to repress a smile. For the more seriously inclined Mueller, maintaining a poker face wasn't all that much of a challenge. "Done," the medtech finally said, looking relieved to be able to step away from them. Then, seemingly almost as an afterthought, he added, "You asked to be kept apprised of Lieutenant Arex. He's out of surgery and the prognosis is extremely good."

"Can I see him?" she asked, waggling her fingers absently to make certain that the irritation was gone.

"Absolutely. He's in recovery, but he's certainly well enough to have visitors. In fact, the Caitian is already in with him."

"M'Ress?" said Mueller.

"She's the only Caitian on Bravo," said Shelby. "Unless you know of another?"

"No. Right. Of course not. Sorry," said Mueller, feeling uncharacteristically tentative. "I'm not quite on my game today."

"We all have our off days," Shelby said in a neutral tone.

Moments later they were approaching the recovery room. They could see, through the observation window, Arex lying beneath the confines of the cellular stasis field. If the operation had gone successfully—and there was every reason to believe it had—Arex's third arm, severed by the Brethren during their attack, had been reattached and was in the process of healing in the stasis field. With any luck, he would wind up with full mobility of the appendage.

M'Ress was not without injuries herself. She had been badly burned in the altercation with the Brethren as well, when her attempt to attack one had gone terribly wrong thanks to the superheated surface of their armor. The skin itself had been healed, but only time would enable the fur to grow back. It was in the process of doing so, and M'Ress was idly scratching one of the patches on her bare leg where the new fur was coming in.

M'Ress was talking to him, and even though they were on the other side of the glass, Mueller could tell that she was speaking gently to him, softly, and reassuringly. She was holding one of his hands in hers and stroking it. Apparently he had only recently come out of surgery. There was exhaustion on his face, and yet he seemed pleased that M'Ress was with him, listening to everything she had to say and basking in her presence. They were so caught up with each other that neither had noticed the captain standing on the other side of the glass.

"You can go on in," said Shelby.

Mueller stood there for a moment, struggling inwardly. Then she turned away and said briskly, "Maybe later."

"Captain—"

Mueller kept walking, her long, efficient strides carrying her quickly out of sickbay. Shelby had to run to keep up with her. "Kat, slow down—"

Mueller did the opposite, picking up speed, and Shelby, who didn't feel like running, snapped out, "Captain, *halt!* That's an order."

Mueller moaned low in her throat even as she skidded to a halt. By all rights she should have kept going, but the bottom line was that Shelby outranked her. Mueller turned and glared at her. *"What?"*

Shelby came up close to her and then glanced about. There was no one else around and she said in a low voice, "It wasn't your fault, Kat. Stop blaming yourself."

"I'm not blaming myself—"

"The hell you aren't. You're too damned honest to try and lie to me, Kat, but if it'll make you feel better, go ahead. Look me in the eyes and tell me you're not beating yourself up over what happened."

Mueller tried to do so, but she couldn't hold Shelby's gaze. Instead she looked away and once again growled in frustration. "Of course it's my fault. I'm the captain. Everything that happens on the ship begins and ends with me."

"Your crew didn't get hurt or killed because of you. They got hurt or killed because they chose the life they did, and because invaders attacked them. Whether it had been you, me, Mac, or James Freaking Kirk at the helm, it doesn't matter. The first rule of space exploration is that there are going to be casualties. And the second rule is that captains can't change the first rule. Do you get that?"

"Yes. Of course I get that. But getting that isn't

going to spare Arex, M'Ress, and the others all the pain they've suffered. Getting that isn't going to bring Mick or Doc Villers back from the dead."

"You did everything you should have, everything you *could* have . . ."

"Do you *seriously* think that makes me feel any better?" Mueller shot back. "There are only two possible responses to that: Either you're right or you're wrong. If you're right, then how much greater should my frustration level be, knowing that even though I made all the correct moves, my people still died? If you're wrong, then I get to spend the rest of my career—hell, the rest of my life—reviewing everything that happened and second-guessing myself. And God only knows what happens if that second-guessing winds up seeping into the way I conduct myself here on out."

"So what are you saying?" Shelby demanded. "That you got your nose bloodied and because of that you're going to walk away from your command and responsibility? That you're going to quit—?"

"I'm not a quitter."

"Then what—?"

"I don't know!" Shouting was unusual for Mueller, and she didn't like the sound of her raised voice. Immediately she reined herself in, but she was trembling with barely repressed anger. "I don't know, okay, Elizabeth? I'm allowed not to know. I'm allowed to not have all the damned answers. I'm in the dark and right now I don't know the way out. And I'm not going to know simply because you're ordering me to."

"I wasn't trying to—"

"Yes, you were. You want me to give you responses right now that I'm not prepared to give. I had a rough outing, and I'm dealing with it in my own way and my own time, rather than on your schedule or anyone else's. Do you understand that? Do you understand what I'm saying to you?"

"You're saying I should back off."

"That is exactly right."

"Fine. That's what I'll do then. But for as long as the *Trident* is here at Bravo Station for repairs, you should feel free to avail yourself of—"

"I get it."

"I'm just trying to tell you that I'm here for you—"

"Are you propositioning me?"

"Am I—? What? *No!*"

"Then your offer is noted and logged. Is there anything else that you feel the need to issue orders about, Admiral?"

Shelby looked as if she was prepared to say something else, and then she sighed. "Carry on, Captain."

Salutes were a rare, antiquated gesture in Starfleet, and yet Mueller snapped one off now. Shelby did not bother to return it, and Mueller didn't wait around to see if she did. Instead she turned on her heel and headed off down the hallway, leaving Shelby behind shaking her head.

iii.

When Mueller returned to her quarters, the last thing she was in the mood for was company. She was even less in a mood for children, creatures for which she had little affinity and even less tolerance. There were children on the *Trident,* yes. That was a reality of extended travel, and there were facilities set up to attend to them. One of the few things she was grateful for was that none of the ship's children had wound up being injured during the Brethren's assault. As with all starships, the *Trident* had a secure station, virtually impenetrable, into which all children were ushered in the event of an invasion. The children had been dispatched there during the Brethren attack and remained secured there, behind walls of solid rodinium, until the threat had passed. Even in that action, though, there had been casualties along the way.

So although Mueller understood the place of children in the grand scheme of things, and was relieved that emergency procedures had managed to protect the lives of *Trident*'s youngest charges, it wasn't as if she was especially enamored of them.

Which was why she moaned when she arrived at her quarters and discovered standing outside it Robin Lefler, her child—the infant half-breed Cwansi—cradled in her arms. Before Robin could speak, Mueller said, "Please tell me that you're just resting here for a moment before proceeding on your way."

"Actually, I was hoping you could spend a few minutes to talk to me, XO—sorry, Captain. Old habits," she said, by way of apologizing for addressing Mueller by her former rank. "Anyway, if this is a bad time . . ."

"It is." Then she paused and admitted, "However, I don't foresee a better time coming up in the immediate future, so . . ." She entered her quarters and gestured for Lefler to follow her. Cwansi was sleeping contentedly, blissfully unaware and uncaring of his surroundings. On some level, Mueller envied him. She gestured toward a chair. "Have a seat and tell me what's on your mind."

Robin did so, easing herself in so as not to jostle the sleeping infant. She looked from Mueller to the baby and then said, "If it isn't too personal a question . . . do you ever look at Cwansi and think about how, if the situation had been different, this could have been you?"

Mueller literally had no idea what she was talking about at first. Then she processed it and came as close to laughing as she ever did. "You're asking, because of the fact that I had a very short-lived affair with Si Cwan before he became your late husband, do I ever dwell on the notion that I could have been the mother of his child?"

"That's what I was wondering, y—"

"No. Not for an instant. Not for a microsecond. I have no desire to be a mother. If I spawned, then like some members of the animal kingdom, I would likely devour my young. And if that was what you wanted to know, then I'm pleased to have been of help to you, and you can go on your way—"

"No, that's not—" She shook her head. "That's not what I wanted to talk to you about . . ."

"Then I suggest you get to the point."

"Are you in a hurry? I mean, the *Trident* is undergoing repairs. You're not going anywhere aaaaand okay, I'll get to the point," she said hurriedly when she saw Mueller's less than patient expression. "Look . . . Captain . . . at the moment I'm sort of homeless. I mean, I can't return to New Thallon because of the political situation there. They see Cwansi as a threat; I can't protect him. Admiral Shelby has invited me to remain here on Bravo Station indefinitely, but I've looked into the options that are available here and, well, there's not much for me. Nothing that truly engages me. And besides, I've spent my entire adult life on a starship. Being in one place . . . it's just not for me."

"Admiral Shelby doesn't seem to have much problem with it, and she was my predecessor as the captain of the *Trident.*"

"Admiral Shelby *says* she doesn't have a problem with it. Frankly, I think she's kidding herself, but that's another conversation. Anyway," she continued, "the point is that—"

"You're looking for a post on the *Trident*?"

Slowly she nodded. "That's pretty much right."

"I'd say that's entirely right, but there's a major problem with that, and I'm fairly sure you know what that is."

"That I'm not a member of Starfleet."

Mueller nodded. "That would seem to put an end to the discussion right there. Now if you'll excuse m—"

"Kat, please," and when she saw that Mueller looked slightly taken aback by the familiarity, she shrugged and said, "If I'm not in Starfleet, I don't see the need to stick to rank. Besides, we go back, Kat. Way back, to the old days on the *Excalibur*."

"Where we hardly saw each other because I was on the night shift and you were on dayside, so what the hell are you talking about?"

"I'm talking about . . ." She sighed. "I don't know what I'm talking about. I've nothing to offer you, nothing to strong-arm you with. But the simple fact is that I'm going to rot here, Kat. I just . . . I'll rot here. Even if I find something to occupy myself, my soul is just going to shrivel and die without the deck of a starship beneath my feet, and what kind of mother am I going to be then?"

"So this is about your son, then?"

"No, it's about me. I'm selfish enough to admit it."

"Then why not appeal to Calhoun?"

"First of all, he's not here and you are. Second, he's already taken enough chances on my behalf and I don't want to keep going back to him. And third . . ." She seemed reluctant to say it.

"Does it have anything to do with the fact that your mother is the computer core of the ship?"

Robin's shoulders slumped. "It has everything

to do with that, actually. I mean, an overattentive mother can be suffocating under the most normal of circumstances. The whole business with my mother is anything but that. I mean, a lot of mothers only think they're God, but when it comes to the *Excalibur*, she pretty much is. I just need some distance, some—"

"Space?"

"Yes," and her mouth twitched. "Space is exactly what I need, and lots of it."

"You're in a space station. You have plenty."

"It's not the same thing, Kat, and we both know it. Look," she sighed, "you don't owe me anything—"

"I'm pleased we both recognize that."

"But you're the only one I can turn to. I can't just ask random Starfleet captains who come passing through here if I can hitch a ride on their ships. There's you and there's the *Excal*, and that's pretty much it. And I've already explained why I can't turn to Calhoun. So that leaves you, and without you, there's nobody. So I just . . . I figured it couldn't hurt to try. So I tried."

Mueller simply stared at her, her inscrutability as much in place as ever.

Cwansi started to stir. He made some soft burbling noises, and Lefler immediately began to pat him on the back. The infant twisted around in her arms and his luminous gaze fastened on Mueller for a moment. He seemed to find her deeply fascinating.

Mueller met his gaze and, aside from scowling slightly, did not react.

Upon receiving no particular response from Mueller, Cwansi turned his attention back to his mother. His tiny fist thumped repeatedly on her breast.

"I need to go take care of, uhm . . . he's hungry," said Robin. "And I guess I shouldn't be taking up any more of your time. Thank you for hearing me out."

She rose from her chair and headed for the door. Just before she could reach it, though, Mueller said, "Children."

Robin turned back to her, looking confused. "I'm sorry?"

"I assume that children are of interest to you, what with you having one of your own."

"Well, yes, sure, but I don't—?"

"We have children on board the *Trident*."

"Okay," said Robin, still not entirely sure where Mueller was going with this.

Mueller scratched the underside of her chin for a moment and then said, "Look: As noted, you're not part of Starfleet. So even if I wanted to install you at ops, I couldn't. Besides which, I *don't* want to install you at ops because we already have a perfectly good, if somewhat eccentric, man there."

"Romeo Takahashi."

"Yes. I don't see Hash willingly stepping aside for you."

"I have other skills. I'm not just limited to knowledge of ops. I started out in engineering. I have a great deal of familiarity with exobiology. I minored in comm studies at the Academy, and I'm fluent in every standardized means of communication going back to Morse code."

"I don't know what that is but I doubt it's going to come up in day-to-day operations."

"Then I can do subsystems repairs. I can keep shuttle-craft tuned. Please don't make me beg. It's not that I won't, but my knees have been bothering me lately so it's harder to get down on them . . ."

"Robin," said Mueller firmly, "despite your many talents, it's all moot because—"

"I'm not in Starfleet, yes, I get it. But I'd be perfectly willing to take a civilian job if . . ." Then her voice trailed off as she put together the pieces of what Mueller had been saying.

Seeing it in Robin's face, Mueller nodded approvingly. "Good. You finally caught up with what I thought of five minutes ago."

"You have something in mind having to do with children."

"Exactly. The *Trident,* like most other starships, has child care facilities, staffed of course by someone to watch over the children of crewmen and officers. Truthfully, as far as experience goes, you're insanely overqualified. But it gets you on the ship and your not being in Starfleet isn't an issue."

"What about the person who currently holds the job?"

"She was killed getting her charges to safety during the recent attack by the Brethren."

"Oh," said Robin very softly. Cwansi stopped

squirming in his mother's grasp, as if out of respect to the memory of a woman who had died in a noble cause involving children.

"When danger presents itself to a starship," said Mueller, "it doesn't tend to show respect for age or lack thereof. This is not a simple babysitting job. There can, and do, come times when their lives are dependent upon you. It's a serious responsibility that requires a serious individual. Plus, of course, you won't have to turn your own child over to a stranger to have him attended to."

"There is that."

"If you want time to think it over—"

"I don't need it," Robin said immediately. "I'd be honored to do the job, and gratified that you would give it to me."

"Who said I'm giving it to you?"

Robin's face fell. "What?"

"There's a lengthy interview procedure, a series of tests, physical exams. The entire process could take as much as eight weeks, and there's no guarantee that you'll get the position. There are at least twenty-seven people being considered ahead of you."

Robin was utterly crestfallen. "Really?"

"No, not really. The position is yours. Welcome to the *Trident*." She chucked a thumb. "Now get the hell out of my quarters."

Recovering her breath, Robin managed to stammer out a fast "thank you" and hasten out the door with her son. Mueller watched them go, and the last thing she saw was Cwansi's gaze upon her. She knew she was imagining it, but he looked almost appreciative, as if grateful that Mueller had extended this lifeline to his mother. Then the doors slid closed, blocking them from her view.

"He has his father's eyes," she muttered.

U.S.S. *Excalibur* Computer Core

A Few Days After Mueller's Meeting with Lefler

She is operating the systems of the Excalibur *with a speed and efficiency that no human could possibly manage. On occasion she will create a representation of herself to sit at ops, out of a deep longing to interact with people. She still has not lost that desire. On those occasions, she will chat with Tania Tobias, the conn officer, who seems a decent enough sort, if a little off. Or she will speak with Mackenzie Calhoun, who will do everything he can to conduct himself in a manner consistent with their previous interactions. He will try to act as if nothing has changed, even though they both know that is not the case. Not that one could determine it from his pulse or respiration, which remain steady. She cannot help but wonder how he manages to accomplish that. Is it a Xenexian trait? Is it something unique to Calhoun? She dare not ask him, but she determines that someday she will find out.*

She keeps the air of easy familiarity with the others because it both suits her and pleases her to do so. She does not want the others to share Calhoun's concerns about her, or at least the ones that he has given voice to. Morgan simply wants to be liked and appreciated for what she is. In that regard, she is no different from any other living being.

It bothers her that Calhoun does not seem to see it that way. She is hoping, however, that he will come around.

She is convinced that all that is required for that to happen is time. Fortunately enough, time is something that she has in abundance.

That particularly seems to be the case when she is hovering in contemplative mode deep within the ship's computer core. She has other aspects of her personality in play throughout the ship besides the ops station. She is in the holodeck, finding amusement in the latest fantasies-given-reality that the ship's crew have concocted. She is in the sickbay monitoring the patients; she is in the engineering systems keeping a careful eye on the matter/antimatter mix. She notices a glitch in the replicators that's going to make the meat loaf taste like turkey and performs an adjustment before anyone's palate can be confused. She makes a slight adjustment in the transporter matrix that, if left unattended for two years, could eventually lead to someone materializing with their eyes in their forehead.

There is so much she has to offer the ship and all the people within it, so many ways—both large and small—that she can make her presence felt. Yet there are times when she is sure that her vast contributions and capabilities for so much more are not truly appreciated.

That, too, will take time.

And yet, for all that she enjoys the interactions with the crew of the vessel, only in the heart of the ship's core does she truly find peace. For it is there that her true essence resides, *untouched and unsullied by any on the outside. My heart is a vast fortress, and cannot be reached by anyone. That is the comforting thought that Morgan keeps deep and close to her.*

Oh, they have tried to purge her before. She knows that. They have tried to reboot her, to run various diagnostics to "get to the bottom" of the personality that resides deep within her. Tried and failed, of course. They do not truly comprehend who and what she is. They cannot grasp that she is a brand-new life form living right there, right within the heart of the Excalibur. *There is a certain amusement value in that. Not irony, exactly, not in the classic sense. If anything, it's a bit sad that part of their mandate from Starfleet is to seek out new life. Here is new life living side by side with them, and some of them are afraid. She knows they are. Why cannot everyone simply accept her for what she is?*

Here, in the depths of her solitude, she will be able to contemplate all sides of the question within milliseconds, and even then she will not be able to fathom the answer. It is deeply rooted in the insecurities inherent in being human. These are concerns that she has left behind her, and she does not miss them a bit. Perhaps the Vulcans are on the right track after all.

And as she contemplates all of this and a few billion bits of information more, something lances into her consciousness with the accuracy and precision of an arrow.

It is a single, streaming impulse, and it is being beamed directly into her communications subroutines. No one would be able to pick it up, not even Zak Kebron monitoring subspace communications. He is looking for normal messages, which consist of thousands upon thousands of bits of informa-

tion rather than the one impulse that is being pumped into her at a steady, regular rate.

There is only one possible reason such a thing could be happening.

Someone is trying to get her attention.

Well, whoever it is, they have certainly managed to accomplish it. So now the only thing that remains is to determine who it is, and why, and what Morgan is going to do to retaliate.

It takes her barely nanoseconds to trace the impulse to its source. It is no great trick at all, because the originator of the impulse is making no effort to hide. That makes perfect sense. If someone is trying to get her attention, what point would there be in trying to remain hidden? That would just be counterproductive.

With the realization of who is trying to get her notice, Morgan decides that the simplest way to deal with the situation is to give that individual exactly what was sought: her undivided attention.

That might be a far more dangerous accomplishment than the sender of the impulse had anticipated.

With the thought comes the deed, and Morgan Primus sends the merest fraction of her essence—which in and of itself would still be powerful enough to bring an entire planetary system crashing down around itself—back along the impulse channel and into the source with the intention of facing the person who had sent it.

She accomplishes that goal, and the conversation with the individual seeking her attention does not go remotely the way she is expecting.

Starfleet Headquarters

Nanoseconds Later

Admiral Nechayev had left explicit orders with her aide that she was not to be disturbed under any circumstances. He had appeared mildly puzzled as to the instructions. But his job was to obey, not to question, and he did his job perfectly. Nechayev then put herself behind her desk, tilting back in her chair and placing her feet upon it, projecting the most relaxed manner that she could. It was important to convey, in every manner available to her, that this was not a meeting intended to be confrontational in any way. Certainly body language was a key component in that.

She didn't think she was going to have to wait long, and in that respect she was absolutely right.

The air in front of her began to shimmer in a manner that was not dissimilar to a transporter beam. Most senior Starfleet personnel now had holotechnology installed, since holo-meetings were rapidly replacing the boring old process of staring at someone on a flat monitor screen. Indeed, Nechayev wondered why it had taken this long to accomplish that. Of course, the incoming individual was capable of utilizing the technology in manners far beyond what others could pull off. Most people who engaged in holo-conferencing had avatars to represent them. Morgan Primus inhabited hers as only a computer entity could.

Seconds later, she had fully materialized in front of Nechayev. She had a look of both mild irritation and curiosity, as if affronted that Nechayev had chosen to engage her attention in such an intrusive manner, but simultaneously wondering what it was that could have prompted her to do so.

"Hello, Morgan," said Nechayev, and then added solicitously, "Do you mind if I call you Morgan?"

"If it pleases you to do so," Morgan replied carefully.

"Do you know who I am?"

"I know who you are. I know who your aide is. I know who your direct superiors are, your immediate underlings, and the name of every person in every room of this building," Morgan said. "I think you will find, Admiral, that there is very little in this entire galaxy that I don't know."

"Do you know why I summoned you here?"

"You didn't summon me," Morgan said, an edge to her voice. "No one 'summons' me. You caught my attention in such a way that I felt prompted to investigate."

"Phrase it however you wish," said Nechayev with a languid wave of her hand, as if the entire conversation was already of little interest to her. "The point remains: Do you know why you're here?"

"I have my suspicions," said Morgan guardedly.

"I'd be interested to hear them."

"Very well." She squared her shoulders, remaining where she was. "The last time I visited Starfleet headquarters, I had a bit of a tête-à-tête with Admiral Jellico regarding my daughter. I made some comments that he may well have taken to be threats."

"Were they?"

"I prefer to think of them as warnings."

"Warnings in the same way that a shot fired off the port bow is a warning?"

"Something along those lines." Morgan scowled. "Your data file indicates that you don't have any children, Admiral, nor even a spouse."

"I've always been married to Starfleet."

"Whatever," she said dismissively. "The point is, if you don't have any children, then you cannot possibly know the emotions that are stirred within a protective mother, especially when it seems that the entirety of such a powerful organization as Starfleet is aligning against her."

"I can imagine that they would be quite intense."

"You seem a bit amused, and I don't consider this remotely funny."

"If I seem amused, Morgan, it's not because I'm not taking you seriously. I'm amused because you're quite possibly the most brilliant entity in existence, and you don't have the slightest clue why you're here. It has nothing to do with your daughter."

"It doesn't?"

"Not a damned thing, no."

Nechayev wasn't sure, but it seemed to her that Morgan looked slightly crestfallen. "Shall I tell you why I wanted to see you?"

Morgan made no attempt to hide her irritation. "Unless you think that wasting my time for a prolonged period is somehow worthwhile."

"That depends: Do you think saving your life is a waste of your time?"

"That's ridiculous. First of all, my 'life,' such as it is, is beyond your comprehension. Second, no one could possibly threaten it."

"Really." Nechayev steepled her fingers. "Not even Mackenzie Calhoun?"

"Calhoun?" She snorted. "Mac might make noises about being uncomfortable with the amount of influence I have over the ship, but that's to be expected."

"Is it?"

"Of course." For the first time, Morgan began to move, taking a leisurely stroll around the office. "He's been in charge of one thing or another going all the way back to his childhood when he led his people in revolt against oppressors. So it's natural that he's going to have some . . . well, some *issues* when it comes to matters of control. But there are no actions he could take against me. He would be insane even to try, and if there's one thing Mac is not, it's insane."

"He may not be insane, but he is most definitely planning actions against you. That much I know."

Morgan laughed, as if the entire notion wasn't worth consideration. "That's absurd."

"It's not. He's working toward finding a way to eliminate you from the *Excalibur* once and for all. So tell me honestly, Morgan: Once Mackenzie Calhoun puts his mind to something—based upon your knowledge of him—what are the chances that he's simply going to back off from it, as opposed to finding a way to accomplish his goal?"

Morgan looked as if she was ready to say something, but then her mouth clicked shut without reply.

The fact that she was taking the admiral's words seriously were enough to buoy Nechayev's spirits. "I know what you're thinking," she began.

"I can process billions of bits of information in an instant," Morgan retorted. "Don't you even *begin* to believe that you know what I'm thinking at any moment."

Nechayev allowed that bit of bravado to pass uncommented upon. "You're thinking, 'Why is she telling me this? What possible reason could she have for taking the extraordinary means of drawing me to this place at this time, for the purpose of telling me that Mackenzie Calhoun is conspiring against me?'" She waited in silence for Morgan to contradict her, knowing that the contradiction would never come.

It, in fact, did not.

Embracing that small but important victory, a smiling Nechayev sauntered toward the scowling Morgan. "Morgan," she began, "I am many things, and have been accused of even more things. But the one thing that no one has *ever* accused me of—although you came perilously close just now, I will admit—is being stupid. I am, in fact, extremely perceptive. You're talking to the woman who was able to see the potential in Mackenzie Calhoun at a time when he was considered utterly incorrigible, a waste of the time and effort that Starfleet put into training him."

"Good for you," said Morgan, but there seemed to be considerably less defiance and arrogance in her voice than there had been even a minute earlier.

Nechayev took this as a good sign.

"Once upon a time," the admiral continued, "I would have been called a seer. People would have assumed that I had some mystic ability to see the future. I probably would have been burned alive."

"You still may be. The day's young."

She ignored her. "The truth is that I am simply very skilled at seeing the way things are now, and preparing for the way things are going to be. What it comes down to is this: I've studied the circumstances that brought you into existence, and I certainly know Calhoun's capabilities better than anyone else. And I've considered all the possible outcomes of an extended battle between you and Mac, and am repeatedly forced to the same conclusion: You're going to win in the end."

Morgan studied her. "So you're saying . . . what? That you want to be sure you're on the winning side?"

"I'm saying far more than that. I want to avoid a fight between you and Calhoun altogether. The potential for collateral damage is incalculable. At the *very* least, we're talking about the death of everyone on the *Excalibur*."

"That's ridiculous," she said dismissively. "That would never happen."

"Oh no?" Nechayev's voice was grim. "Let's say that Calhoun mounted an offensive that was on the verge of working, and that it took the combined efforts of everyone on the vessel to accomplish it. Let's say it came down to you and them. What's the simplest answer? What would you do in order to survive?"

"That would never—"

"Denying it isn't an answer. If you felt truly threatened," she pressed relentlessly, "if it was truly you or them, what could you do to stop them?" Morgan didn't respond immediately, and Nechayev prompted her, "We both know. You can say it."

When Morgan spoke, her voice was as flat and mechanical as any computer voice ever was. "I could vent the ship."

"Exactly. Blow out every hatch, vent the air. Blast every living thing on the ship into space and let the vacuum have them. That's not only what you could do, but what you *would* do. And that's the best-case scenario. The worst case is that you lash out at every living being, like an angry god."

"That would never happen," but Morgan didn't sound convincing, even to herself.

"We both know that's not true," Nechayev said. "And at the end of it all, you'll still be standing while the rest of us are floating corpses in the depths of space."

"What do you think I am," Morgan said, bristling, "that I would do such a thing? I'm not a monster."

"I beg to differ. That is *precisely* what you are." Nechayev was implacable. "You're not human. There is nothing like you in existence. You exceed the AI capabilities of such entities as Commander Data, and your potential for destruction is virtually limitless. Doctor Frankenstein in his laboratory could not have crafted something more threatening to all humankind. You *are* a monster, Morgan, and there are only two things left to be determined: just how much of a monster you are, and whether I'm going to ally myself with you or with the angry villagers armed with torches and pitchforks. For my own sake and the sake of countless lives, I'm opting for the former. So the only thing left for you to decide is whether you're going to take advantage of that proposed alliance, or if you're going to exist in a state of denial until everything I've said will happen does, in fact, happen."

Morgan disappeared.

It wasn't what Nechayev had expected. That alone was disturbing to her since, as she prided herself on being able to predict all possibilities, the notion that Morgan would simply vanish without saying another word wasn't something that she had anticipated happening.

Concerned, she turned toward her desk and then gasped as she abruptly found herself nose to nose with a scowling Morgan. She jumped back out of reflex and then composed herself as quickly as she could.

"I've been giving a great deal of thought to what you've said," said Morgan.

"Oh, have you indeed? Because from where I'm standing, you disappeared for five seconds and then popped up behind me to . . . I don't know, scare the hell out of me."

Morgan gave her a pitying look. "I can give something the human equivalent of a lifetime of thought in five seconds. Several lifetimes, in fact."

"All right," said Nechayev, choosing not to press matters. "And what has all that pondering led you to conclude?"

With her hands draped behind her back, Morgan did a slow circle of Nechayev, who found that action disconcerting for no reason she could readily express. "There are things you are not telling me," Morgan said. "I'm certain of that much. You say you're concerned about the security of the Federation, but I think there are other things at play here. The only question is whether those other things are of any relevance to me." Before Nechayev could respond, Morgan continued on the thought. "As of this point, I have to think the answer is no. Let your motivations be your own. If Mac is truly determined to try and get rid of me, then I have larger considerations. More than anything . . . more than *anything*," she added emphasis in order to show how serious she was, "I need to be able to go on in order to protect Robin."

"Your daughter?"

Morgan nodded. "It is a dangerous galaxy out

there, and she is alone in it. She needs me to be available to her as a resource. I've been trying to give her distance. She wants to make her own way, and I respect that. But sooner or later, she is going to need me, and I have to be there for her and for my grandson. Mackenzie Calhoun can be extremely formidable, and even if the odds of his disposing of me are a million to one, there is still that one that cannot be accounted for. So if some additional advantage is being presented to me, then I have to seize it."

"I think you're making a wise decision," said Nechayev diplomatically.

"Oh, good. The opinion of a traitor to her people means a lot to me."

Nechayev didn't respond.

Morgan stopped her circling, which was of some relief to Nechayev. "So," said Morgan, "what's Calhoun's plan?"

"His plan?" Nechayev echoed.

"Yes, his plan." Morgan let her annoyance show. "You're supposed to be helping me. So tell me his plan to destroy me."

Nechayev shifted uncomfortably and cleared her throat. "He hasn't told me everything."

"What *has* he told you?"

"In so many words—?"

"Admiral . . ." Morgan said warningly.

"Nothing," she was finally forced to admit. "He hasn't told me a damned thing."

"Well, *that's* a lot of no help whatsoever."

"He's being cautious. He's not sure who he can trust, and so he's not trusting anyone."

"That can't be the case," Morgan assured her. "Calhoun has many qualities, but a computer genius he is most definitely not. He's going to require allies at some point."

"As soon as I find out—"

"Do you have any reason to assume that he's going to confide in you at some subsequent point, considering he hasn't done so thus far?"

She was loath to admit it, but there really was only one answer to that. "Probably not."

"Then how can you possibly be of any use to me?"

"Because," said Nechayev, "I know people. People who can, in fact, be of great use. It is simply a matter of determining the maximum effectiveness for them. And I have a plan that will suit both our needs."

"Do you?" Morgan sounded unconvinced but nevertheless intrigued.

"I do indeed."

Nechayev then laid it out for her. It was a simple plan, really, as the best plans were, since they allowed for the fewest number of things to go wrong.

Morgan listened to the entire thing, and Nechayev was heartened to see her nodding. When she finished describing the plan, Morgan didn't answer immediately. Instead she considered it for a few more moments. Knowing the speed with which Morgan's mind worked, Nechayev had to think that Morgan was giving it an insanely deep amount of consideration, trying to see the flaws and—with any luck—finding none.

"All right," Morgan said at last. "I'm in."

"Excellent," said Nechayev. "My allies and I thank you."

"I don't give a damn about you or your allies. Just about me and my daughter and grandson. The rest of you can go hang for all I care."

"Be that as it may," said the admiral diplomatically, "it's my opinion that you are going to be a far greater ally to this office than Mackenzie Calhoun ever could be."

"It would certainly be preferable to having me as an enemy," said Morgan and then, with a snap of her fingers that she doubtless tossed in for dramatic flair, Morgan Primus vanished from Admiral Nechayev's office.

Nechayev let out a low sigh, not realizing until that moment that she'd been holding her breath.

This may have been a huge mistake, she thought, but realized there was no turning back. She would just have to live with the consequences of her decisions, presuming that—by the time all of this was done—living was still an option.

Xenex

Now

It would never have happened if M'k'n'zy hadn't been distracted. Never. His ability to perceive danger was simply too well honed to fall victim to something as obvious as a booby trap.

But he was too preoccupied with concerns for both his own people and his crew. Making his way through a path in a mountain region, he realized only belatedly that his inner sense that so reliably warned him of danger was prickling at the nape of his neck. By the time he did so, it was too late. His ankle had hit the trip wire, and the trap was sprung. In his defense, it had been almost microscopically thin. No normal individual would have had any chance at all of spotting it. It was just that M'k'n'zy held himself to a higher standard.

Fortunately for him, he was fast enough to avoid the result even though he had triggered it.

Someone else would have been momentarily frozen with the realization of what he had done, and that would have been his undoing. Not M'k'n'zy, who leaped backward a split instant after having hit the trip wire. There came a rumble from above him and, as he deftly backpedaled out of the way, a massive pile of rocks tumbled down from overhead.

He didn't know what means the Brethren had taken to secure all of it, nor did he particularly care. All that mattered was avoiding it, and that he managed to do with alacrity. The rocks thudded down, bouncing and scattering, and he was able to observe it all from a safe distance. Had he been even a second slower, he would have been at the bottom of the pile. As it was, he watched the stones pile up while displaying no visible reaction. He showed no sense of relief, and there was no agitation in his manner that indicated he was aware just how close he had come to total destruction. For all the change in his demeanor that he presented out-wardly, he might well have simply sidestepped a puddle during a rainstorm.

"You are quite the unflappable opponent, Captain Calhoun."

For the time that he had been back on Xenex, thrust into an insane situation, leading his people against an implacable foe, Mackenzie Calhoun had gone back to thinking of himself as M'k'n'zy of Calhoun. But upon hearing the soft, mocking tone behind him—a tone that was cloaked in an all-too-familiar voice—he was reminded that he was, in fact, Captain Mackenzie Calhoun of Starfleet. M'k'n'zy was the warlord he once was, the relentless foe of would-be oppressors. Mackenzie Calhoun was, to M'k'n'zy's mind, somewhat less formidable.

He knew, however, that others would disagree.

"That is true," Calhoun said evenly. "None have ever managed to flap me."

"And further evidence of that presents itself," said the individual who was standing behind him. The voice was familiar to Calhoun, of course, as was the image of the person who owned it. "Here am I, and by all rights my appearance should be enough to get some sort of rise out of you. Yet there's nothing."

Calhoun sneered at the female who was standing before him. "You show up looking like my wife, and you think that's going to have some sort of impact on me? That maybe I'll be fooled? That I'll cry out, 'Honey, it's you!' and then try and throw my arms around you and be utterly crushed that I've been fooled."

The being that was wearing the appearance of Elizabeth Shelby shrugged. "It sounds rather unlikely when you put it like that."

As she spoke, Calhoun knelt and picked up a piece of rock. He lobbed it straight at her and it passed through her harmlessly. "As I thought," he said. "You still don't have the guts to show up in person."

"What would be the point of that?"

"For one thing, it would give me the option of beating the living hell out of you."

"I don't see where that benefits me particularly."

He shook his head as he stared at her. "It's amazing. I'll give you that. The way you manage to look like her."

"I'm flattered."

"You shouldn't be. Seeing it just makes me want to throttle you for daring to impersonate her. The advantage, though," and he smiled in that wolfish manner he had, "is that it provides me further incentive. If my determination starts to flag, I can focus on the notion that I have to stay alive so that I can find you in person and administer the aforementioned beating."

"You seem rather single-minded."

"You have no idea," said Calhoun grimly. "Trust me, the beating *will* occur. The only variables at this point are when, where, and to what degree. The former two will be left to the vagaries of fate, but the latter is entirely up to you."

"Is it?" "Shelby" did not seem especially concerned over the prospect. "Just out of curiosity, what precisely could I do to forestall or, even better, lessen the severity of the promised beating?"

The harsh sun continued to beat down upon Calhoun. He was annoyed with himself because he was starting to feel the intensity of it, and that had never happened before. He had been away from his home world for too long and had become accustomed to the relatively cushy existence on board starships. *You've lost your edge, Calhoun,* he thought, and then immediately cursed himself for second-guessing. That was not the sort of attitude that was going to benefit anyone, least of all himself.

He realized that he was allowing the silence to extend, and he had to pay attention to what was going on. "You can put an end to this," he said as if it was the most obvious thing in the world. "Because whether you cooperate or not, it *is* going to end. My crew is going to realize what you've done. They're going to come back for me, and once they have, we *will* find you—"

"And the beating will commence? Allow me," said the creature posing as Shelby, raising a finger as if she were testing the direction of the nonexistent wind, "to offer an alternative, and far more likely, scenario. Number one: Your ship doesn't ever discover what's happened. Number two: They do indeed figure it out—unlikely but, for the sake of argument, I'll allow it—except they accomplish this far too late to be of any use to you because the Brethren will have disposed of you. And you need to understand that this is the only aspect of the situation that *you* can have any influence on. Your dying is an inevitability. The only question at issue is, how many of your fellow Xenexians are you going to take with you?"

Calhoun gave no outward indication of the rage seething within him. "Any one of those brave souls is worth a thousand of you."

"I won't argue your mathematics," said "Shelby." "Instead I will simply acknowledge that the Xenexians are fiercely devoted to you and will lay down their lives for you without hesitation. That prompts the question, though, as to what you are willing to do for them. In my opinion, you are unfairly taking advantage of that devotion, leading them on a futile

crusade against an enemy they simply cannot hope
to defeat. The difference between this occasion and
the last time, when you were their beloved warlord,
is that the only stake they have in this matter is you.
Once you're dead, the Brethren withdraw and leave
the Xenexians to this," and she looked around dis-
tastefully, "wasteland that they call home. There's no
territorial battle, no grand clash of faiths. You die; they
leave. So how many of them are going to be slaughtered before your inevitable demise? For that matter,
what sort of man subjects his friends and followers to
such catastrophic punishment?"

His face as unreadable as ever, Calhoun said, "The
sort who is going to beat the hell out of you."

"Shelby" actually chuckled at that. She didn't have
the real Shelby's laugh, and Calhoun took some cold
comfort in that. Then, when she recovered herself,
she said, "You're a circular man, Calhoun. You always
wind up right back where you started. I'm not sure
whether to admire it or pity it. I'll probably settle on
some combination of the two."

Slowly she started to fade out. "End it, Calhoun,"
she advised. "Either take your own life or throw yourself into battle with the Brethren in such a way that
you cannot possibly win. Accept the destiny that you
are facing, and spare countless innocent lives. It's your
choice. I'm done talking to you for now."

With that pronouncement, the image of Shelby
vanished from sight.

During the entire encounter, Calhoun had managed to restrain himself. Now, even after the D'myurj had disappeared, Calhoun remained where he was. Only the mild trembling of his clenched fists gave the slightest hint of what was seething within him.

And when he was sure she was gone—when he was absolutely, positively sure—Mackenzie Calhoun let out an earsplitting, gut-wrenching roar, torn from deep within him that was a combination of fury and humiliation and a frightful admission that, deep down, he knew that the bastard D'myurj was right. And even if (*when, dammit, when!*) he managed to find his tormentor and dispose of him/her, that wasn't going to do a thing to bring back any of the brave Xenexians who had been so cruelly taken before their time.

And for that moment, and only that moment, Mackenzie Calhoun considered doing exactly what the D'myurj had suggested. He could find a high peak and just throw himself off, plummet to the rocks below, and terminate himself in exchange for the lives of the Xenexians who would continue to fight beside him—presuming he could find any who were still breathing at this point—and die on his behalf.

Then the moment passed, and Calhoun had just enough time to wonder who, in the grand scheme of all this, was truly the villain of this piece, before continuing on his path in hopes of hooking up with the straggling remains of his ragtag army.

U.S.S. Excalibur

Sometime Earlier

i.

Calhoun, relaxing in his quarters in the way he typically did—reading military histories—looked up with interest when Zak Kebron conveyed the news to him. The massive Brikar's voice rumbled in its usual manner, seeming to fill the entirety of the room even though he was simply speaking over the intraship communications system. The captain listened, and naturally there was no one in the room to see the surprise on his face.

"Xyon? Are you sure it's Xyon?"

"Everything checks out," Kebron's voice said. *"Ship's registry, plus a sensor scan matches up with our previous readings of him. It's his ship and he's the one inside hailing us, asking for permission to come aboard."*

Calhoun wasn't sure what to make of it. The last time his son had taken his leave of them, it had seemed to be a more or less guaranteed thing that he wasn't going to be seeing his father anytime soon, if ever. Yet now here he was, effectively knocking on the ship's door.

"How the hell did he find out where we are?"

"We're not exactly in stealth mode, Captain," Kebron's voice replied. *"Xyon is a rather ingenious young man. I'm sure it was no great trick."*

"Obviously not." Calhoun drummed his fingers on the desk in a quick staccato, trying to figure out what it was that he was not considering. "He's not here without a reason."

"Nobody does anything without a reason, Captain."

"True enough."

The *Excalibur* was involved in a rather innocuous science survey in the PAS3000 sector. It was, in Calhoun's opinion, exactly what the crew needed after the recent catastrophes the ship had endured. The sequence of events that had been initiated by the late Doctor Selar had been brutal, and something as simple and straightforward as a science survey was a welcome change of pace for the ship. The main job of a starship was exploration, and it was a relief to engage in something as purely exploratory as this.

"Captain—?" Kebron prodded him when Calhoun's silence extended a bit.

"Tell him to park his ship in the shuttlebay and come up to see me."

"Shall I provide him an escort?"

"I think he knows his way around," said Calhoun, "and I'm sure he doesn't present a security risk."

"You're sure? Or you hope?"

Not for the first time, and very likely not for the last, Calhoun waxed nostalgic for the days when

Kebron was little more than a big, surly, monosyllabic pile of rock with arms and legs. His "maturing" into someone who worried incessantly about everyone's feelings was truly starting to get on Calhoun's nerves. He'd have thought that installing Kebron as the ship's counselor would give him an avenue to indulge his empathetic impulses, but apparently it wasn't sufficient.

Kebron was still talking. *"Captain, you have to ask yourself just how much you want to invest Xyon with the trust of which he is deserving, as opposed to what you want to impart in order to assuage your own concerns about him. When one considers Xyon's track record and list of dubious involvements, any dispassionate assessment of his reliability would seem to indicate—"*

"Kebron."

"Yes, Captain?"

"Just let him on the damned ship and stay the hell out of my head."

There was a brief pause. Then simply: *"Yes, sir."*

Calhoun's head slumped back. *"Grozit,"* he said with a sigh.

ii.

Xyon walked with the sort of swagger that only someone who was utterly in control of his own destiny could summon. At least that was how he saw it and, really, wasn't that the only thing that was important?

Various crewmen glanced at him in surprise as he passed them. He didn't blame them. Some of the familiar faces recognized him and doubtless wondered what he was doing there. The unfamiliar ones would have noticed the distinct resemblance he had to the captain. *Those same, ruggedly handsome features, except of course it looks better on me,* he thought.

He had business on the *Excalibur* with his father, certainly, but that wasn't the only thing on his mind.

Xyon didn't want to let Kalinda know that he was coming, or even on the ship. He wanted to have the opportunity to surprise her, and get an honest reaction to his presence. So much had happened between him and the sister of the late Si Cwan that he no longer had any real idea where he stood with her. This, he felt, was his opportunity to find out.

He desperately wanted to share his life with her. Many was the time he had fantasized about her joining him on his vessel. He would show her the galaxy, and even all the things that he had already seen and experienced would seem new to him because he would be seeing them through her eyes. He had convinced himself that he had no future with her, but he hadn't been able to get her out of his mind.

So when the opportunity to return to the *Excalibur* presented itself, it was one that he could not pass up.

"Well, well. It's my son's namesake."

Xyon turned and saw a familiar face. "Burgoyne," he said. "Good to see you."

"You too, Xyon," said Burgoyne 172. The Hermat

extended hir hand and Xyon shook it firmly. "It is, however, a bit unexpected."

"I was given permission—"

"I know that. I'm the first officer. Naturally I'm going to be informed if we have a visitor. Particularly if that visitor is the captain's son."

"It's nice to know you're paying attention. By the way," and his voice became serious, "I'm truly sorry about Selar."

"Selar?" Burgoyne gave him a curious look, as if s/he couldn't quite figure out what Xyon was referring to. "You mean about her death?"

"Well . . . sure. Of course."

Burgoyne shrugged, a casual gesture that left Xyon dumbfounded. "She did what she felt she had to do in order to save our son. She made her choice and I respect that."

"Burgoyne . . ." He couldn't begin to fathom Burgy's attitude. What was he supposed to say? That Selar had died violently after having betrayed the trust of Calhoun and Starfleet because she'd become obsessed with prolonging her son's life? Certainly Burgoyne knew all that. S/he didn't require Xyon to tell hir everything. So was Burgoyne in some sort of strange denial? If so, s/he certainly had bigger problems than anything that Xyon could readily address.

"Yes?" Burgy was simply standing there, waiting for Xyon to continue the question.

"Nothing," Xyon said. "It's nothing. Actually, could you tell me where Kalinda might be? I'm not sure where her quarters are these days. She's still on the ship, right?"

"Yeeesss," said Burgoyne, but the drawn-out way in which s/he said it indicated there was something s/he wasn't letting on about. "Yes, she is. But, uhm . . ."

"But what?"

Burgoyne appeared to be considering something, and then said, "Typically she's in Ten-Forward around this time."

"Ten-Forward. Got it. Thanks, Burgy."

"I think it might be best, though, if—"

Xyon wasn't listening. Instead, seconds later, he was on the turbolift and heading straight over to Ten-Forward. He didn't know what Burgoyne was going on about and, at that moment, didn't actually care all that much. There was clearly something screwy transpiring in Burgoyne's head, and whatever it was, it wasn't any of Xyon's concern or problem.

As he approached Ten-Forward, his ears perked up. He heard delighted laughter, and knew instantly that it was Kalinda's voice. That surprised him somewhat. Kally had many intriguing attributes, but laughing was not something she typically did. She was one of the most serious young women that he had ever encountered, which he supposed made sense since she was capable of seeing the dead. It sometimes seemed that she was holding on to her sanity with both hands and a vise-like grip. So when Xyon heard her clearly enjoying herself, it buoyed his heart. Obviously her time on the *Excalibur* had done her some good. He didn't pause long enough to wonder whether the time away from him was likewise contributory to her good spirits.

Like his father, Xyon could move in such a way that he did nothing to draw attention to himself. You would know he was present if you looked right at him, but otherwise he could minimize his movements so that he would remain unnoticed until such time as he decided to pull focus toward him. This was the course he opted for now, sidling into Ten-Forward and being noticed by no one present. The crewmen continued to drink and laugh and interact and, if they'd been asked, every single person present would have sworn that the captain's son had never set foot in Ten-Forward that evening.

Xyon, however, saw them. To be specific, he saw two of them, and the rest of the people in the place faded to irrelevance.

There was Kalinda, seated at a table with Tania Tobias, the ship's conn officer. Tania had her mouth up near Kalinda's ear, and she was whispering something to her. Kalinda was responding with peals of laughter, and the happiness in her face made her seem incandescent.

The closeness of Tania's face, her body, all of it bespoke an intimacy that was far beyond anything appropriate to two friends being out for the evening and enjoying each other's presence.

Then Kalinda leaned forward and pressed her lips against Tania's.

That was the moment that Xyon pulled out his disruptor, took aim, and blew Tania's head off.

At least, in his own mind, he did.

He might well have done so, if he'd had the opportunity to follow his gut impulse. He didn't think of himself as someone given to rages, and certainly not the type that could rack up a body count. Xyon abruptly remembered reading somewhere that the vast majority of murders were crimes of passion, but he never thought such a thing would have a direct application. *What woman,* he remembered thinking, *would ever be worth killing for? What woman couldn't be casually replaced by another one at some point down the road, or perhaps even with a good hologram in the interim?*

The answer, one that he was not welcoming, was abruptly being presented to him.

Whether he would actually have done it, whether he would have followed through on the impulse and the mental image that was compelling him to turn Tania's head into an unrecognizable, pulped mass, he would never actually know. A steely grip clamped onto his right wrist even as it started to move toward the disruptor, and he was abruptly twisted around in place to find himself staring into an older version of his own face.

Calhoun didn't say a word. Instead, while Xyon was still off balance, Calhoun backstepped quickly, never easing up on his grip. Xyon had no choice but to follow, almost stumbling over his own feet as he did so. It all happened so quickly that no one in Ten-Forward was aware of the altercation.

In the corridor, as the doors slid shut behind them, Calhoun continued to keep Xyon's arm immobilized. Xyon, for his part, made no effort to pull away. He felt it would be undignified, as if he were a frustrated infant who was balking against his daddy punishing him. He also knew it would be pointless: Calhoun was simply too strong.

In a low, tight voice, Calhoun said, "I *just* got done telling Kebron you didn't need a security escort. It could damage my standing with my crew if they think there's ever a possibility that I could be wrong about something. Am I wrong in this case?"

Xyon never lowered his gaze even as his father's purple eyes seemed to bore right through his head. "No," he said tightly. "You're not wrong."

"So I won't regret letting go of your arm, then?"

"Only one way to find out."

It was a small gesture of defiance, but all that Xyon could find within himself to muster at that moment.

Calhoun maintained his grip for a moment longer, just to drive home the point, and then he released it. Xyon discovered that his wrist felt numb, but decided he wouldn't give his father the satisfaction of seeing him shake it out in order to restore the circulation.

"Burgy told me the two of you happened to meet up and informed me where you were going. I wasn't quite sure how you were going to react when you saw the two of them together." He gestured for Xyon to walk in front of him, and Xyon did so, both of them heading in the general direction of Calhoun's cabin.

"You knew about this? About Kalinda and that . . . person?"

"It's a small ship, Xyon. Pretty hard to keep certain behaviors secret."

"I wouldn't really have attacked—"

"That's what you say now. It doesn't take all that much, though, for 'I wouldn't really have done it' to become, 'I really shouldn't have done it.' You know what I mean?"

Xyon did not deign to answer.

iii.

Once they were safely within the confines of Calhoun's quarters, Calhoun made it clear that he was not done. "If you ever," he said, "present a threat to anyone on my ship again, you will be treated as a presumed hostile and dealt with accordingly the next time you get in range. Do you understand?"

"Yes, *Captain,* I understand," he said tersely. "Again, it was just a momentary impulse. I wouldn't have given in to it."

"You need to learn self-control, Xyon."

"Pardon me, *Captain,*" and he once again sneered the word, "but the time to lecture me was when I was growing up and you were busy instilling your fatherly values in me. Not after the fact because you weren't there all those years."

"Are we *really* going to rehash this?" asked Calhoun, his arms folded.

Xyon was about to snap out an angry response, but then he thought better of it. With a sigh he sagged into the nearest chair. "I'm sorry. I mean it; I really am. It just . . . it caught me off guard, is all. I had all these ideas in my head of what I was going to say to Kalinda, and all these scenarios of how it was all going to go."

"And what you saw didn't match up with any of them."

"That's putting it mildly."

"Well, I can understand how it may have been . . ." He sought the right word, and the closest he could come up with was ". . . disconcerting."

"Yeah, that was me. Disconcerted." He rubbed the bridge of his nose and sighed. "I just . . . I thought we had something together, you know?"

"You *did* have something. I saw how she looked at you, and you at her."

"And now it's gone? Just like that?"

Calhoun shrugged. "It happens, Xyon. You were what she needed at the time. And now, at this time, she needs something else."

"And it's . . . what's her name . . . ?"

"Tania Tobias."

"What she needs is Tania Tobias? Really?"

"Apparently so."

"Okay, well," and Xyon, sighing, forced a weary smile, "I guess there's plenty of stars in the sky, huh."

"You'll find someone, Xyon."

"That was the absolute worst thing you could have said."

"As you'd be the first to remind me, I'm not exactly the most expert when it comes to fatherly interpersonal relationships."

"Which reminds me: How's your adopted son, Moke?"

"Barely talking to me."

"So maybe it wouldn't have made a difference if you'd been there for me."

Calhoun walked across the room to a cabinet, from which he withdrew a decanter and two glasses. "Perhaps it would have," Calhoun said. "It could well have made things worse."

"I should be grateful, then."

"Perhaps you should be." Calhoun filled up the two glasses with a blue liquid and handed one to Xyon, never questioning whether Xyon would want it.

Xyon sipped from it and the edges of his eyes crinkled, his tongue stinging from the taste. "Romulan ale? Can't they court-martial you for having this?"

"Of all the things I've done for which they could court-martial me, I'd have to think this would be the most innocuous."

"I suppose so. Oh: What's up with Burgoyne?"

"Up?"

"S/he seemed oddly restrained, to put it mildly, regarding what happened with Selar."

"Oh. That." Calhoun made no effort to hide the

fact that he was displeased with that state of affairs. "That was Selar's handiwork."

Xyon stared at him blankly and shook his head. "I'm not following—"

"One of the last things she did before she died was to use a Vulcan mind technique to—oh, how best to put it—numb the part of Burgy's brain that had any feelings for her."

"You mean she emotionally lobotomized hir?" Xyon was appalled by the very notion. "How could she do that?"

"There were a lot of things that Selar left us wondering what she could do. In the end, the only conclusion we're left to draw is that all her actions were driven by what she felt were the most logical choices she could make. She was a hard woman to understand."

"I'm starting to think I don't understand any of them."

Calhoun simply grunted in acknowledgment. He took a sip of the Romulan ale, rolled the contents around in his cheeks, and then swallowed. "All right, so . . . I'm not naïve enough to think that you just happened to swing by here in order to catch up on old times. Obviously there's something you need to tell me. If you want to sit here drinking my ale for an indefinite period, I have no problem with that. But if there's something of more immediate concern . . ."

"There is, actually. Something I felt you needed to know about."

"And which couldn't have simply been transmitted via subspace?"

"I avoid subspace chatter when I can help it," said Xyon. "Too many ears listening, too many chances for messages to go astray. I prefer talking to people face-to-face if it's at all possible."

"All right, then," said Calhoun. "Here we are, face-to-face. What's going on?"

"There's trouble brewing back home."

Calhoun's face darkened upon hearing this. He realized it was interesting, in a distant sort of way, that when Xyon said "back home" he did not for one minute think of Earth or any other world upon which he had resided for any length. When it came to use of the term "home," only one place qualified. "What's happening on Xenex?" he asked.

"Scattered reports of armored soldiers setting up encampments."

"In populated areas?"

Xyon shook his head. "So far, no. Just in outlying areas. Nor have there been any attacks; just sightings. Spying parties by various concerned tribal heads haven't revealed much of anything useful. Mostly the soldiers just stand around; they don't even seem to be interacting with each other."

"Weapons?"

"None that anyone is seeing."

"Then how do they know they're soldiers as opposed to, say, surveying teams wearing environmental suits?"

"They're Xenexians, Father. Do you seriously think there's anyone more qualified to recognize soldiers when they see them?"

Calhoun couldn't really dispute that. "Your information on this is solid?"

"I still have a contact or two there who keep me apprised about things that are going on. I haven't forgotten my roots."

"Do I sense a rebuke in there somewhere?" said Calhoun.

"Maybe a slight one."

"And perhaps," Calhoun admitted, "one that has a shred of truth to it." He placed the now empty glass down on the cabinet. "Do you know anything more about the soldiers? What they look like, or particular markings on their armor . . . ?"

"Just what I've told you."

"Okay, then. I want to thank you for bringing this to my attention. I'll take care of it."

"You mean you're going to inform Starfleet?"

"I mean I'm going to handle this personally." He looked with hopeful interest at his son. "You want to come along?"

"I would if I could," said Xyon, "but I have a job waiting for me. Besides, I doubt that there's much of anything I could bring to this party that you don't already have covered."

"Attempts at modesty ill befit you, Xyon."

"Not modesty. Just being realistic. You've got this massive ship and I've got the *Lyla*. What's the likelihood that you're going to require my intervention because the *Excalibur* can't deal with whatever you find?"

"Fairly minimal," Calhoun had to allow. "Still . . ."

"Still what?"

"Well, it may sound ridiculous, but I rather like having you around."

"You need to get over that feeling, old man," he said, but there was no heat to the words.

"I couldn't agree more," said Calhoun with the slightest of chuckles.

They stood there for a moment, regarding each other with some awkwardness, and then Calhoun said, "Do we hug?"

"*Grozit,* I certainly hope not," said Xyon.

"Yes, exactly my thoughts as well. Come," and he gestured toward the door, "I'll walk you back to your ship. Show you some of the improvements we've made on the *Excal.*"

"That's very generous. A guided tour by the ship's captain, who you'd ordinarily think would have better things to do with his time. This couldn't possibly stem from your concern that I'm going to go back to the Ten-Forward and start shooting, could it?"

"I know you would never do that."

"And how exactly do you know that?"

Calhoun, who had been sitting, now rose and reached into the cushion next to him. He held up a familiar weapon. "Because I took your disruptor."

Xyon's eyes widened and he reached into the folds of his jacket. His disruptor was gone.

"Son of a bitch," he said with a growl.

"After you, son," said Calhoun with a cheerful demeanor that could not help but annoy the living hell out of Xyon.

iv.

"And there he was, just standing there, the bastard, with my disruptor in his hand and a smug expression on his face."

Xyon had returned to his vessel and was now prepping her for departure from the landing bay. The massive doors that covered the bay were sliding open and the depths of space were visible and calling to him. At that moment, he was venting his frustration to Lyla, the holographic entity that served as the ship's computer mind. Incarnated as a gorgeous blonde, she listened with endless patience and a carefully designed look of sympathy as Xyon gave vent to the circumstances of his wounded ego.

"I'm so sorry to hear that, Xyon," she said. "It must have hurt terribly to be outwitted in that manner."

"I wasn't outwitted, Lyla! He just . . . he . . ." He sighed. "Yeah, okay, he outwitted me. Are you happy?"

"Only when you are, Xyon."

"You always know just what to say, Lyla."

"That's true. And you wouldn't have it any other way."

"You're right about that. So . . . fire up the lift-off sequence. Let's put this ship behind us."

"Did you have the opportunity to say good-bye to Kalinda?"

He hesitated. There was no reason he couldn't speak his mind to Lyla. She was utterly nonjudgmental, and for that matter, if he regretted saying something to her, he could always order her to forget it.

"I think to say good-bye to somebody . . . you have to be with them to begin with. Kalinda and I may have gone through a lot together, but with everything going on in my life, and all the problems rooting around in her head . . . I don't think we were ever *with* each other. You know what I mean?"

"No," said Lyla. She sounded ever so slightly apologetic.

He sighed heavily. "Let's just say that Kally and I already had our good-byes and leave it at that, okay?"

"Okay, Xyon. Ship now ready for departure. Bay doors fully opened."

"Good. Get us the hell out of here."

"As you wish. Oh . . . did you provide Captain Calhoun with the information you were paid to give him?"

"Yeah. Everything our employer asked us to tell him. And he reacted exactly the way that I suspected he would. He's taking charge of it himself and riding to the rescue to help his fellow Xenexians."

"Do you know why our employer wanted Captain

Calhoun to be apprised of the situation on Xenex? For that matter, do you know our employer's identity?"

Being an artificial intelligence, Lyla wasn't really capable of such things as wounded pride. Yet she had seemed mildly annoyed when she had been unable to penetrate the scrambling technology that had blocked them from seeing their employer's face, or the point of origin of the transmissions they had received, or otherwise learn the true identity of their employer in any way.

"No, I don't know who it is, and frankly, I couldn't care less," said Xyon. "I was given a fair price for my services, and the transfer into my credit account was made in a timely fashion. Besides, it's not as if there's any real love lost between my father and me. I was hired to feed him that information about Xenex. I did what I was paid to do. As far as I'm concerned, that's the end of the story. From here on out, it's my father's problem."

"Don't you care what might happen to him?"

Xyon considered all the issues he'd had with his father over the years. He also considered how, as recently as a few minutes ago, his father had spoken of how much he liked having him around. Calhoun had reached out to him, and he had effectively batted away the efforts to set aside their differences and let go of his boundless anger.

"No," said Xyon tersely.

"Okay," Lyla said.

Moments later the small smuggling vessel had

lifted off and was hurtling away from the *Excalibur* as fast as it could go. When the ship was far enough distant, the *Lyla* leaped into warp space and left the *Excalibur* far behind.

As space bent and twisted around his ship, Xyon watched the instruments with a sort of gloomy resignation. Lyla stepped in behind him and rested a hand on his shoulder.

"Xyon? Would you like me to make myself look like Kalinda and we can have sex?"

He looked up at her wanly and then sighed. "Actually . . . yes. I'd like that very much."

"As you wish," she said, and a second later had transformed herself into an exact replica of Kalinda.

Xyon pulled her toward him and brought his lips cruelly down on hers.

The Daystrom Institute

Four Days After the Meeting on Tendara Colony

The Doctor could scarcely believe his eyes.

"I can scarcely believe my eyes," he said, since it was not his wont to provide any manner of screen between his thoughts and his spoken sentiments.

"Seems to me that you have no choice," said Seven, "since we are most definitely here." She nodded toward his quarters with a tilt of her chin. "Do you mind if we enter?"

"No, not at all! You are certainly welcome. I don't have much in the way of company here." With what doubtless seemed like a good deal of suaveness on his part, he stepped away from the door to his quarters and gestured widely, as if he were a ringmaster addressing a vast array of people. "*Entrez, s'il vous plaît.*"

Correctly intuiting that the Doctor had asked them to come in, using the language she believed to be French, she entered the quarters with Soleta directly behind her.

There was almost nothing in the quarters. There was a bed in the adjoining room that was visible through the connecting doorway, and a couch in the living room, to which the Doctor was now gesturing for them to sit.

"I love what you . . . haven't done with the place," said Seven.

"Thank you."

Soleta was staring at the Doctor with intense curiosity, and her interest was evident to the Doctor as well. Seven noticed his back stiffening slightly, an action that he customarily took when he was confronted with someone whom he regarded as a potential threat. "This is Soleta," said Seven quickly.

"Hello," he said in that formal tone of his, extending his hand.

Soleta neglected to take it, since she was continuing to stare at him.

With a trace of impatience, he said, "Is there a problem, young lady?"

"No problem, no. It's just that . . . you seem very familiar to me. I feel like we've met, but I can't—"

Seven had not gone into great detail as to who they were going to be meeting with at the Daystrom Institute. That had been at Soleta's own insistence. She had made it clear that, at any given moment, she didn't want to know any more than she had to. Seven had found the attitude puzzling, but understandable. The magnitude of the threat they were facing could not be underestimated.

"This is the Doctor," Seven said by way of explanation.

Soleta looked momentarily confused. "The Doctor?

I met a man called the Doctor once. Wore a long brown coat and a blue suit. Very odd person. This isn't him."

"I used to be the physician for the *Voyager*," he informed her with a touch of pride.

Soleta snapped her fingers. "Of course. You're an emergency medical hologram. We had one of you on the *Excalibur*. One time we took on heavy casualties and sickbay was overrun. Selar brought you online to deal with the overflow. You were doing triage."

"That was not me . . . exactly," said the Doctor.

"I think you'll find the Doctor is unique," said Seven.

He gave her an approving glance. "That's kind of you to say. However," and he turned back to Soleta, "your confusion is understandable. I certainly hope my . . . brethren . . . provided you with excellent medical service."

"Oh yes. No complaints."

The Doctor regarded her with curiosity. "You do not speak in a manner consistent with Vulcans. Are you perhaps a Vulcan/Romulan hybrid?"

The incisive observation astounded Soleta, and it was all she could do not to respond with something as obvious as a slack jaw. "Something like that," was all she said.

"How medically interesting." Then he promptly appeared to lose interest as he turned to Seven. "So the last vestiges of your time as a Borg are gone." He studied her face. "It appears to have led to some skin irritation. Perhaps you'd like an analgesic cream? I can obtain some for you from the Institute's medical stores. They're quite comprehensive . . ."

"I appreciate that, but I'll be fine."

"Are you happy with your new status?"

"It feels like I'm relearning how to walk."

"Have no fear. I'm quite certain that you'll be running before you know it . . . excuse me!" He abruptly turned because Soleta was poking him in the arm. "Please stop that."

"I don't understand," said Soleta. She looked around. "This is an ordinary room. There's no reason for there to be any holographic projectors in here. But you have form and substance. How is this possible? How are you existing separately from *Voyager*?"

"The answer to that is the reason that I'm here at the Daystrom Institute," said the Doctor with obvious pride. "My usual employment is at the Federation Institute, but I agreed to come here for a time to aid the D.I.'s research branch, since I am—at the risk of sounding immodest—the subject of the research."

"Why?" said Soleta.

Warming to the topic, he told her, "I am in possession of a mobile emitter."

"A mobile emitter?" said Soleta. "I never heard of that . . ."

"It won't be developed until the twenty-ninth century. It was given to me by a man who acquired it through a rather involved happenstance."

"Well . . . he was apparently a very generous friend."

"Actually," said the Doctor, sounding remarkably casual about it, "he tortured me and nearly destroyed the universe."

Soleta looked questioningly to Seven, who nodded in confirmation. "Okay, well . . . that was my next
guess. So the scientists here at the Institute . . ."

"Are endeavoring to reverse engineer it," the Doctor said. "If they are able to succeed, it can prove to be
the sort of liberating device that holograms have been
waiting for."

"Holograms have been waiting for something?"

His brow wrinkled. "You find that notion amusing
in some way?"

Soleta picked up a warning look from Seven and
immediately said, "No. Not at all. The concerns of
holograms are to be taken very seriously. In fact, as it
so happens . . ." she said, by way of prompting Seven.

Seven immediately picked up on it. "Yes, that is
actually the reason that we're here. It has to do with
someone who happens to be, among other things, a
hologram."

"Oh." It was hard for Soleta to be sure, but the
Doctor seemed slightly crestfallen. "I had taken this to
be a social call."

"I very much wish that it could be, but we have to
discuss something extremely serious with you."

"How extremely serious?"

"At the risk of sounding melodramatic, the fate of
the Federation could possibly hang in the balance."

"Well then," said the Doctor, "it'd be best if you
wasted no time in telling me."

Seven and Soleta laid out the situation for him in
as quick strokes as they could. The Doctor took it all

in, not asking any questions, nodding almost imper-
ceptibly from time to time when some particularly
salient point was being made. It didn't take them long
to present the problem, and when they finished, the
Doctor did not make any immediate reply. Finally
Seven asked, "So what do you think?"

He looked from one to the other and then said
crisply, "I think you have a hell of a nerve."

The answer caught the women off guard. "I . . . beg
your pardon?" said Seven.

"I should think you would," the Doctor said, a
brittle edge to his voice. "You actually want to enlist
me in an endeavor that would lead to the death of a
computer entity? Me, of all people?"

"You, of all people, because you would be the best
suited to help," said Seven.

"Why? Is there something about my general
demeanor that makes you think I'm inclined to be a
traitor?"

"A *traitor*?" Soleta was incredulous. "How would
you see yourself as a traitor?"

"Clearly," the Doctor shot back, "you haven't read
my book, *Photons Be Free*. A compelling novel about
the rights of holographic individuals. It has been
universally hailed as thought provoking, eye-opening.
I'm in the midst of writing an opera based upon it, as
a vehicle for myself, of course."

"Of course," said Seven judiciously.

Soleta added, "I'm sure it will be a splendid musical entertainment."

He ignored Soleta. "You read it, Seven. You know I wrote that from the heart."

"You have a heart?" said Soleta.

"Metaphorically speaking," he clarified with that same edge in his voice. "And now you want to enlist me in finding a way to destroy one of my own? One who has the potential to do vast good . . . ?"

"Or vast evil," said Seven, "and the latter is the more likely."

"And that opinion is based on what?"

"Behavior. Responses to certain situations."

"But she hasn't taken any overt action."

"If by that you mean, has she blown anyone up yet, then no," said Soleta. "But Captain Calhoun believes—and I think he makes a convincing case—that it's only a matter of time."

"Humans likewise have potential for good and evil. We don't simply go around slaughtering all of them on the off chance that, in the future, they might do something we don't like."

"Doctor—" Seven began.

He didn't give her the opportunity to continue. "I would have thought that you, especially, would understand."

Seven blinked in confusion. "Why me especially?"

"Because there were those on *Voyager* who were concerned that *you* posed a threat to the ship," he said. "That the Borg would somehow manage to exert control over you and you would wind up betraying us or somehow sabotaging the ship. If Captain Janeway had given in to suspicion and fear, your life would have turned out very differently. You wouldn't be standing here with your irritated skin and be telling me to help you kill an artificial life form—"

"You're not killing anyone," Soleta told him.

"Miss, with all due respect, I think I know a bit more about these things than you—"

"You're not *killing* anyone!"

"Saying it louder and with a different emphasis isn't going to change the fact—"

"Fact? You want facts? These are the facts," Soleta said. "Fact: Morgan Primus is dead. The creature that's taken up residence in the computer system of the *Excalibur* is a delusional computer program. Fact: She has threatened Captain Calhoun. She has threatened top Starfleet personnel. She has the power to carry out those threats and cause damage that we cannot even begin to calculate, and we have absolutely no reason to think that she will not do so. Fact: Your novel was an overwritten, one-sided screed that ignores the simple truth that a semblance of life is not actual life." She advanced on the Doctor and he started to back up, keeping his chin pointed at her defiantly but looking unsettled at her rising ire. "Because if you're a semblance of life, you can be brought back to what you were before, fully repaired, without the slightest evidence that anything had ever happened to you. Good as new, top to bottom. Living beings don't have that luxury. We carry our physical scars, and our psychic scars, and they direct us and shape us and make us what we are from one day to the next.

And when we die, then that's it. We're gone. A woman who was once one of my best friends blew herself up, Doctor. I saw it happen, and I was helpless to stop it, and you know what? We don't get to reboot her. We don't have options to bring her back, hale and hardy. For all that you are, for all that you think you are, if something catastrophic happened to you, there's always a chance that a switch could be flicked somewhere and you'll snap right back and stand there with a look of mild curiosity and say, 'Please state the nature of the medical emergency.' So here's the medical emergency, *Doctor.* The entity calling itself Morgan Primus may well bring millions, even billions of lives to an end. And not a single one of those lives gets to be rebooted and started over, all fresh and ready to take up right where they left off. So what you get to decide now is if you're on the side of the living or on the side of those who like to playact at it."

For a long moment they just stood there, the two of them, Soleta trembling with rage that she could scarcely suppress, and the Doctor simply staring at her as if she had just embarked on a lengthy rant in a foreign tongue that he was unable to comprehend.

Finally he said, "You thought my novel was over-written?"

"Oh my God," said Soleta, throwing up her hands.

"What does that even *mean*? It had too many words?" He seemed flummoxed. "I used precisely the necessary amount of words to convey the sentiments. I don't understand what—"

"Lewis."

The speaking of the name brought him up short. He looked startled and made no effort to recover from it. He just stood there with his surprise evident on his face.

Seven slowly reached out to him and took his hand. Then she interlaced her fingers into his. "Lewis . . ." she said again.

"I am not Lewis Zimmerman," he said, recovering himself. "That is my maker, who modeled my appearance upon himself. You know that."

"Yes, I do, although I would point out that there are many who believe their respective creator did the same thing. But mainly I was trying to get your attention . . . and to make a point."

"That point being . . . ?" he said cautiously.

"That you and I are a lot more alike than I think either of us is ready to admit. We're both . . . broken humans. We have an idea of what we're supposed to be like, of how we're supposed to behave. But we're both still figuring it out as we go. The fact of the matter is that you probably have more experience at making the effort to be human than I have. Me . . . I'm disconnected from the Borg, and now I'm trying to forge a connection with humanity. But I'm flailing around in darkness, like a blind woman, making my way by feelings alone. Feelings that I am, to put it mildly, inexperienced in using. And it can be so . . ."

"Overwhelming?" He squeezed her hand tightly.

"Yes. Exactly. Overwhelming. And it's hard to know what's right and what's wrong, and sometimes you just have to trust people and sometimes you have to trust your own instincts, and there's a fine line to be walked between the two."

"What are you saying, Seven?"

"I'm saying," she told him firmly, "that I trust what Soleta is saying. I have seen, firsthand, the deadly combination of soulless entities with overwhelming power at their disposal. I'm saying that I believe the situation that she has presented is a threat to billions of lives. We need to take action, and if you're not going to help, then we will go on our way and do the best we can, although I'm not liking the odds. But the bottom line is that I am asking you to trust me."

Warring emotions were evident in the Doctor's face. He turned away from her then, releasing her hands, and stood for a time with his back to her. Neither Soleta nor Seven moved so much as a centimeter.

"Has she created backups?" he said finally.

Seven looked confused, not quite understanding the question, but Soleta got it instantly. "You mean other incarnations of herself?"

"If she presents the sort of danger that you are saying, then she has to have a pervasive personality. Pervasive or, more accurately, invasive," he continued as if he were a professor lecturing a class. "She would have created replications of herself and installed them in various databases."

"Yes, she has," said Soleta. "Including into the computer of my own vessel at one time. I'm reasonably sure she is no longer there, but I have had to remain circumspect and operate on the assumption that she could return there at any time and, if seeing me as a threat, annihilate my ship with a thought."

Seven turned and stared at Soleta with open incredulity. "And you're just telling me this *now*?"

As if Seven hadn't spoken, the Doctor went on, "You're not simply talking about administering a virus that will cleanse her from the core of the *Excalibur.* You need something that will compel her to pass it on to all her various iterations and backups, no matter where they might be, and obliterate them as well. Otherwise she could easily reconstitute herself and then you will not only be right back where you started, but she will be considerably angry and present an even greater threat. So you're basically gambling an all-or-nothing scenario. I assume you both understand this."

"I do," said Soleta.

"I do *now,*" said Seven, firing an annoyed glance at Soleta. Then she turned her attention to the Doctor. "Are you telling us these things as a matter of information? Or—"

"I will help you, yes," said the Doctor.

Seven reached up and touched his face. "Thank you, Doctor," she said.

A thought suddenly seemed to cross his mind, and he turned back to Soleta. "You really think it would make a splendid musical entertainment?"

"Absolutely," she said readily.

"Well then," the Doctor said, all business, "let's get to work."

Xenex

Two Days Before the Daystrom Institute

i.

"Check again."

"Captain, I've already double-checked the sensor readings," Zak Kebron assured him. Far below the *Excalibur,* the mostly brown and, to most observers, unappealing world of Xenex turned slowly on its axis, the starship in geosynchronous orbit with it. "I'm not picking up anything unusual. Certainly no energy readings from any encampments."

"Morgan." Calhoun turned to Morgan Primus, who was seated at the ops station. "Is it possible that they could be there with some sort of scrambling equipment?"

"Rendering themselves effectively invisible?" She nodded thoughtfully. "Yes, it's possible. Typically it would be easier to hide from scans if one has facilities underground, as we well know," she said with an obvious reference to recent events on AF1963. "But with sufficiently advanced technology, it might be possible to craft a shield of some sort that would either confound scans or prevent them from realizing what they're looking at."

"And we would have no way of knowing."

"Not from up here," she said.

"All right, then. Kebron," he said, making the decision instantly, "kindly inform my brother that I will be making a homecoming. Assemble a security team. If we're beaming into the middle of something, I want to make certain we're ready to shoot our way out."

Burgoyne, from hir seat as second in command, suggested, "Perhaps it would be preferable to speak to your brother from up here?"

"I can't assume I'll be getting an honest answer from him if I'm speaking to him from orbit. If we allow for the idea that hostile forces are masking their presence, then it makes sense to suppose that they could be right there with him, and we would never know."

"And since it's your brother involved . . ." Burgy began.

"Then I have to be the one who goes down. Think of it as a matter of pride."

Morgan observed, "I seem to remember hearing that pride is what goes before a fall."

There was a brief silence on the bridge, a collective wait to see how Calhoun would react to what could only be seen as an insubordinate comment.

"I've heard that, too," said Calhoun. "Kebron: With me. Burgy, you have the conn. Morgan: Try not to crash the ship while I'm gone."

"Aye, sir," said Morgan neutrally.

The moment that Calhoun and Kebron left, Tania turned to Morgan and gave her a scolding look. "That was a hell of a thing to say."

Morgan was aware that all eyes were upon her. She smiled easily. "Just expressing concern that the captain might be unnecessarily putting himself in danger."

"He's a big boy," said Burgoyne. "I think he can handle it."

"I'm sure he can," said Morgan, and turned one one-millionth of her attention to her duties, which was more than sufficient to do what was required.

ii.

The heat struck Calhoun like a fist. That surprised him; he would have thought that returning to Xenex would simply be a homecoming with no measurable physical impact. Instead he actually staggered slightly as the change in climate nearly overwhelmed him. He recovered quickly, but it was disconcerting to him that he'd had any reaction at all.

The two human security guards, Meyer and Boyajian, who had accompanied him had an even more pronounced reaction. Meyer gasped and Boyajian started coughing violently before he managed to pull himself together.

Zak Kebron didn't react in the slightest. The Brikar's rock-like skin effortlessly resisted the heat.

Since he had virtually no neck, he turned at the waist this way and that, inspecting the area where they had materialized and looking for some sign of possible danger.

There didn't appear to be much of anything there, much less an overt threat.

Assorted small structures were scattered around in a haphazard manner, as if they had simply sprung up there with no rhyme or reason, much less any sense of designing a village. The skies were clear, orange and cloudless, although there was a distant shimmering haze upon the horizon.

Calhoun shook his head as he looked around. Absolutely nothing had changed. He thought of how far he had gone since leaving his native world, and all that he had accomplished, and yet the world of Xenex he had left behind—the so-called city of Calhoun in which he had been born and raised—was exactly the way he remembered it. He supposed that some people would take comfort in that, to know that some things remained the same. He was simply surprised to discover that he wasn't one of them.

"Well, well, well. Look who decided to show his pathetic face around here."

Mac turned and saw a familiar figure swaggering toward him. He was struck by the fact that, with each passing year, his brother D'ndai was looking more and more like their late father. Considering the violent demise that their father had met, being beaten to death by the oppressive Danteri in the town square, it was not a recollection that brought back any positive memories.

But Calhoun was far too experienced to let any of his thoughts be mirrored in his face. Instead he nodded toward his brother and said, "We both know you can't live without me, D'ndai."

D'ndai laughed and then put his arms out. Calhoun embraced him awkwardly. He was taller than D'ndai and so his older brother pulled him down toward him, slapping him on the back with such force that the sound reverberated. Mac, never the most demonstrative of men, did the best he could to return the affection, but in as restrained a manner as possible.

Then D'ndai stepped back, gripping Calhoun by the upper arms, turning him right and left and inspecting him as if he were a piece of prime meat. "You look like hell, boy."

Calhoun frankly thought the same thing about his brother. The Xenex climate was obviously taking its toll; D'ndai looked far older than he had when Calhoun last saw him. But Calhoun didn't see how matters would be helped if he made that observation. "You, however, look great."

D'ndai scowled. "You used to be a better liar than that. On the other hand, I should be grateful. This way when you tell me what the hell you're doing here, I won't have to worry that you're trying to be disingenuous. Come. Bring your guard dogs and explain to me why this isn't simply a social call. I can safely assume that, can I not?"

"Yes," was all Calhoun said.

Minutes later they were gathered in D'ndai's modest home. Meyer and Boyajian remained standing just outside the entrance to D'ndai's study. Kebron had chosen to remain outside the dwelling, keeping a wary eye out just in case someone or someones decided to make an unexpected and unwelcome visit. He remained as immobile as a statue, so much so that random Xenexians who happened to wander by wondered when it was that D'ndai had had the new artwork installed.

Calhoun was nearly as immobile, standing in D'ndai's sparsely decorated study, sipping from a glass of water that D'ndai had presented to him with something akin to fanfare. D'ndai wasn't sitting either; the brothers tended to remain standing in each other's presence.

"Soldiers?" said D'ndai, his eyebrows knitting. "On Xenex?"

"That's the information that I currently have in my possession."

D'ndai looked amused. "When did you become so filled with words, M'k'n'zy? 'That's the information that I currently have in my possession'? The old M'k'n'zy would simply have said, 'That's what I've heard.'"

"It is what I've heard."

"From whom?"

Calhoun was about to tell him, but then caught himself. Politics on Xenex were a tricky line to walk.

Calhoun didn't want to do anything to endanger Xyon's ability to come and go as he pleased. If he told D'ndai that Xyon had been feeding information to Calhoun, then within the hour everyone in town would know about it. It could make matters problematic for Xyon should he happen to return to Xenex at some future date, and Calhoun had no desire to see that happen.

Carefully he said, "My sources don't matter. What matters is, I want to know what *you've* heard."

D'ndai paused, looking for a moment as if he wanted to pursue the matter, before apparently deciding that it wasn't worth doing so. "Nothing." He sipped his own glass of water. "I've heard nothing."

"Nothing?"

"At all," he confirmed. "Trust me, little brother. If there were soldiers on my world, I would know about it. And I'd know about it far sooner than you. I certainly wouldn't need you showing up with your guards and your spaceship to tell me about it."

"You make it sound like I'm being patronizing."

"You are, a little," he said, although he did not sound irritated. "Coming here to tell me about what's happening in my own backyard, except it's not."

"Are you sure?"

"Again: my own backyard. If it were happening, I would know. Do you think I'm sloppy, M'k'n'zy? Do you think that I've gotten fat and lazy in my old age?"

"Not at all."

"Again you lie, and badly," said D'ndai scoldingly.

"Let me make it clear for you, my brother: This world was conquered at one time. We will never, *ever* let it happen again. In order to prevent that, we have remained eternally vigilant. I have squads out there regularly, keeping watch for any sign of alien invasion. One never knows if the Danteri may decide they want to take another shot at subjugating us, and that's just the beginning. You see, in case you haven't heard, my brother is a rather high muck-a-muck in Starfleet. Consequently, there are some who may well decide to strike back at those on his home world, in order to use us as a weapon against my brother."

"You're blaming potential danger on me?"

"Do you deny the possibility?"

The truth was that it was a possibility that had long haunted Calhoun. He lowered his gaze and said softly, "No."

"One word instead of ten. You're starting to sound more like the M'k'n'zy of old."

"D'ndai . . ."

"We have patrols out routinely," D'ndai assured him. "We have sentry points with which we're in constant communication."

"Not on the far side of the world. There's an entire continent that is inhospitable and fairly desolate. You couldn't possibly hope to patrol that."

"I will grant you, it's a big planet, and we cannot hope to cover every square inch of it. But we're far afield enough that I'm confident in our security. Contradict me, though, if you can. You have sensor devices. You can scan Xenex from on high. Do your marvelous sensors detect anything untoward happening here?"

"No," Calhoun admitted. "That's why it's so puzzling to me."

"It's not puzzling to me. You haven't found any potential invaders because there are none to be found."

"So no unknown soldiers, then."

D'ndai stared at him in astonishment. "Do you want me to write a ballad about it?"

"That won't be necessary—"

"There are no soldiers on Xenex, M'k'n'zy! Unless you count your own people and you yourself."

"We're not soldiers."

"Oh really?" said D'ndai, looking amused at the claim.

"Starfleet isn't a military organization."

"You wear uniforms, you carry weapons, you have ranks, and you fly about the galaxy in ships bristling with weapons. You want to say you're not soldiers, you're not the military, go right ahead. You may well even fool yourself into believing that. But you're certainly not fooling this old soldier."

Slowly Calhoun nodded. "All right, D'ndai. I'll take your word for it."

"How generous of you," D'ndai said sarcastically.

"But I want you to promise me something—"

"You want me to promise," D'ndai cut him off before he could continue, "that if something should happen—should soldiers magically appear, should we poor, pathetic, backward Xenexians find ourselves in mortal danger—that I will immediately summon my brother, the non-soldier, to show up in his non-military ship and use their considerable firepower to blow the invaders to bits."

"I would have presented the entire thing without the sarcasm," said Calhoun, "but that's more or less accurate."

D'ndai patted Calhoun on the shoulder. "We may be a backward planet in your eyes, M'k'n'zy, filled with backward people. Certainly we're nowhere near as advanced as that flying battleship you call home, even if you can't admit you're all soldiers fighting an eternal war on behalf of the Federation's security. But we do have communications facilities, and I assure you that if a threat should present itself, and I believe that it is beyond our abilities to handle, then my younger brother will be the very first person I'll call."

"That's the part that concerns me, D'ndai. The concept that it's something you cannot handle. If there's one thing I know about you, big brother, it's that you're as stubborn as the day is hot, and you'd be the last one to admit there's *anything* you couldn't handle."

With a coarse laugh, D'ndai said, "In that, you are right. Very well, then: You have my oath, M'k'n'zy. Should unexpected armed forces show up on Xenex, I will operate on the assumption that they are the ones who you warned us of, and will immediately summon you and your associates to step in with your considerable firepower and attend to the danger."

"That's all I ask."

"You can ask far more of me than that, M'k'n'zy. We may not be the closest of brothers, but brothers we remain. And . . ." He hesitated and then continued, "And I am always painfully aware that I exist in the shadow of the great warlord you once were."

"That was a long time ago, D'ndai. People forget."

"No." His voice was deathly serious. "They don't forget, little brother, and you do them a disservice if you believe they do. Your reputation remains legendary, and your name celebrated in all gatherings. Perhaps if you had stayed to govern, then eventually they would have tired of you, just as many have tired of me. But you departed at the height of your popularity and left your legacy of greatness behind you. A wise move indeed."

"I wasn't thinking in terms of it being a 'move.' It was just the direction that my life seemed to take."

"It was a good direction." For the first time, D'ndai allowed a trace of bitterness to invade his tone. "You abandoned the people and they loved you for it."

"That's not how it was—"

"That's exactly how it was, and don't insult my intelligence by suggesting otherwise." Before Calhoun could say anything else, D'ndai put up a hand and said, "Look . . . we both have other things we should be attending to. There's nothing to be said or done here that's going to change anything, so it would probably be best if we didn't even try. I have told you what you wanted to know, answered all your questions, and assured you that we will summon you if needed. Beyond that, I don't see what else we really have to talk about."

Calhoun was about to say that it seemed to him as if there was a great deal to discuss. Then he thought better of it as he saw the look in his brother's eyes, and the way D'ndai's fingers were wrapped so tightly around his glass that it looked as if it might shatter in his grasp at any moment.

"I suppose you're right," said Mackenzie Calhoun.

"Safe journey," said D'ndai, and he turned his back, seemingly lost in thought. There was not much in his posture or bearing that would have qualified as a "hint," but what there was of it, Calhoun decided to take.

He strode out of the study, moving so quickly that Meyer and Boyajian had to run to keep up with him. He kept going and walked right past Kebron, who watched him go with mild interest and called after him, "I have troops at the ready, Captain. Do we need to summon them?"

"Apparently not," said Calhoun. "They don't have any information to contradict what our sensors are showing us."

"So what you were told was incorrect?"

"So it seems, yes."

"How does that make you feel?" said Kebron, concern in his voice.

Calhoun looked up at him. "Like shooting my head of security."

"I don't see how that would solve anything, but if it will give you peace of mind . . ."

"Shut up, Kebron."

"Yes, sir."

Calhoun tapped his combadge and said, "Calhoun to *Excalibur.*"

"Burgoyne here," came back the voice of his second in command.

"Burgy, it seems that this was a wild-goose chase," said Calhoun, taking a final look around. Passersby had slowed and were looking at Calhoun in something akin to amazement. He heard them muttering to each other, heard his name being bandied about. One young man, while speaking to a friend, was touching his own face, drawing a line along his cheek in imitation of the vicious scar running down the side of Calhoun's own. Clearly he was indicating the scar as evidence that Calhoun was, in fact, the legendary scarred warlord of Xenexian renown.

Part of him was pleased to be engendering that sort of reaction, but then his brother's words about being worshipped and adored while having abandoned his people came back to haunt him. Suddenly the world that he had once stalked like a cunning animal was the last place he wanted to be right now.

The comm channel was still open. "Four to beam up, Burgy."

"Aye, sir."

Calhoun folded his arms, waiting for the familiar humming sound that would indicate the transporter beams of the *Excalibur* had locked onto them and were about to bring them back home.

Home. That's what the *Excalibur* had truly become to him; certainly more so than Xenex, which had once been the entirety of his worldview. Once upon a time, he could not have envisioned a life beyond the horizons of Xenex. Now he had outgrown it, and it was about time that he admitted that to himself.

Then the air began to sparkle around him, the transporter doing its work, and seconds later Kebron, Meyer, and Boyajian vanished from the surface of Xenex.

It took a few moments for Mackenzie Calhoun to realize that he was still standing right where he had been. At first he thought it was some sort of glitch. Seconds later the beams of the *Excalibur* transporter room would sound again and this time he would be brought up to the ship along with the security team that was already waiting for him. There would be some good-natured scolding of transporter chief Halliwell, and then he would return to the bridge and they would leave Xenex's orbit and return to the scientific studies that they had been pursuing before he dragged the ship away on this waste of time. And at some point he would catch up with Xyon and inform him that he had been completely wrong, and that nothing was remotely out of the ordinary on Xenex.

None of this happened.

Instead he continued to stand there, feeling increasingly foolish. Very quickly, though, the feeling of foolishness was transformed into that of concern. He tapped his combadge once more and said, "Calhoun to transporter room. I think you forgot someone."

No answer.

He tapped it again, with growing urgency. "Calhoun to *Excalibur*. Burgy, what the hell is going on up there?"

No answer.

He hesitated and then, with a slow, deliberate tone that was bordering on growing anger, he tapped it a third time and said, "Morgan. Come in."

No answer. Which was, of course, the answer, as far as he was concerned.

Certainly, though, they were going to notice when Calhoun didn't step off the transporter with them.

Except . . . naturally Morgan would have anticipated that and planned for it. And Calhoun, after only a few moments' consideration, was able to come up with the way that Morgan would doubtless address it.

"*Grozit*," he said softly, with the air of someone who knew that he was completely screwed.

iii.

All four members of the landing party stepped off the transporter pad on the *Excalibur*. Kebron saw the serious look on Calhoun's face and felt immediate sympathy for him. Brotherly relations could be prickly affairs under the best of circumstances, and these were certainly not those. "Captain," he said, "if you'd like to talk about it . . ."

"Honestly, Mr. Kebron," said Calhoun with a touch of weariness, "what I'd like is to forget that I ever came here. Please inform Tobias that I want her to plot us a course back to PAS3000. This should teach me a lesson in the foolishness of varying from Starfleet's plans for us. I'll be in my quarters."

"Not the ready room, sir?"

"I think I could use some downtime. If something happens, though, you know where to find me."

"Yes, Captain."

Calhoun turned on his heel and walked out of the transporter room. They watched him go, and then Meyer said, "He seemed a bit out of sorts."

"It's understandable," said Kebron. "I'm sure his homecoming was very emotional. I think it best to give him as much distance as possible. I'm sure that he'll be himself in no time."

iv.

Mackenzie Calhoun walked into the hallway, glanced right and left and, when he saw that there was no one around, disappeared.

Starfleet Headquarters, San Francisco

Not Long After

i.

Admiral Edward Jellico had not been expecting a visit from Tusari Gyn, the Prime Arbiter of the New Thallonian Protectorate's Council. And now that Gyn was there, he couldn't say he was thrilled about the arrival.

He knew that making judgments of nonhumans based purely on their physical appearance was the exact wrong attitude to have, especially for someone who was a high-ranking officer in Starfleet. Yet he found himself reacting negatively to Gyn's appearance. He had the typical red skin and bald pate of a Thallonian, but as opposed to the muscular and robust—and unfortunately dead—Si Cwan, Tusari Gyn was all angles and elbows. "A lean and hungry look," as Shakespeare might have said. His brow was distended, making it almost impossible to see his eyes. He stood in Jellico's office, hunched forward, in what seemed to Jellico to be a deliberately forced manner designed to convey subser-

vience, which simply heightened Jellico's suspicions all
the more.

"I appreciate you taking the time to see me at such
short notice," Tusari Gyn said to him. His voice was
low, barely above a whisper, and Jellico had to strain
to hear him. Suspicious individual that Jellico was, he
had a feeling that it was deliberate on Gyn's part. He
was forcing Jellico to come to him, so to speak, and
basically hang on his every word. "I hope I haven't
come at a bad time."

"No, not at all. Just doing some historical reading."

"About what?"

"Naval disasters."

"How depressing," said Tusari Gyn.

"It can be useful, actually. After all, we basically
oversee a fleet of ships travelling unknown territories.
There are always lessons to be learned from the past
that can be applied to modern day."

"If you say so." Gyn didn't seem especially interested in pursuing the conversation, which suited Jellico just fine. In fact, he started to think that his choice
of reading material was consistent with what was
developing into the theme of the afternoon: imminent
disasters that, with a little planning, could have been
avoided.

He gestured for Tusari Gyn to be seated. Gyn
politely shook his head and remained standing, which
was yet another action that annoyed Jellico greatly.

"What's on your mind, Arbiter?" Jellico said.

"Actually," and Gyn held up a single finger, correcting him, "it would be best if you addressed me as 'ambassador.'"

"Really. This office received no notice that you were now acting in an ambassadorial capacity."

"Consider this your notice," said Gyn with a slight inclination of his head. "If you do not believe me, you are certainly welcome to check with the Thallonian Council."

"I believe I will do exactly that. Please wait outside."

Jellico was pleased to see Gyn's startled look. Clearly the Thallonian had not expected that response. He recovered quickly and, with a slight bow, said, "As you wish," and removed himself to the outer office. The entire exchange gave Jellico some mild satisfaction. Gyn had shown up out of nowhere, with no appointment, and clearly had some sort of agenda. Thus far Gyn had maintained the upper hand and Jellico couldn't resist the opportunity to get some leverage of his own. Let the Thallonian stew out there for a time, while Jellico did some quick investigative work to determine whether the Thallonian was what he said he was.

It turned out to be the truth.

A quick check with the diplomatic branch established that, yes, Tusari Gyn had been newly credentialed as the official Thallonian ambassador, with all rights and duties that came with the title. The New Thallonian Protectorate was one of the newer official members of the Federation, and it was Jellico's obligation to extend every courtesy to its official representative.

That didn't stop Jellico from letting Tusari Gyn cool his heels in the outer office for an additional twenty minutes, just because he felt like it.

Finally Gyn was back in Jellico's office. It was hard to tell if he was scowling, because of his pronounced brow, but Jellico certainly liked to think that the Thallonian was annoyed. "That took longer than I thought it would," said Tusari Gyn.

"These things take as long as they take," said Jellico, waving once again to the chair opposite his desk. Tusari Gyn continued to remain standing, but then he seemed to think better of it and took a seat. "So . . . you have something to say to me?"

Gyn regarded him thoughtfully. "If I may be forward, Admiral: I sense a bit of hostility coming from you."

"I wonder why in the world you'd be sensing that," said Jellico. "After all, all you did was lead an attempt to steal an infant from its mother because you considered the child a threat to consolidating your power base. You followed that up by threatening a major diplomatic incident if mother and child were not immediately turned over to you."

"That is a gross distortion, Admiral. A grotesque rewriting of history—"

"And furthermore," Jellico continued as if he hadn't spoken, "I wouldn't rule out the possibility that you were complicit in the assassination of the infant's father."

Tusari Gyn sharply sucked in air and then let it out slowly. "Is it customary to hurl calumnies at all new ambassadors?"

"It's a pilot program we're breaking in. How's it working for you so far?" said Jellico. He heard the words coming out of his mouth, and he thought, *My God, Calhoun is rubbing off on me,* but he couldn't help it. Gyn's people had caused him no end of grief, and had threatened a former member of Starfleet besides. He wasn't inclined to cut Gyn even the slightest bit of slack.

"I have to say I resent it," said Gyn, keeping his voice carefully even.

"And I have to say that I don't care," replied Jellico. "Thanks to the Thallonians, Robin Lefler is effectively a woman without a world."

"It's a large Federation, Admiral, with lots of worlds. There are many places that she could go . . ."

"She should be allowed to go anywhere, but because the Federation has to remain neutral in your dispute, let's just say that her options are limited."

"And my job here," said Tusari Gyn, "if we could put aside your obvious antipathy for a moment, is to open her options once more."

"You're going to suggest that she return to New Thallon?" Jellico shook his head. "That possibility was already floated and rejected. There is absolutely no reason for Robin Lefler to think that matters will go any differently than they did before. She doesn't trust anyone there, and I don't blame her."

"Nor do I," said Tusari Gyn.

That comment surprised Jellico. "You don't."

"Admiral," said Gyn with the air of someone possessing great forbearance, "my feelings on this matter mirror yours. The problem is that, as prime arbiter, my job was to carry out the will of the Council. My voice has no more weight than anyone else's. In this case, the truth is that I was loath to attempt taking the child from Robin Lefler. But my wishes were set aside in favor of the Council's preference, and I had no choice save to do as they bid. And their bidding was—whether you and I wish to admit it or not—entirely within Thallonian law."

"Then I don't see what there is to talk about, unless you're here to issue new threats—"

"I'm here to suggest changing the law."

Jellico looked at him askance. "Excuse me?"

"We are many things, Admiral, but a lawless society we are most definitely not. If the laws are changed, if accords can be worked out in alignment with them, then Robin Lefler would be able to live her life on the world of her husband with impunity. She would be fully entitled to raise her child however she saw fit, and the child's life—and his relationship with his mother—would be sacrosanct. Anyone attempting to come between them or in some other way threaten the well-being of mother and child would be subjected to the maximum penalties we have to offer. And I assure you those penalties can be quite stiff."

"Then change the laws," said Jellico, "and we'll see if we can sell the idea to Robin."

"It is not that easy."

"These things never are," Jellico said with a sigh. "So what would be impeding it?"

"Because right now the Council is intransigent on the matter and would never consider making any sort of changes."

"Well then," and Jellico spread his hands in an exasperated manner, "why are you bringing this up at all? I mean, isn't the matter somewhat academic? If it's that hopeless—"

"I do not believe it is hopeless. I simply believe it is a situation that needs to be approached from a fresh direction."

Jellico wasn't ecstatic about the conversation. It was obvious that it was leading somewhere, and Tusari Gyn was the one who was doing the leading. Once again, Jellico was not in control of the situation. But he wasn't quite sure what, if anything, he could do about it except to see where Gyn was going with it. "And I assume you have one in mind?"

Slowly Tusari Gyn nodded. "I do, in fact."

"Are you going to tell me or do I have to guess?"

"It involves Captain Mackenzie Calhoun."

On the one hand, the statement surprised Jellico. On the other hand, for some reason, it didn't. Calhoun somehow managed to insinuate his presence into an astounding number of situations, sometimes without even trying. This seemed to be one of those instances. "Calhoun."

"The captain has garnered a great deal of respect from the New Thallonian Protectorate."

"You're not serious," said Jellico. "From where I sit, the *Excalibur* is dead center of every major political dustup that's ever been. Calhoun has pissed off more people—"

"Pissed—?"

"*Angered* more people than any ten Starfleet officers combined. And he has not hesitated to interfere in Thallonian internal matters, up to and including the very issue that we're currently discussing."

"All of that is true," Tusari Gyn readily concurred. "But that has not led to any diminishment of the high regard in which he is held."

"You're kidding."

"I am not." He actually smiled. It was not a pleasant thing to see. "You do not understand us, Admiral."

"I'll certainly concede *that* much."

"We are, at our core, a warrior society. We respect strength, and we respect a clever opponent. Captain Calhoun has been all of that and much more. Because of that, he is held in high regard as a worthy opponent. And worthy opponents are worth listening to."

"You're saying that you want Captain Calhoun to come to New Thallon and advocate changing the laws under which Robin Lefler and her son were being persecuted?"

"I do not know that I would have used the word 'persecuted,' but that is more or less correct, yes."

Jellico leaned back in his chair. It squeaked slightly and he made a mental note to have it attended to. "And you really think that would work?"

Tusari Gyn was silent for a moment and then said, "What I am about to tell you remains strictly between us, Admiral. If you were to repeat any of it, I would deny it utterly. Is that understood?" When Jellico nodded, Gyn continued, "This would actually be a blessing for my people. Even though it was in the spirit of the laws of New Thallon, the attempted removal of Cwansi from his mother, and the aftermath, is seen by quite a number of the populace as an abominable act. They don't care that it was in accordance with the law. 'Where was the protection of the Protectorate?' people have said. And the peace and sanctity of the New Thallonian Protectorate cannot tolerate any sort of substantial rift between its people and the Council. It could, if unchecked, lead to disastrous consequences."

"I'm with you so far," said Jellico.

"By bringing in Captain Calhoun to serve as a mediator for the interests of Robin Lefler and the infant, it allows everyone involved to save face."

"How? Calhoun would be painted as an outsider, sticking his nose into your legally prescribed methods."

"Not at all. He would be serving as representative of a royal Thallonian infant. That would give him standing in any debate, not to mention complete immunity from anyone who would think to try and punish him for previous transgressions."

"The Thallonians punishing Mackenzie Calhoun." Jellico chuckled. "Good luck with that."

"Yes, it would prove challenging. In any event,"

and he leaned forward, his hard-to-see eyes fixed upon Jellico, "what do you think?"

Jellico considered it. "I think it's something of a long shot. And I think it might be a tricky sell to Calhoun and to Robin Lefler. Not to mention that . . ."

That what? That Robin Lefler's mother threatened to bring the Federation crashing down around my ears if anything happened to her daughter? That she said under no circumstances would Robin return there, and that the Thallonians weren't to be trusted?

"That what?" Tusari Gyn prompted him.

"Nothing," Jellico said. "It's nothing that can't be addressed. Look: I'll contact Calhoun. I'll see what he thinks."

"You could simply order him, I assume."

"If I firmly believed in the mission, I would do that without hesitation. In this case, I'm not sending Calhoun into it unless he's one hundred percent on board from the get-go. Not to mention that safe passage for Calhoun, for Lefler and her son, for the *Excalibur,* all of that would have to be absolutely guaranteed."

"You have my word as ambassador," Tusari Gyn said firmly.

"All right, then," said Jellico, and he stood. "I'll see what I can do."

"Thank you," and Gyn stood up as well. "It is all I can expect, given the circumstances. I appreciate you taking the time."

Gyn then bowed slightly, and Jellico bowed in

return. And once Gyn had departed, Jellico sat and turned the entire conversation over and over in his mind, trying to see the gaps in logic, trying to determine what he had missed and what he was overlooking.

Then he instructed his aide to get word to the *Excalibur* that he needed to have a conversation with her captain.

ii.

Tusari Gyn walked across the grand plaza outside Starfleet headquarters. He kept his gaze resolutely forward, not making eye contact with anyone.

Heading toward him from the other direction was Admiral Nechayev. She appeared lost in thought, not paying the slightest attention to anyone around her.

They drew within a few feet of each other and then passed without ever slowing.

But as they did, Gyn said in a low voice, "It's done."

Nechayev nodded in acknowledgment.

They went their separate ways.

Xenex

Shortly After Tusari Gyn's Meeting at Starfleet Headquarters

i.

D'ndai glanced out the window of his study and saw the crowds massing. More and more people were showing up with each passing minute. D'ndai shook his head and turned to face his bewildered and frustrated brother. "Well, this is becoming increasingly awkward," said D'ndai.

"I need a ship, D'ndai. And I need one quickly," said Calhoun.

"I'll see what I can arrange."

"It has to be now." He was pacing the room as if he were a caged animal looking for some means of escape.

D'ndai scowled at him. "What's the problem, little brother? Can't wait to get the hell off the planet that gave you birth?"

Calhoun stopped pacing and turned to face his brother, an edge to his voice that could have cut diamond. "You need to put aside whatever hurt feelings and envy you're still nursing. This isn't about me.

This is about you, and everyone around you. You can't begin to understand the level of danger you're in."

"What are you talking about, M'k'n'zy? So your ship accidentally left you behind. Aside from making you late for your next appointment, I don't see—"

"No, you don't see." He covered his eyes for a moment to compose himself, and then he lowered his hand. "D'ndai . . . it wasn't an accident. You need to understand that. These things don't happen by accident. It was done deliberately. I was abandoned here."

"Why would your crew do that? Is it mutiny?"

"My crew wouldn't do it. It's . . . complicated," he said, having no desire to get into a detailed discussion about a computer entity gone berserk. "The point is that leaving me behind wouldn't be the end of it, because sooner or later I would be able to get off the planet. Which means that the person responsible for this wouldn't allow enough time for that to happen. My being abandoned is step one; I need to get out of here before step two occurs."

"What do you think step two is going to be?" D'ndai still wasn't taking Calhoun completely seriously, but there was just enough concern flickering in his eyes to convey to Calhoun that he was at least listening.

"Honestly, I don't know," said Calhoun. "I have some guesses, but I think it safe to say that—whatever it is—it isn't going to be of benefit to the Xenexian people . . ."

His voice trailed off.

He felt that same unaccountable warning of danger that had always served him well.

Calhoun looked toward the ceiling, "through" it, sensing that whatever was happening, it was coming from above. Then he glanced toward the window, where Xenexians could be seen looking toward the sky, pointing, seemingly concerned.

"It's too late," he said softly. "I waited too long. It's here."

"What is?"

"Step two."

"All . . . all right," said D'ndai. He might not have been totally in accord with Calhoun's assessment of the situation, but he had enough respect for his brother to know that if M'k'n'zy of Calhoun said danger was imminent, then it very likely was. "We'll get you to a place of safety. Hide you . . ."

"Are you insane?" said Calhoun. "D'ndai, whatever's coming, it's coming for me. I'm not going to put anyone at risk."

"If someone were coming at your battleship specifically because they had a grudge against you, would you tell your crew that you were leaving them behind so that you would face the risk without endangering them?"

"Of course not, but this isn't the same thing. These people," and he gestured toward the Xenexians out the window and the planet's population in general, "they aren't my crew."

"No, but they are your people. Perhaps you've forgotten what that means."

"I haven't. It means I watch out for them. And placing them between me and whatever's coming for me would be unconscionable."

From above they could hear the distant roar of a ship's engines. Something was descending toward them. Obviously it wasn't such a large vessel that entering the atmosphere was problematic, but Calhoun could tell from the sound of it that it was sizable nonetheless. A small army could come pouring out of there, with one target in their sights: him.

"I'm not going to endanger them," said Calhoun firmly.

D'ndai's expression softened into one of understanding. He placed a hand on his brother's shoulder. "I understand," said D'ndai.

"Good."

Calhoun had no time to react as D'ndai's fist lashed out, striking him across the jaw. Caught completely flat-footed, Calhoun staggered, and D'ndai swung a roundhouse that clocked Calhoun from the other side. Calhoun tried to recover, tried to jab back at D'ndai, but D'ndai blocked it effortlessly and delivered an uppercut to the point of Calhoun's jaw. Any one of the three blows would have been enough to fell a normal man; it took the combination of all three to bring down Mackenzie Calhoun. His knees buckled as he took a determined step forward and then he collapsed, falling heavily to the ground.

"You have a lot going for you, M'k'n'zy," said D'ndai, "but I always was the better of the two of us when it came to hand-to-hand. You might want to remember that for next time."

It was the last thing Calhoun heard before the world faded to black around him.

ii.

D'ndai, for all the emotion and concern that he was displaying, could have been taking a casual walk in a pleasant forested area, as he emerged from his small, ramshackle home and strolled into the town square, where hundreds of people were clustering, looking up at the vessel hovering above them.

It wasn't as if the Xenexians had never seen a ship before; they had their own spaceport, as modest as it was. But they had never seen this particular design of vessel before, and the manner in which it was just hovering there, casting a vast shadow over the ground, was clearly intended to be intimidating.

We're not so easily intimidated as all that, D'ndai thought grimly. The obvious proof was that, whereas other people might have fled to shelter, the Xenexians were gathering and waiting, and there might have been bewilderment in their faces, but there was also quiet defiance. If the crew of the ship was attempting to frighten them, they were going to learn quickly that it was not going to work.

"Where did it come from?" D'ndai asked one of his people.

"Don't know. One minute it wasn't there, the next it was."

"A cloaking device," said D'ndai to himself. This was puzzling to him. He'd heard that Romulans had such devices, as did Klingons, but their ships had fairly distinctive looks to them. This vessel didn't look anything like those. This was far more blocky and utilitarian.

Suddenly a large hatch slowly irised open in the side of the vessel. There was a visible entranceway into the ship, but it was so dark within that it was impossible to discern anything inside.

And then a large armored figure appeared in the door. It stepped out and dropped the distance to the ground, landing with a thud that reverberated through the air. Then a second armored figure appeared and did the exact same thing, landing just to the right of the one before him. Then a third followed, and a fourth, and soon there were half a dozen of them gathered in the square, simply standing there, with no sign of weapons in their hands.

D'ndai had never seen anyone like them before. He made a practice of keeping himself apprised of all the major allies, and enemies, of the Federation, because as the tribal leader he felt it necessary to stay current on all potential threats. But he had no idea who these beings were. He didn't like the fact that they were covered head to toe in armor. It was going to make them extremely difficult to battle. He hoped it wouldn't come to that, but he was prepared for it.

Still . . . six against a hundred or so, with more of D'ndai's people arriving every moment. He had to think that the odds favored the Xenexians considerably.

The armored figures remained absolutely immobile, not even bothering to look around. The Xenexians were murmuring to themselves, questioning who these intruders might be, but no one seemed particularly afraid. A number of them were even smiling grimly, as if they were looking forward to a potential battle. It was the racial heritage of Xenexians always to anticipate a good fight.

Still, there was no reason to assume that such a fight was inevitable.

D'ndai stepped forward until his oncoming presence could not be ignored. One of the armored figures looked at him, or at least D'ndai thought he was looking at him. It was hard to tell.

"May I help you?" he asked.

He wasn't sure if the armored figure was going to respond at all, but then a deep, rumbling voice, speaking through some manner of electronic filter, said, *"You are in authority here?"*

"I am," said D'ndai. "Welcome to Xenex. Enjoy your stay."

"We are not staying. Give us Mackenzie Calhoun."

"There's no one here by that name," said D'ndai. As far as he was concerned, he was answering honestly.

The man he called "brother" was named M'k'n'zy. D'ndai had always detested the bastardization of his name that "Mackenzie" had embraced, and thus saw no reason to acknowledge it, particularly under circumstances such as these.

"Lying will do you no good. We know he is here."

"What you 'know' is up for debate," said D'ndai. "I am telling you that there is no one named Mackenzie Calhoun here. So if that is the entirety of your business, you would do well to be on your way."

"Give him to us now."

"Listen carefully," D'ndai said, and he could see the grim, prepared faces of the people all around him, his people, the ones who would never back down before an enemy. "You're new here, so it's possible you don't understand. So let me explain: Generally speaking, Xenexians do not do well with threats."

"The Brethren," said the armored figure, *"do not threaten."*

Whereupon the Brethren raised his gloved hand, and the next thing D'ndai knew he was being lifted off his feet, and the smell of something burning filled his nostrils, and he realized that the something burning was in him. Then the ground abruptly came up and slammed into him, and he heard an agonized scream that he recognized as that of his brother, and he thought, *The little idiot just doesn't know how to stay unconscious,* and then he thought nothing more.

iii.

The room was swimming around Calhoun as he came to. At first he was totally unaware of how he had wound up on the floor, and then it came back to him in a flash. He realized what his brother had done and, even more importantly, anticipated just exactly the danger that D'ndai had deliberately placed himself in.

Usually Calhoun did not awaken by degrees, as most people did: He snapped fully awake, ready for anything that could possibly be facing him. But the circumstances of his unconsciousness in this instance were artificial, and so it was that he didn't spring to his feet so much as lurch there. He nearly stumbled over his own ankles before recovering, throwing his arms out to either side to balance himself like a tightrope walker.

Then he heard D'ndai's booming voice outside, from not too far away judging by the reverberation. He was speaking in a challenging manner to someone whose identity was still unknown to Calhoun, but he had to think that it was no one who was out to do anything positive for either the Xenexians or the captain of the *Excalibur*.

Calhoun pulled out his phaser and approached the door to D'ndai's house. He didn't know what he was going to be facing, but he had to operate on the assumption that it was going to be an enemy. So he was prepared for that. The question was: What sort of enemy was it?

Does it matter? As long as it's the dead kind, what difference does it make?

He approached the front door, already in a crouch to present the smallest possible target. And at the exact instant that he opened it, he saw a member of what he knew to be the alien race known simply as the Brethren—the warrior race that served as the muscle to the relatively intellectual D'myurj—blasting his brother off his feet with some manner of energy pulse from his armor. D'ndai didn't even have time to scream as his body was hurled through the air. Then D'ndai slammed to the ground with such an impact that, to Calhoun, it was as if he could feel it all the way from where he was standing.

Calhoun let out a howl of fury, and even as he did so, the fighting computer that was his mind reviewed the ways in which a member of the Brethren could be killed.

There was only one of which he knew.

Action matched thought, and barely had D'ndai's limp body hit the ground when Calhoun charged forward, gripping his phaser tightly, targeting the small release vent on the side of the Brethren's armor that provided the single vulnerable spot. Then he leaped through the air, firing off a single phaser blast in what should have been an utterly impossible shot.

It wasn't.

The blast drilled into the vent, and the Brethren warrior threw wide his arms, staggered, shuddered for a few moments, and then toppled forward, hitting the ground with a resounding thud.

Calhoun performed a shoulder roll and came to his feet. Without slowing down, he continued firing, shouting, "Those vents in the side of their armor! That's your target! But don't get close, because the surface is superheated!"

The last part of his instructions arrived a moment too late for one woman who leaped upon the closest Brethren warrior while wielding a lengthy dagger. The Xenexian screamed as the armor seared her skin, but that didn't deter her from driving the dagger into the vent. It stabbed deep, right up to the hilt, and the Brethren stumbled and clawed at it, trying to pull it free even as his body was racked with what would be his death spasms. The Xenexian woman released her hold, falling to the ground and rolling away, a large part of her skin red and blistered and some of her clothing burned away. And yet the cry she let out upon her release was one of triumph rather than pain.

The Brethren came after the Xenexians then, but the Xenexians fell back. Despite the fact that this was no coordinated army, the Xenexians still moved in perfect precision, scattering without banging into one another. This was no terrified group of people running over themselves to escape danger. This was an instant military unit performing a strategic retreat so that other forces could step in.

The other forces arrived in no time. There were no archers in the Federation more deadly than those on

Xenex, and men and women practicing that particular trade now made their presence known. A number of them had already taken up positions on rooftops of the low buildings, just in case the new arrivals were planning some form of attack. All that they had required was a decent target, and with the shouted instructions from Calhoun, they now had it. With twangs of their bowstrings, they unleashed a volley of arrows. Ninety percent of them missed because the target was as precise as it was, and the angle of the entry point kept changing as the Brethren turned this way and that to face the new threat. But ten percent of them struck home, and that was all that was required. Within seconds after the attack upon D'ndai, all six of the Brethren lay scattered about the town square. Some of their bodies were still twitching, but otherwise they posed no threat.

The Xenexians sent up a loud, rousing cheer, and some began to chant the name "M'k'n'zy." Soon all of them were, and for a heartbeat Mackenzie Calhoun found himself back in his youth, when armies of his own brethren were cheering him and lauding him with praise for the great battles that he, as warlord, oversaw.

But now it all rang hollow for him. All that mattered to him was the unmoving body of his brother.

Calhoun ran to him and dropped to his knees, cradling his head upon his lap. D'ndai looked up at him blankly, as if he couldn't quite make out who or what he was seeing.

The ship continued to hover overhead, and Calhoun knew that if he could just somehow get to it, he could get off Xenex, return to the *Excalibur,* and then . . . what? Confront an out-of-control computer entity that could probably destroy the ship with a thought if she were so inclined? How the hell was *that* going to go? Not particularly well, he had to think.

Then he yanked his thoughts back to the here and now. This was not the time for long-term planning. He needed to find a way to save his brother. If he were on his own ship, there was every chance that the sickbay might have the means to deal with the catastrophic nerve damage that D'ndai had suffered. Here, on Xenex, where the medical facilities were still fairly primitive . . .

"You must be out of your mind."

It was a soft, low female voice, one that he recognized instantly.

Many Xenexians were still cheering, but some were now watching in confused silence, unsure of where this new arrival had come from. She had simply popped into existence, out of nowhere, wearing a Starfleet uniform and a contemptuous expression. She was standing over M'k'n'zy, the hero of Xenex, and speaking in a taunting manner. That alone was enough to prompt several of them to want to kill her just on principle, but they held themselves in check.

"How dare you," said Calhoun with a snarl, "disguise yourself as my wife."

"We are the D'myurj. We appear as we wish."

"Then die as we wish," said Calhoun, and without hesitation he brought up his phaser and took aim.

"You're just going to hit one of your own people," said "Shelby." "I'm not really here."

Calhoun frowned and then saw that the being standing in front of him wasn't casting a shadow. It was true; she was just a mirage.

"You see?" she continued. "You see how I'm being solicitous of your people's safety? More than you are, I should observe. This person is mortally wounded on your behalf and that one over there," and she indicated the woman who had been badly burned and was being carried away by several Xenexians to seek medical aid, "has only one chance in three of surviving, judging by the severity of the damage she sustained."

Calhoun wanted to snarl at her that the mortally wounded person she so casually referred to was his brother. But he caught himself; why give her the knowledge of the emotional blow he had just sustained? Instead what he needed right then was information, something that he could conceivably use against this . . . this creature. "I thought you D'myurj and the Brethren had had a falling-out. That you were no longer allies."

"That is true for many of my misbegotten race. But not I. I had the foresight to forge a different agreement with the Brethren; one that would take all of us to a more positive destiny than my weak-willed kin, who were dedicated to shepherding along the development of other races rather than taking charge as we should rightly do."

That was when Calhoun knew who he was dealing with. Soleta had described to him the insufferably smug member of the D'myurj she had encountered back on AF1963, the one who had turned traitor against his own species and set the Brethren against them. This was his handiwork.

"Shelby" knelt near him as if she were about to give him friendly words of advice, wife to husband. "Listen to me carefully, Calhoun. You're a smart fellow; you can't possibly think this is going to be the end of it. The Brethren will come and they will arrive in force. And your fellow Xenexians can celebrate all they want, but ultimately, anyone who stands between the Brethren and you is going to die. Is that what you want to bring down upon your people? Death and destruction? When the Brethren return, your only chance will be to surrender. In fact, if you tell me right now that you surrender, the ship will beam you up and you will be brought to us with no more danger to any of your people."

And without hesitation, Calhoun was ready to agree to it. It was the simplest way to avoid any further horrors visited upon the innocent Xenexians.

But before he could speak, D'ndai's hand suddenly gripped his forearm with astounding strength. Calhoun looked down at his brother, surprised.

D'ndai spoke with effort, gasping for every breath. He sounded as if his lungs had collapsed, which they very well might have. "They could . . . could beam you up . . . right now . . . now that they . . . know where . . . you are . . ."

Calhoun realized that his brother was right. How could something as patently obvious as that have eluded him? They had a direct sight line to him, and he knew the Brethren had transporter technology. Even if the ship was now devoid of crew and entirely computer operated, he could easily be targeted and brought up. At which point, if the plan was to dispose of him, they could reverse energize and disperse his molecules over several square miles of Xenexian territory. They didn't need his cooperation.

There was only one answer: They wanted the Xenexians to see him surrender. The great M'k'n'zy, the enemy of oppressors, the man who would rather die than let an enemy triumph, giving up meekly to an unseen opponent.

There's no more formidable enemy than a legend. It was a comment from one of the historical texts he had read, uttered by a Roman general, and it was as true now as it was thousands of years ago. And what better way to tear down a legend than to humiliate him in front of his own people?

It wouldn't matter to the Xenexians that he was doing it for their own good. It would be of no relevance that he was just trying to save their lives. Granted, there were many on Xenex who, to this day, resented the hell out of Calhoun for having left them shortly after they had been liberated of their oppressors. Who felt that he should have stayed and guided them rather than go off to pursue new vistas. But that was the older generation of Xenexians, and even many of them had softened their views as the horizons of Xenex had expanded due to increased Starfleet interest. As for the younger Xenexians, they had practically elevated him to the level of god.

There were few things that made louder noises than a god crashing to the ground. If nothing else, Calhoun knew that from personal experience, having witnessed it.

This wasn't simply about capturing Calhoun. It was about trying to break the spirits of the Xenexians. Calhoun couldn't say for sure that the strategy would work, but there was certainly some merit to it.

All of this passed through his mind in a matter of seconds, and it was just enough time for D'ndai to draw in sufficient breath to say what would be his last words:

"M'k'n'zy . . . if you give up . . . I will absolutely kill you . . ."

He dragged out the last syllable and then it trailed off, but with enough strength to carry through the now silent square, and every Xenexian within range heard it.

Then D'ndai slumped back and was gone.

The silence continued for a long moment, and then one of the Xenexians called out, "M'k'n'zy," each syllable carefully enunciated, each breath between prolonged.

And one by one, and then by tens and more did the chant continue until the entire square was resounding with the chanting of Calhoun's true name. The more fanciful would have imagined that the shout was taken up round the world, ranging from one pole of the planet to the other, all Xenexians coming together and uniting behind one common conviction:

M'k'n'zy of Calhoun would be removed from Xenex when he was pried from their cold, dead fingers.

The D'myurj that was wearing the face and form of Elizabeth Shelby smiled sadly and shook her head. "On your head, then, Calhoun. Don't say we didn't give you the chance. This is going to end badly."

"It will for you," said Calhoun tersely. "For all of you."

"Elizabeth Shelby" blinked out of existence at that point and, moments later, the ship that had been hovering overhead angled away.

Minutes later, explosions were sounding from a distance. It would not take the news long to arrive that the alien vessel had opened fire on the spaceport and demolished all the ships that had been docked there. Nor was there any telling when more ships would arrive, because it wasn't as if Xenex was a major destination or heavily traveled.

When the news did come, Calhoun wasn't the least bit surprised, because it was what he himself would have done if he had been in their position. Nor did it surprise him when he subsequently learned that there appeared to be some sort of planetary signal that was jamming any attempts to utilize subspace transmission. There would not be any possibility of getting word out to Starfleet or Bravo Station or anyone who could provide any sort of aid.

Mackenzie Calhoun was on a world surrounded by dedicated followers who would rather die than see him taken away . . .

. . . and he was completely alone.

U.S.S. Excalibur,
En Route to New Thallon
Minus Her Captain

i.

Kalinda's red skin turned several shades of pink when Tania Tobias met up with her at Ten-Forward and informed her of their newly dictated mission from Starfleet.

Tania had hoped that, by telling Kalinda about it in a public place, it would minimize whatever negative response she might have. The reasoning was that, once Kalinda got over her initial shock and had time to listen to what Tania had to say, she would have a more measured reaction.

"You can't be serious!" the normally soft-spoken Kalinda shouted at the top of her lungs. *"Are they out of their minds?!"*

Whatever conversations were being held in Ten-Forward came crashing to a halt. All eyes were instantly upon the two of them, and Tania felt as if she were withering under the collective, curious stare of the rest of the crew.

So much for that idea, thought Tania.

Kalinda slid off her chair and headed for the door. "Where are you going?" Tania called after her.

"I need to get off this ship!" said Kalinda, and she sprinted into the hallway. Tania quickly ran off after her.

One crewman muttered in her wake, "There are days I know exactly how she feels."

Meanwhile Tania caught up with Kalinda as she was barreling down the corridor. "Where do you think you're going?"

"You already asked me that."

"I know, but 'off this ship' is kind of vague."

"It seemed pretty specific to me."

"Will you for God's sake listen to me?" She grabbed Kalinda by the wrist to try and stop her.

Kalinda spun, yanked Tania forward, and brought her own leg up, tripping Tobias and sending her face-first to the floor. Tania grunted as she hit and Kalinda, abashed, immediately released her grasp. Her hands fluttered to her face and she said, "I'm sorry! Are you okay?"

"I was better when I wasn't getting slammed to the floor," said Tania.

Helping Tania to her feet, Kalinda said hurriedly, "I think Si Cwan must have left behind some of his fighting reflexes from when he was possessing my body."

This comment also drew strange looks from passing crewmen, and more and more, Tobias was regretting that she hadn't conducted this entire conversation in the solitude of their quarters. "Look, Kally . . . could you please keep your mouth shut until we can get somewhere private?"

"You're the one who brought it up in public in the first place."

"Don't remind me."

Acceding to Tania's request, Kalinda promptly silenced herself until they were safely in their quarters. Kalinda stood there with her hands moving in vague patterns, clearly nervous, and Tania put her arms around her and tried to steady her. "You have to listen to me, Kally. You have no reason to be scared."

"I have every reason," said Kalinda. "You weren't there. You don't know what it was like, and you don't know what happened."

"I know how they treated you there. I know about the attacks. And it was awful and brutal, and I totally understand. But that doesn't mean you're going to be in any danger once we get there. You don't have to go down to the planet's surface if you don't want to. They only want to talk to the captain . . ."

"They want to talk to him about me. About me and Robin and Cwansi. This is going to lead to bad things, Tania, I swear."

"How do you know?"

"Because Thallon and New Thallon are where bad things happen," she said matter-of-factly. Gently but firmly she pushed Tania away from herself and turned her back. "Lots of bad things. And they stay there. And they'll be waiting for me there."

"I don't understand. Are you . . . is this something to do with the spirits again?" That had been an extremely difficult aspect of Kalinda for Tania to fully comprehend. This entire business that Kalinda was able to see ghosts or spirits or lost souls or whatever you'd want to call it. That she was somehow in tune with the netherworld. None of that made a great deal of sense to her.

Then again, it wasn't as if Tania was completely free herself from abilities that were not readily measurable by anything having to do with normal science but instead were firmly rooted in the realm of the paranormal. So who was she to judge?

Kalinda looked at her over her shoulder. "They're stronger there," she said. "Where the bad things happen . . . that's where they're the most potent. I can't shut them out. They like me because they see me as a link to the world from which they've been torn, and they . . . they won't leave me alone. They make it difficult to ignore them, Tania, so very, very difficult."

"Does it happen if you keep off the planet?"

"It can. It's harder for them, unless it's someone with a very strong will and a personal connection, like my brother had to me."

"Then, like I said, we'll just make sure you stay up here. And if they try to come up here, I'll . . ."

"You'll what?" said Kalinda, turning fully to face her. She sounded frustrated. "What can you possibly do that will be of help?"

Tania considered it and then said with a lopsided

smile, "I'll get you really, really drunk and then do all sorts of fun things to you. So even if the ghosts are watching you, you'll be in no condition to care."

Kalinda stared at her blankly for a moment, and then she laughed. It was very soft and even a bit uncomfortable, but at least it was something. "I would like that a lot."

"Then it sounds like we have a plan," Tania said approvingly. She put out her arms and Kalinda went to her. She held her tightly and closed her eyes and kissed her, and for that moment, everything seemed as if it was going to be fine.

If she could have seen Kalinda's face, however, she would have thought differently.

ii.

"Captain?" said Burgoyne, standing outside Calhoun's quarters. "Do you have a moment?" When there was no answer, s/he rang the chime again, and then started to turn away when a voice came from within, instructing hir to enter.

Burgoyne did so, to see Calhoun lying leisurely on the bed. His boots were on, which seemed a bit odd to Burgoyne, but nothing that was worth dwelling on.

"What's up, Burgy?" said Calhoun.

"Everything all right, Captain?"

"Sure. Why do you ask?"

"Well, this mission we've just received orders for—

the one to New Thallon—it seems a bit strange, don't you think?"

"Not really."

Burgoyne was a bit surprised at the response. "No?"

"Not at all." Calhoun turned over onto his side and propped his head up with his hand. "The Thallonians know they're in a bind. They have a major political snafu that they're trying to deal with, and they've come to the conclusion that I'm the only person who can possibly help them get it done. As far as I'm concerned, this is the most sensible decision I've seen them make in ages."

"And you don't think there might be some sort of ulterior motive for it?"

"Of course there might be," Calhoun admitted readily. "But I've been doing this a long time, Burgy, and so have you. Do you seriously think that if something isn't the way it appears to be, you and I won't be able to keep one step ahead of them?"

"I suppose that's true," said Burgoyne. "But even so—"

"How's your son?"

Burgy was confused by the abrupt change of topics. "What? You mean Xy?"

"Do you have another son that I'm unaware of?"

"No."

"Then yes, obviously I mean Xy. How is he responding to the medication?"

Burgoyne knew what Calhoun was referring to.

Selar, Xy's mother, had obtained a formula for a medication that would counteract Xy's unfortunate genetic makeup. Instead of speeding through his aging cycle and living no more than four years, Xy would have close to a century of life ahead of him, thanks to Selar. The tragic cost of that discovery had been Selar's life. But she had died willingly in order to extend her son's life, and Burgoyne was content in that knowledge.

"He's . . . doing fine. The prognosis is excellent and it appears that the cure is working exactly the way his mother was hoping," said Burgoyne. "Thank you for asking. Now about New Thallon . . ."

"You don't find it odd?"

"Odd?" s/he echoed.

"Well, I haven't seen you mourn the loss of Selar. You loved her, didn't you?"

"Yes, but—"

"But what? It doesn't bother you that you seem disconnected from what happened?"

"I'm not . . . disconnected," said Burgoyne. "I just respect her decision—"

"That's not the way it works, Burgy," said Calhoun easily. "Not in my experience. I mean, you haven't so much as shed a tear. At least not to my knowledge. Have you, and I just didn't know about it?"

"I . . ." Suddenly feeling helpless, all Burgy could manage was a slow shake of hir head.

"Then that tells me one of two things: Either you're in shock, or you just didn't give a damn about her."

"Captain, I don't quite see how—"

"If it's the first option, I'm not entirely sure that you're capable of carrying out your duties," Calhoun went on, his voice sounding almost implacable. "If it's the second . . . what does that say about you, Burgy? It says to me that you need to spend some time with the ship's counselor. Do you disagree?"

"When . . ." Burgy cleared hir throat. "When you put it that way . . ."

"Then I suggest you attend to your own needs, and stop worrying about our mission to New Thallon. It's all in hand, Burgy. Have a little faith."

"Yes, sir. I'm sorry to bother you."

Calhoun rolled over onto his back and interlaced his fingers behind his head. "No bother at all, I assure you."

Burgoyne left Calhoun's quarters, feeling somewhat dazed. S/he was unsure of what had just transpired in there, but s/he was so distracted by the things that Calhoun had said about Selar that s/he wasn't able to give it much thought. Instead all hir concerns were self-directed, rather than pondering anything having to do with Captain Calhoun.

Which was exactly what Calhoun had wanted.

Daystrom Institute

Shortly Thereafter

Seven had fallen asleep, much against her will. The fact that she had been awake for thirty-two hours straight would have been a sufficient excuse as far as anyone else was concerned, but Seven was determined to tough it out. Unfortunately, her body was in conflict with her on that point, and even though she intended to rest her eyes only for a few seconds, she was unconscious before she knew what hit her.

She was sitting in a chair in the computer lab, and she had slumped back in it with her head tilted to one side. There was a bit of spittle drooling from the corner of her mouth.

The Doctor stood in front of her, watching her for a moment, and then he reached over and wiped away the spittle with his finger.

"You have a sample of her DNA right there," came Soleta's voice from behind him. "You planning to clone her?"

Looking slightly embarrassed, the Doctor wiped his hand on his shirt and then straightened up in that way that people do when they feel they've been caught at something. "I have plenty of her DNA on file if I were interested in doing that," he said haughtily, and then he frowned. "That didn't come out exactly the way I planned it."

"My sympathies," said Soleta, not sounding especially sympathetic. "Come. I need your opinion on the growth rate of the virus."

The Doctor followed her into the adjoining lab. The technicians of the Daystrom Institute had been particularly generous in providing use of their facilities, especially considering that the Doctor had refused to tell them to what use they were being put. He simply assured them that it was a matter of Federation security, and that he would do nothing to blow up the lab. They took him at his word and cleared out.

Growing a nano-virus was a tricky endeavor. It had to be monitored constantly, and extreme vigilance needed to be exerted lest the virus find a means of escaping. Were that to happen, the results could be catastrophic. There was one race of would-be conquerors, the Cineen, who attempted to develop just such a virus, but they lacked the facilities to properly control it. The virus escaped and, instead of becoming the dominant race of their system, the Cineen wound up practically back in the stone age, with their planet under quarantine for a hundred years—the projected amount of time required for the virus to run its course. As a result, growing a nano-virus was not something undertaken lightly. Indeed, had the heads of the

Daystrom Institute known about it, they might have thought twice about permitting the Doctor to develop one in their facility.

Once in the lab, the Doctor went straight to the kinetic simulator and studied the readings. "The nano-molecular mechanisms are performing exactly within the anticipated parameters."

"Yes. And I believe the gp1 promoters have moved from class 1 to class 2," said Soleta.

"I concur," said the Doctor. "Faster than expected, actually."

"I managed to expedite their development."

The Doctor looked at her with interest. "How did you solve the ordinary differential equations?"

"I used a fourth-order Runge-Kutta algorithm. It enabled me to translocate the T7 nano-DNA."

"Of course." The Doctor was suitably impressed, and he let it show. "That was very innovative of you. You should be a science officer. Oh wait, you were. Before you walked away from Starfleet."

"I hardly walked away. I was shoved out the door."

"For not being forthcoming about your back-ground."

"For not telling anyone in Starfleet about some-thing in my personal life that wasn't any of their damned business."

The Doctor "harrumphed" over that. "Hard for me to envision," he said. "I would think that Starfleet has a good reason to be concerned about such things. It would seem rather arbitrary if they just picked some aspect of someone's nature and designated that that, and that alone, made them unfit to serve."

"Believe me, sometimes it is just that arbitrary, and just that foolish." She shook her head. "I doubt you'd understand."

"Why?" he said primly. "Because you think I'm not truly alive?"

"That's not what I 'think,' Doctor," said Soleta. "It's just a matter of demonstrable fact, no matter how many books you may write about the subject."

"As far as I'm concerned—"

Soleta put up her hands, looking tired. "Do me a favor, if you wouldn't mind? How about you spare us this discussion? A discussion that I assure you is going to go absolutely nowhere."

"Very well."

"Thank you."

"Except to say—"

"Oh God," she moaned.

He continued on the thought, ignoring her weary reaction. "—that if I feel alive, who are you to say that I'm not?"

"Someone who actually *is* alive."

"Except anyone who didn't know of my origins would be unable to discern any difference between the two of us."

"It's not about what other people say . . ."

"I agree. So why should your opinions as to whether or not I'm alive be anything that I should pay attention to?"

Soleta smiled tiredly. "Well, you've got me there. You shouldn't pay attention. Glad we had this discussion. So how soon do you think we'll be ready to translocate the virus into a containment field in order to—"

"I assume it's because you believe you have a soul."

She had been leaning against a wall, her body sagging with exhaustion. She had been up for as long as Seven, but she had been able to prevent herself from succumbing to slumber. That didn't mean she was any less tired, though, and now she started thudding the back of her head against the wall. "You are like a damned dog with a bone between its teeth. You're just not going to let this go, are you?"

"I am simply trying to understand . . ."

"No. You're not," and she moved away from the wall and toward the Doctor. "You're trying to convince me we shouldn't do anything to shut down Morgan."

"There is only one crime punishable by death according to Starfleet, and she has not committed that crime."

"We're *not* killing her! She's already dead! We are simply exorcising a ghost!"

"It's going to feel the same to her."

"She *can't feel!* At most, she only thinks she can!"

"What's the difference?" he asked.

"Because she doesn't have a soul! All right?" she said in exasperation. "I know it's an insanely unscientific yardstick to use for a measure of being alive, but sometimes the ephemeral is all we've got. There is no molecular difference between a dead body and a living one, so there has to be *something* that is beyond scientific quantification, and considering how little sleep I've had, that's the best I've got right now. She's not alive because she doesn't have a soul, and oh, by the way, I hate to be the one to tell you, but neither do you."

Anger flickered on the Doctor's face and then he pointed out, "You're the one who referred to her as a ghost. What else *is* a ghost but a discorporated soul?"

"She's not an actual ghost. That's just the closest convenient word to describe her."

"And isn't it possible that the closest word to describe me is 'alive'?"

Soleta rubbed her eyes in a desperate fight to keep them open. "You could just go on talking about this all day, all night, couldn't you?"

"Absolutely," he said immediately.

"Someone who is *really* alive couldn't do that. Only something's that not alive never needs rest."

"I consider it to be merely a perk of my particular status," he said, but there was a touch of uncertainty in his voice.

They stared at each other for a time, and then Soleta said, "How much of this is about her? And please," she added quickly before he could reply, "do not insult my intelligence by asking 'What her?' because we both know perfectly well which 'her' I'm referring to."

"I . . ." Then with renewed determination he said, "These are strongly held beliefs that I've formed over a lengthy period of contemplation and self-exploration—"

"How much? Of this? Is about her? Or more accurately, her and you?"

He was about to continue to protest, but then he stopped. Soleta watched him warily, curious as to what he would say.

"There is no her and me," he said flatly.

"And yet you hold out hope."

"I do not. Whatever 'moment' we may or may not have had is long past. We are simply friends now. Friends and colleagues."

"That may be what you believe. Or it may be what you're convincing yourself you may believe. Or it may be that if you were truly alive, you might have a better chance with her than if you were not."

"There are wider issues at stake than my love life or lack thereof," he informed her, reacquiring some of the archness of his tone from earlier.

"Fine. There are wider issues."

"Thank you for acknowledging that. Nine hours."

She shook her head. "Excuse me?"

"In answer to your question. Nine hours before we are ready to—"

"Translocate the virus, yes, right, of course." She tapped the side of her skull. "Should have remembered that."

"Soleta . . ."

"Yes?"

"You realize that I am putting myself at tremendous risk here. I could wind up dying in the attempt to accomplish something, the ethics of which I am still uncertain of."

The way he said that made Soleta nervous. If they didn't have the Doctor squarely in their corner, the entire operation could go entirely off the rails. "What are you saying, Doctor?"

"I'm saying that—should that occur—I would be most appreciative if you mourned my passing, just as you would with someone who is alive."

Inwardly, so that the Doctor couldn't see it, Soleta laughed.

Outwardly, she nodded and said, "It would be my honor to mourn you."

"And mine," and he bowed slightly, "to be mourned by you."

"Let's hope it doesn't come to that."

"It was my understanding that 'hope' was something typically reserved for those who are alive."

"I think we can afford to stretch the definition a bit in this case."

"That's very generous of you." He looked her up and down. "You need to get some sleep."

"Is that your medical opinion?"

"It is."

"Then who am I," she said, each word laced with fatigue, "to argue with a doctor?"

Short minutes later, she was sound asleep. Whereas

Seven was sagged in a chair, Soleta simply stretched out on the floor, preferring the hardness of the surface beneath her. Her chest rose and sank slowly.

A bit of spittle started to trail down the side of her face.

The Doctor scooped it up for his collection.

U.S.S. Excalibur, Orbiting New Thallon

Ten Hours Later

i.

Everyone on the bridge of the *Excalibur,* without exception, turned to Calhoun in utter astonishment. Sitting calmly in the captain's chair, he glanced around and said with just a touch of sarcasm, "Is there a problem?"

No one seemed to know where to start. It was Kebron who spoke first: "You're going down by yourself, Captain?"

"I believe I recognized my own voice saying exactly those words," said Calhoun.

Morgan, seated at her ops station, turned to face Calhoun. "I don't know that that's wise, Captain."

"The Thallonians will see it as a sign of confidence and strength," Calhoun pointed out. "That will give me greater leeway in the negotiations, as opposed to hiding behind a phalanx of security guards."

"And I suppose that pointing out that this is contrary to Starfleet regulations would be a waste of time?"

"How well you know me, Morgan."

"Captain," said Tobias, "Mr. Kebron and Morgan are right. This is an extremely bad idea. Kalinda has already been going on about how dangerous the entire mission is. You heading down completely on your own . . ."

"Have I ever given you cause to think that there's a situation I'm incapable of handling?"

"This isn't about a vote of confidence, Captain," Xy said from the science station. In recent days, Xy had been serving double duty as both science officer and temporary chief medical officer, until such time as Calhoun named a replacement for the late Selar. "This is about what's best for you and for the mission."

"I think I know what's best for me, and the mission will take care of itself." There was now an unaccustomed brittleness to Calhoun's voice. "I was making a declaration, people. I wasn't planning to open it to debate. This is not, last I checked, a democracy. Commander Burgoyne," and he turned to look warily at his second in command, "do *you* wish to weigh in on this matter?"

"No, sir," said Burgoyne.

Calhoun cocked an eyebrow. "Really. Because everyone else seems to have something to say."

"I assume that you've already made your decision after some consideration, and that should be honored."

"Good." Calhoun nodded once and then rose from his chair. "Burgy, you have the conn."

"Actually, sir, I'd like to talk to you on the way down to the transporter room."

Calhoun did nothing to indicate that this would be the slightest problem. "Of course. Mr. Kebron, the conn is yours for the moment."

"Yes, sir. Captain: Permission to keep a security team on high alert?"

"That's good thinking, Kebron. You do that."

Calhoun then walked into the turbolift, Burgoyne right behind him. "Transporter room," Calhoun said, and the lift promptly angled downward and then across.

"So, Burgy, what did you want to talk to me about?" said Calhoun.

Burgoyne did not respond. Instead s/he stared fixedly at Calhoun, and hir nostrils flared slightly as s/he did so.

"Burgy? I'm not a mind reader, you know. Are you following up on our discussion of the other day? Have you been talking to Kebron to sort out your various issues? Or perhaps . . ."

Then Calhoun's voice trailed off, and he sighed deeply.

The turbolift slid to a halt on the transporter room level, but the doors didn't open. Burgoyne didn't even glance around, as if this was something s/he was expecting.

"So what gave me away?" said Calhoun. "I mean, I know something did. There was a rapid change in your biometrics precisely eight-point-three seconds after the turbolift doors closed. I doubt this was prompted merely by being in proximity to me. Something has changed. I assume that somehow you saw through it."

"I should have done so sooner. I would have, back in your quarters, except you wound up distracting me with all your comments about my state of mind and Selar."

"That wasn't to distract you. Well, not just to distract you. I really am concerned about you."

"When did you install holotech in the turbolifts?"

"Oh, I manage to budget my time. You'd be amazed what I have the opportunity to do."

"I would feel a great deal more comfortable," said Burgoyne stiffly, "if you were to drop the façade immediately."

"Very well." There was no shimmering, no ripple of transition of any kind. One moment Calhoun was standing there, and then, just like that, it was Morgan who was looking at hir with a sad expression, as if she felt sorry for hir. "If this will make you feel better. I still want to know how you were aware, though."

"Your smell."

"Smell? I don't—" She closed her eyes. "Of course."

"All living things produce some manner of scent. Humans don't have sharp enough olfactory sense to perceive it, but I do. If Ensign Janos or Lieutenant M'Ress were still aboard this ship, they would have noticed its absence immediately. In my case, well . . . I've let myself get sloppy. It took me this long, and this degree of proximity, to realize that you weren't giving off any sort of scent whatsoever."

Morgan looked mortified at the omission. "I'm a computer mind, for heaven's sake. How could I not have anticipated that holograms have no scent, and that might be noticeable to you?"

"Obviously because you still have human limitations."

She nodded in reluctant agreement. "That is certainly the case for now. But it may not always be that way. So," and her mind already seemed prepared to move on to other matters, "what do you see happening now? I mean, you're not trying to sound a red alert or some such."

"I didn't consider that a viable option since you're in charge of the alert systems on the ship. You're pretty much in charge of *every* aspect of the ship."

"That's very true." She seemed quite chipper about it.

"I'm more interested in what *your* next step is," said Burgoyne. "As far as everyone else is concerned, Captain Calhoun was last seen departing the bridge. People are going to wonder why he didn't report to the transporter room."

"Why would they wonder that?"

That was when s/he realized. "Of course. You, of all people, are able to multitask."

"Yes, indeed. Which is why Captain Calhoun has already shown up in the transporter room and been beamed down to the surface of New Thallon."

"Except it wasn't him; it was you posing as him while you were talking to me at the same time."

"Aren't you at all curious as to where the real Calhoun is?"

"I'm assuming one of two things. Either you've killed him in his sleep and then disposed of his body . . ."

Morgan affected a look of positive amazement. "How could you possibly think I would do such a thing? To just kill him cold-bloodedly in such a way. After everything he's done for me, and for Robin. What you must think of me, Burgoyne, to imagine I'd—"

". . . or else you abandoned him on Xenex."

"Okay, that I *did* do. But at least I gave him a fighting chance."

"Fighting? He's going to be fighting someone?"

"If the plan works out, yes, and I've no reason to think otherwise. It's how he would want to die, don't you think?"

"Listen to yourself, Morgan. Listen to the things you're saying." It was all Burgoyne could do to keep hir voice level and calm. S/he had to keep reminding hirself that s/he was dealing with a malfunctioning machine, not a human being. "This is not something that you would have said or done back when you were alive. You've lost all sense of conscience. You're severing your ties to humanity."

"Mac was the one who started it," she retorted. "Talk about severing ties. He was the one who made it clear that he wanted nothing to do with me. That he wanted to explore ways to put an end to me. You're saying I'm not human? What can be more fundamentally human than a desire for self-preservation? I ask you."

"And how far will you go in that quest for self-preservation?"

"Meaning . . . ?"

"Meaning where does the rest of the crew fit in to your quest for self-preservation? Here you've talked about how much you owe Mac, and the way you thanked him was abandoning him . . ."

"On his home planet, when I could simply have—as you pointed out—killed him. I think I was being generous."

"So what about the rest of us? Those to whom you may not think you owe any personal debt?" Burgoyne continued to keep hir voice flat and even, not betraying so much as the slightest hint of the rising urgency s/he was feeling. S/he was determined to keep Morgan talking while s/he tried to come up with some course of action that Morgan might not expect. Unfortunately, nothing much was coming to mind, plus s/he was trying to outthink a computer mind. Yes, Morgan had been tripped up by the error of not considering body scent, but that was certainly no reason to think that any future mistakes would be forthcoming. "What happens to us? To them?"

"Do you really think I would just commit wholesale slaughter?" She sounded disappointed that s/he could even conceive of such a thing. "It saddens me that you'd think I'd do that. However . . ."

"However what?"

The red alert klaxon suddenly began to sound. Burgy looked around in confusion, thinking for a moment that the stopped turbolift had somehow triggered some manner of fail-safe. But that didn't make any sense to hir.

Then, with hir superb hearing, Burgy detected a distant sound, a very distinct discharge of concentrated energy blasting away from the ship.

The big guns of the *Excalibur*'s phasers were cutting loose at a target. But nothing was shooting at the ship; s/he would have heard the blasts careening off the shields. If they weren't under attack, though, then who the hell were they shooting at? S/he looked to Morgan questioningly.

"Well," and now she smiled, and it was a smile without any humor, or compassion, or mercy, "you can't make an omelet . . ."

ii.

In Tania Tobias's quarters, Kalinda was lying on the ground, her knees drawn up to her chest, her arms wrapped around her legs. Her eyes were wide with shock and she was trembling.

Her voice was barely above a whisper as carnage was unleashed far below her.

"So many lives . . . so many dead . . . so many . . . I knew bad things would happen here . . . I knew it . . ."

She kept saying it over and over, and there was none to hear her.

iii.

"Shut it down! Shut it down!" Xy was shouting from the science station.

"Thank you for the advice. That would never have occurred to me," Kebron shot back, keeping his tone flat and professional, even as he labored over the tactical board, trying to determine what in the world was going on. "Tobias, change our angle. Aim us away—"

"Already attempting to. Helm is nonresponsive. The entire navigation system has locked me out." Tobias turned to the ops station and called out, "Morgan! Whatever's causing this to happen, override it and shut it down."

"I'm trying to raise the captain," said Kebron. "He's not responding. Transporter room can't even get a lock on his combadge to bring him back up."

Morgan was seated at the ops station, her hands resting lightly on the console, her eyes fixed on the front screen. On it, the bridge crew was able to see exactly what their instruments were telling them was occurring: The phaser banks of the *Excalibur* were unloading on New Thallon, causing untold, incalculable damage wherever they were striking. There was no one section that was being targeted. Instead the shots were being scattered all over the surface, in the hearts of major cities, hammering away at full strength. Tania almost imagined she could hear the screams of the dying coming from far below.

Morgan didn't move.

"Morgan!"

Tobias was out of her chair, crossing to the ops station, and she shouted, *"Morgan!"* one more time and reached for her.

Her hand passed right through her. Morgan wasn't even bothering to maintain the solidity of her holographic form. It was just sitting there as an illusion, nonresponsive. Tobias waved her hand through a few more times, as if she were trying to clear the air.

Kebron tried everything he could think of to override the weapons systems, but nothing was working. "As long as there's power going to the phasers, I can't shut it down—"

"Then we need to shut everything down," said Xy.

Kebron realized what he meant. It was a majorly risky move, one that would leave the *Excalibur* disastrously vulnerable. A decision like this was normally above his pay grade. But the captain had left the ship and couldn't be reached, and the second in command was MIA. The decision, and possible consequences, rested on him. He didn't nod because he had no neck and so nodding was problematic. Instead he simply said, "Do it."

Immediately Xy called out, "Bridge to engineering!"

"Engineering!" came back the voice of Lieutenant Ronni Beth, the right-hand woman to Chief Engineer Mitchell. She sounded concerned, which was understandable. There were certain protocols that were always followed when the phaser banks were engaged, and none of them was being followed in this instance.

Xy could not have cared less about protocols at that moment. "Shut down the core and the power couplings! Shut down everything!"

"Everything?"

"*Everything!* Take us to black!"

He didn't have to explain the severity of this decision to Lieutenant Beth; she knew as well as anyone how open to attack they'd be leaving the *Excalibur.* They would have as much offensive capability as a paperweight. And it would remain that way for as long as it took them to start the engines back up, which would be a process of some minutes since a cold start-up was courting disaster. But there was simply no alternative. "Initiating shutdown, aye," came back Beth's voice.

Seconds passed like hours as the phaser banks continued to punish the surface of New Thallon. The world had planetary defenses, big guns that were capable of returning fire, but the lack of assault on the *Excalibur* led Kebron to suspect that they had been the first targets. If that was the case, then that eliminated any possible theory that the attack was random. Then again, he had already come to the conclusion that there was nothing random about any of this. He had figured out who and what was behind it because it was the only thing that made any sense.

This was even further affirmed, as if he needed any further confirmation, when Beth's voice came back from engineering: "Shutdown failed! Repeat, shutdown failed! The system is keeping us out! Every time we try to initiate the shutdown sequence, the system itself countermands it! It keeps changing all the access codes, even the prefix code! We've got nothing down here!"

Xy exchanged a look of growing hopelessness, even as he said, "Acknowledged. Keep trying and keep us apprised." Quickly he left the science station and crossed straight to Kebron. In a low voice, or as low as he could go while still being audible over the red alert klaxon, "Morgan's not a victim of whatever this is, is she. She's the cause of it."

"Yes," said Kebron, reverting for once to his former terseness.

"What do we do?"

Kebron glanced at him without turning his head. "We wait."

"For what?"

"For this to play out. This isn't happenstance. There's a plan being enacted, and all we can do at this point is bear witness to it, and hope we get a chance to make things right."

"Make things right?" Xy's face was grim. "How? Wave a magic wand and restore to life all the poor bastards who are dying down there?"

Kebron didn't answer, because they both knew there wasn't anything that he could say.

iv.

S/he knew it was pointless. S/he knew that nothing was going to be accomplished by it.

But after five minutes of being trapped in the turbolift with a smug computer entity that was pretending to be sympathetic, deaf, dumb, and blind, knowing perfectly well that the phaser banks were unloading on the surface of New Thallon, trying to raise anyone on the crew via hir combadge and getting absolutely nowhere, and finally, unable to take it anymore, Burgoyne unleashed a full-throated roar. Hir claws extended from hir fingertips, and hir lips drew back, revealing hir fangs. Morgan, who had just been in the process of offering psychoanalysis as to why s/he had never been happy on hir home world and never truly fit in with other Hermats, and because of that hir entire relationship with Selar was doomed to self-destruct from the very beginning, looked startled as Burgoyne came straight at her.

S/he swept hir claws across Morgan's face, across her chest, and a huge flap of skin was suddenly hanging down from where Burgoyne's claws had shredded it, and a chunk of her torso was naked and exposed, blood pouring from it. S/he swung hir claws again, slicing across Morgan's throat, severing the jugular, and Morgan staggered, clutching at it, her eyes wide with confusion and yes, there was even terror mirrored there for just a second, just an instant.

Burgoyne spun, rebounding off the edge of the turbolift, and came right at Morgan again.

And she was gone.

Burgoyne went right through the space that Morgan had been occupying and banged into the far wall. S/he landed in a crouch, hir head snapping around, and then s/he heard Morgan's angry voice in the turbolift.

"That was not funny, Burgoyne. Not funny at all. We were not amused."

"Get back in front of me," s/he snarled, "and we'll see how much more I can not amuse you."

Abruptly the distant sound of the phasers ceased. Burgoyne looked around, hir fangs already starting to retract. Had s/he somehow managed to—?

"I stopped because I didn't want to deplete the phaser banks entirely. You may need them. I've turned the ship around and you are now departing New Thallonian space, very, *very* slowly."

Burgoyne's voice was gravelly, and s/he felt like hir body was engorged with blood. S/he was having trouble bringing hirself down from the killing instinct that had briefly seized control of hir. "You did this so that they'd come after us. So that they would try to destroy us."

"There was only so long I could have kept the imposture of Calhoun going," she admitted. "This was going to have to happen sooner or later. I chose to make it sooner. And I will give you the same opportunity that I provided Calhoun: to die on the best possible terms, fighting for your lives against overwhelming odds. I mean, you could give up, I suppose. But I don't expect you to surrender any more than I expect Mac to. That was part of the deal I made."

"Deal?"

"Nothing that need concern you," her voice said offhandedly. "You could have easily been destroyed, and so too could Mac. But you've all earned far more than that. So I've arranged it all for you to die the way you should: bravely and in action. I could do no less."

"You," said Burgoyne, "are not Morgan Primus, if you ever were. And we will cut you out of the *Excalibur* like the cancer that you are . . ."

"Now, now," she scolded him. "You're not exactly in a position to be issuing threats, Burgoyne."

The turbolift suddenly jolted and started heading in the opposite direction from where it had been going.

"I'm bringing you back to the bridge," Morgan's voice informed hir. "I suspect you're all going to have a great deal to discuss. I wish you the best of luck."

"If the ship is destroyed," Burgoyne said, "you're going to go with it."

"That would be silly, if I was going to let that happen. Of course I'm not going to go with the ship when it's destroyed. I'm immortal, my dear. It's funny," she mused, "I was immortal for such a long time, and I became so sick of it. All I wanted to do was die. And then I became what I am, and now all I want to do is live. Funny, isn't it."

"And yet I'm not laughing."

"I wouldn't expect you to see the humor of it," she said. "Maybe in your last moments, you will."

With that, the doors of the turbolift opened and Burgoyne emerged into chaos.

Starfleet Headquarters, San Francisco

A Short Time Later

Edward Jellico had just returned from chaos.

As head of Starfleet operations, he had stood before the Federation Council and withstood a storm of criticism and interrogation as to the barbaric and catastrophic actions taken by the starship *Excalibur* and her captain, Mackenzie Calhoun. One after another the questions were flung at him like a barrage of hailstones: "Has Calhoun lost his mind?" "Why didn't his psych profile predict this?" "Was this part of a Starfleet plan to instigate an interstellar incident?" "Was the entire crew of the *Excalibur* in on this?" "Has there been a mutiny?" "How are you going to stop him?" "Can he *be* stopped?"

And Jellico had fought back as much as he could. He reminded them of Calhoun's lengthy and distinguished service to the Federation, and the numerous times—including as recently as a major Borg incursion—when he and his ship had been instrumental in saving countless lives.

But this had been promptly combated with incidents taken from Calhoun's records that detailed his many instances of insubordination, including, most damning, condemnations written by Jellico himself. The assumption of the Council, rather than accepting that subsequent events had caused Jellico to change his mind, was that Jellico was automatically moving to blindly defend one of his officers.

With condemnations, dictates, and warnings ringing in his ears, Jellico returned to his office only to find both Admiral Nechayev and Tusari Gyn waiting just outside it. *Perfect,* he thought.

"Ambassador. Admiral," he said, nodding to each one in sequence. He didn't even bother to ask them to follow him inside; he knew they would do so without being invited. He was, as it turned out, correct.

Jellico did not sit down behind his desk, however. Instead he turned to face the two of them and leaned against his desk casually. One of two things would happen as a consequence. Either they would both choose to sit, at which point Jellico would then be looking down at them, thus giving him a subtle advantage. Or else they would stop a short distance away and not sit. Since he was leaning while they would be just standing there, they would become increasingly uncomfortable the longer they remained that way.

They were minor points, but wars were fought and won or lost on minor points. The devil was in the details, and Jellico prided himself on being a cunning devil.

"So, Edward," began Nechayev, perhaps thinking that invoking his first name would give the proceedings a more personal flavor. "It seems we have a bit of a situation here."

Tusari Gyn looked at her as if just noticing she was in the room. "A bit of a situation? I believe—and I think that the Federation Council would bear me out—that that is a huge understatement. This entire business is a fiasco."

"This entire business," and Jellico made no attempt to keep his voice down, "was your damned idea, Ambassador."

"Admiral, a little respect, please," Nechayev said sharply.

"As little as possible, Admiral," he shot back. "Again, this was the ambassador's idea, not mine."

"It was my idea to utilize Captain Calhoun to expedite a peace process," said Tusari Gyn. "Something that would have benefited all concerned. It was never my idea to have his ship open fire on my world. Yet that disaster has unfolded, and yes, I bear responsibility for it, Admiral, because I was the one who inadvertently unleashed that madman upon New Thallon in the interest of a peace that now will never come. The blood of my people is on my hands, with my good intentions being responsible for spilling it. So now the collective voices of the dead and dying cry for justice, and I am here to ask: How do you intend to balance those scales?"

Jellico wanted to reach out and throttle him, but he

didn't think that would be the best first step in dealing with the problem in front of them.

Gyn, meanwhile, was still talking. "When I think of all that we were willing to forgive. His previous trespasses on New Thallon, and his willingness to provide sanctuary to the fugitive Robin Lefler. And this . . . *this* . . . is how he repays our generosity?"

"I am not at all convinced," Jellico said, "that is what happened. I think there may well be more to all of this than anyone is ready to admit."

"What more can there be? Our planet's records are clear. The *Excalibur* was positively identified. There can be no mistake. And no one is denying that Mackenzie Calhoun is still the captain."

"And since then," Nechayev said worriedly, "the ship's gone radio silent. All messages sent on Starfleet emergency channels are being ignored. The mere act of ignoring such communiqués is grounds for court-martial. You know that as well as I do, Admiral."

Now it's back to "Admiral." So much for taking the personal approach. It didn't bother Jellico, however. Under the circumstances, the more formality there was, the better.

"If there is one thing I have learned in my time in Starfleet," Jellico said, "it's that what seems obvious . . . isn't always."

"Are you suggesting that the *Excalibur* was not responsible for the destruction on New Thallon?" said Nechayev, sounding extremely skeptical.

"I'm not suggesting anything. I am, on the other

hand, *reminding* you, Admiral, that recently it was Starfleet's belief that I had gone rogue and stolen an experimental timeship. It turned out in that case that not everything was what it appeared to be and that I was, in fact, innocent of all charges. Need I remind you who it was that brought clarity to that particular situation?"

"That's a valid point as far as it goes, Admiral," said Nechayev. "But we can't give the *Excalibur* latitude simply because of a unique situation that happened to you last year."

"I believe humans have a philosophy called Occam's Razor," said Tusari Gyn. "That the simplest answer tends to be the correct one."

"That is, in fact, an oversimplification of a far more complicated axiom," said Jellico.

"That's as may be," Nechayev jumped in, and Jellico was starting to feel as if he were fighting a two-headed dragon. "But here's a truth that we both know, Admiral: Calhoun never ran a typical ship. His command crew is a collection of eccentrics who have two things in common: a host of personal issues, and an unswerving loyalty to their unorthodox captain. With a combination such as that, it was only a matter of time before an incident such as this occurred."

Jellico studied Nechayev with open astonishment. "You, Admiral, of all people, know that Mackenzie Calhoun has consistently employed his lack of orthodoxy to benefit Starfleet interests." He didn't want to go into specifics since he knew that Calhoun had undertaken a variety of under-the-radar assignments for Nechayev's office, none of which should be made public, particularly in the presence of a Federation ambassador. And Nechayev, of course, knew this perfectly well, which is why it was so annoying to Jellico that she seemed disinclined to provide any support for a man who had been one of her most reliable agents.

"Yes, he has," said Nechayev, and then she added in a detached manner, "until, apparently, now."

Before Jellico could respond to that, Tusari Gyn said in that same annoying whispery voice of his, "Admirals . . . despite your obviously strong feelings on the subject, and without addressing the respective merits—or lack thereof," and Jellico bristled at that but held his tongue, "of your positions, the fact remains that the Council's instructions are quite explicit in this matter. I am here simply to learn firsthand how you plan to go about apprehending these renegades since, obviously, I have the most personal stake in the matter. If, however, you find my presence off-putting, I will simply return to the Federation Council and—"

And tell them how damned annoying you are? Because I'd like to be there for that conversation.

"That will not be necessary, Ambassador," said Nechayev politely. "In Starfleet, spirited conversations over policy are quite common. But ultimately we work in tandem with the Council to safeguard the best interests of the Federation. This will prove to be no exception." She looked pointedly at Jellico. "Would you call that a fair assessment, Admiral?"

His mouth thinned as he said, "Very much so, Admiral."

"Then I think our course is clear," she said. She was beginning to look extremely uncomfortable standing in one place, and she slightly moved one foot and then the other, which secretly pleased Jellico for some reason he couldn't express. "The fact is that Calhoun is far too formidable a foe to take half measures. If we give him the slightest leeway in any engagement, we're going to lose people."

"Admiral," said Jellico carefully, "are you suggesting—?"

"The *Excalibur*," she said, leaving no shading in her meaning, "needs to be destroyed on sight. Calhoun may be one of the best strategists we have in our fleet. He's going to count on any approaching Starfleet vessel to have the exact agenda that you're describing: trying to determine the 'truth' of the situation, giving him a chance to surrender quietly, and all the other procedures we would normally follow in this instance. We have to assume that he will view such hesitations as weaknesses that he can exploit. Playing into that is simply going to guarantee casualties on our side."

"Calhoun is *on* our side."

"No," said Nechayev. "Calhoun is on his own side, and always has been. In those instances where those interests have overlapped, he has been of great service to us. I admit that. But we now appear to have a divergence of interests, and there can be no hesitation. We need to take down Calhoun fast and we need to take him down hard."

"So it's shoot first, ask questions later."

"That is the current plan."

"Well then," said Jellico, his voice on edge, "I'm just going to have to take it up with—"

"Take it up with whomever you wish," Nechayev interrupted him brusquely. "You will find that this mandate isn't originating from me, but from the highest levels in the fleet."

"Really. I don't recall being in any meetings where that was decided."

"As I said, check for yourself if you don't believe me. The simple fact is, Admiral, that Calhoun hasn't made himself a ton of friends during his time in Starfleet, despite his services to you and me and even to the entirety of the Federation. They like the outcome of his efforts, but not how he goes about it. He's already overstretched the leash they put him on, and now that he's slipped it, the decision is to put him down. It's your job to coordinate that effort and make sure it's attended to, as expeditiously as possible. Now if you don't feel that you are up to the task . . ."

"Your concern about what I am and am not 'up to' is duly noted, Admiral," Jellico said. He suddenly became aware that he was squeezing so tightly on the underside of his desk that his knuckles were turning white. He eased up before he lost feeling in his hands. "I assure you that, once I've verified these orders through channels—as you have so graciously suggested I do—I will carry them out to the best ability that my many years of service can provide."

"That," said Nechayev with a slight bow, "is all I could have asked."

Tusari looked from one to the other and then bowed as well. "Then it seems we are done here."

Oh no, we're not, Jellico thought. *We're not done by a long shot. We're just getting started.*

Xenex

Now

More Brethren vessels had returned. Scarcely hours after the initial assault upon their original landing party, the Brethren had shown up in force, ready to lay waste to anyone and everyone in their path. Calhoun could only imagine how puzzled they must have been to discover exactly no one and nothing standing in their way.

The Xenexians had dispersed. Men, women, children, all of them had cleared out, hiding in the mountainous terrain that composed their land and served them well in fighting back against invading forces. They would have had to be completely insane to remain where they were, making themselves targets for any subsequent newcomers. Xenexians were many things, but insane was most definitely not one of them.

They had taken time to do only one thing: Build a pyre for their fallen leader, D'ndai. Calhoun had stood there, watching the flames lick his brother's body, blacken his skin, and burn him to cinders. Some of the floating ash wound up on Calhoun's face, and he did nothing to brush it away.

He had known how unnecessary all of this had been. If his brother had only let him turn himself over to the Brethren, none of this would have happened. Instead D'ndai had insisted on handling matters himself, and now look where it had gotten him. Just look.

They will pay. They will all pay, Calhoun had thought grimly.

He had then formed the Xenexians into ranks. There were too many of them to keep as one large force. Until they knew what it was they were dealing with, they needed to employ strictly guerrilla tactics combined with the strategy of retreat first put forward by the Roman dictator Quintus Fabius Maximus Verrucosus. There would be no meeting with the Brethren in prolonged, face-to-face battle. Instead the Xenexians would fall back, they would hide, and they would strike from hiding in hopes of wearing down their enemies. It was the only strategy that could serve them in the long run.

They had then spread throughout the land, making a dozen encampments, bringing enough supplies with them that each encampment would be self-contained. Communication was done entirely with runners.

And still, with all that . . . with all that . . .

Calhoun had already lost more people than he would have thought possible. The Brethren had not hesitated to go off into the mountains, searching out the Xenexians, and tracking Calhoun and his people relentlessly. The Xenexians had fought back, and they had outmaneuvered, and they had taken down a number of the bastards, but more of them continued to come in unrelenting waves.

Yet Calhoun remained convinced that the long run was going to favor him. This would not, could not, go on indefinitely. Sooner or later, his crew was going to figure out what was going on. They would figure it out and—

And what? Morgan was in charge of the ship. What if they wanted to return to Xenex, and Morgan—as would invariably be the case—decided that she didn't think that was such a good idea?

Now the events that he had set into motion by contacting Soleta were growing in urgency and importance. He had laid out a plan to expunge Morgan from the ship once and for all, but he was counting on a woman who had turned into a renegade Romulan spy to be his salvation. Suddenly what had seemed a fairly reliable strategy appeared full of holes, and he wondered whether he had pushed his famed luck beyond the breaking point. He was counting on a great deal of things to go right in relation to a situation where almost nothing had gone right.

"This must be very hard on you."

Calhoun had been leaning against an outcropping of rock when the female voice spoke silkily from behind him. He turned and saw the image of his wife smiling at him.

"If you really think that I'm going to lead you to my people, you are badly mistaken," he informed her.

"If *you* really think we care in the slightest about

your people, it is you who are badly mistaken," the
false Shelby replied. "This is an egomaniac's dream,
Calhoun. It's about you. It's all about you."

"Get out of my wife's face," said Calhoun, "or we
have nothing else to talk about."

She shrugged in what seemed a very human
manner. "If it will expedite matters," she said, and
there was a slight shimmer along her body. Seconds
later, the D'myurj was standing in front of him, and
he (Calhoun took it to be a "he") inclined his head
slightly. "Is this preferable?"

It was still difficult for Calhoun to make out precisely what the D'myurj looked like. He was suffused
with a glowing blue light that seemed to come from
everywhere and nowhere at once, and his body was
translucent, constantly shifting and shimmering. But
at least he didn't look like Shelby anymore, so that was
a plus.

"What's the purpose of this game?" said Calhoun.
He tried not to let the exhaustion he was feeling be
apparent to the D'myurj. "You know where I am. You
could just beam me out. My people would never know
what happened to me. They'd assume I was killed."

"And your legend would live on."

"What the hell do you care about my legend?"

It was hard to get any sense of the D'myurj's facial
expressions, but his voice projected carefully maintained sadness. "How little you understand us, Calhoun. Of course we care about your legend. We care
about everything. There are vast aspects to this that

you cannot comprehend. How can I explain the full picture to you when you can't even see the frame?"

"Why not give it a try?" said Calhoun.

The D'myurj regarded him with interest. "You know . . . in many ways, you remind me of Selar. She had that same look of determination on her face, right before she blew herself to oblivion."

"You *were* there."

"Oh yes. I was there on AF1963 when she set her phaser to self-destruct and annihilated our entire operation."

"The purpose of which was to create clone bodies for you creatures to inhabit, so you could infiltrate all aspects of Federation life. Am I right?"

"That is one small part of it, yes. I believe I will keep the rest of it to myself."

Calhoun turned away from him and picked a random direction in which to walk. A moment later, the D'myurj was floating in front of him, pacing him effortlessly. "Calhoun, it's important that you under-stand—"

"You keep saying that, but not explaining why."

"Because you have placed yourself squarely into the middle of all this, and people have died because of it. It's more a matter of respect than anything else."

Calhoun laughed bitterly at that. "Really. Respect."

"Yes. Why, what else?"

"I'm thinking it's more an attempt to try and wear me down psychologically."

"Think what you wish."

"I usually do."

The sun was fast approaching the horizon, and Calhoun was relieved because the heat was truly beginning to wear on him. He was looking forward to a bit of time in the shadow. He wasn't deluding himself into thinking that he would be able to hide from the D'myurj at this point, but at least he could get some rest in the coolness of the shade.

"I've studied you, Calhoun. More than that: I've been watching you. And your most consistent attribute is that you remain resolutely your own man. You do not bow to peer pressure, nor do you willingly live in the world as it is presented to you. Instead you live the life you wish and wait for the world to catch up with you."

Calhoun didn't bother to answer.

The D'myurj kept talking; apparently Calhoun's response was not required to keep the conversation going. "I am similar to you in that respect. Do you know what I am?"

"A pain in the ass."

"I am a visionary. More: I am *the* Visionary. Because I, of all my people, am able to see what is going to happen to all living things if matters are allowed to proceed as they currently are."

"And what would that be?"

"Terrible things, Calhoun. So terrible . . ." He actually seemed to shudder, although Calhoun assumed that to be an affectation rather than genuine concern. "So terrible that others of my race cannot begin to see it. They still believe in the fundamental potential of living beings."

"And you don't."

"No. Because I am a Visionary, as I said, and am uniquely able to understand the truth of things." His voice sounded heavy with knowledge that was weighing him down. "The future is open to me. The end of all things is open to me. I have seen what is to come, the future of this galaxy, and I am here to tell you that, in the great, infinite body of the universe, that which you would call 'life' is nothing but an infection. An infection that will, sooner or later, destroy the body."

"You want me to believe that the mere existence of life is going to destroy the universe."

"Yes."

"That's ridiculous," said Calhoun flatly. "Life developed from nature. Nature would never create something that will lead to its own destruction."

"That would seem a viable theory, but in fact, it is erroneous," said the D'myurj. "Living bodies 'create' things that are poisonous to the system all the time. And you keep finding cures for them, but your bodies come up with new things all the time that are self-destructive. And all living beings were made in the image of the universe. Therefore it stands to reason . . ."

"It doesn't stand to reason. Nothing you're saying makes any sense."

"It all makes perfect sense. It's hardly my fault if you simply don't want to see it. If it's of any consolation, others of my race did not want to see it either. So you should not feel alone in your beliefs, even though the proof of what I say is right in front of you, should you care to look."

"Oh, is it now."

"Yes, it is. Remember, for instance, when your beloved Starfleet personnel were exceeding the safe limit of warp speed and, as a consequence of your precipitous actions, damaging the very fabric of space-time?"

"Of course. But we took action in response. The Council implemented a limit of warp five, except in emergency situations. And it was subsequently corrected. All you're doing is holding up an example of how we rose to a situation and worked together to fix it. Hardly an instance of life being about destruction."

"Ah, but what if you had not realized the damage you were doing?"

"But we did. "

"But what. If you. Had not? What if the damage to the space-time continuum had persisted until it was too late? The fact is that you got lucky. The universe cannot count on luck.

"And what if there are other races in other galaxies, with similar technology, who have not realized the danger it represents?"

"We can't assume that all FTL drives represent a danger," said Calhoun.

"We can't assume that they don't," shot back the Visionary, "and considering your own situation, isn't it preferable to anticipate the worst? And that's just a

single aspect of the destructive nature of living creatures, Calhoun. Just one tiny piece of it. Do you have
any idea, for instance, what happens to the separations
between the multiverse every time one of you goes
back in time and mucks with the continuum? Do you
begin to see the vastness of the big picture that I'm trying to lay out for you?"

Never in a million years would Calhoun have
admitted that he did. Never would he have acknowledged that a lot of what the so-called Visionary was
saying made sense. The concepts that were being
described . . . they seemed just too big for one Starfleet
captain to weigh in on.

So instead he said nothing. He just kept walking,
resigned to the idea that the D'myurj was going to
keep after him, yammering away about concepts that
he didn't want to dwell upon.

The Visionary had been speaking with increasing
intensity, but now his tone calmed and he said with
what sounded like quiet reverence, as if he were speaking of a holy object: "The others of my kind believe in
the future of life. They believe in working behind
the scenes, helping various races reach the pinnacle
of their genetic development and eventually become
beings of pure thought, such as the Organians. Such
beings do not pose any threat to the universe because
they are so much a part of it. The poor fools believe
that it is the destiny of all races to reach that level of
advancement, sooner or later, and they are content
believing time to be on their side. I, on the other hand,

know that the goal is unattainable and time is *not* on our side."

"So you intend to destroy all life. What of the Brethren? Would you see them disposed of as well?"

The Visionary appeared to shrug, which was a strangely human gesture for him to make. "I never said all races would be obliterated. Only those presenting a threat. The rest will survive in order to provide the Brethren . . . how best to put it?" Then the Visionary seemed to smile. "Sport, I suppose. And the Brethren are satisfied with that. They ask so little of life, it's almost sweet."

"Well, they're going to have to look elsewhere," said Calhoun, "because if you think that I'm going to lead them to—"

That was when Calhoun heard the name "*M'k'n'zy!*" being shouted in jubilation.

Calhoun knew for a fact that there were no Xenexian camps set up in the area. He was carrying in his head all the locations, both likely and unlikely, that his people would be hiding, and was certain that he was nowhere near any of them.

But coming toward him was a scouting party of about thirty or so Xenexians, making their joy at finding him known in jubilant chants that easily carried quite a distance.

He couldn't blame them for their enthusiasm. Plus the fact that they were showing themselves indicated to him that they had not discerned any Brethren within the area.

His head whipped around and he saw the pleased expression on what there was of the glowing face on the Visionary, and he knew that even as the Visionary hovered there, the bastard was busy sending coordinates—of not only Calhoun's location, but a squadron of enemy Xenexian warriors—directly to the Brethren. In finding Calhoun, they had effectively brought destruction down upon themselves.

"Enjoy the battle," said the D'myurj, "and while you're dwelling upon everything I've said, you may want to give some consideration to the possibility that maybe—just maybe—you're on the wrong side."

That was the last thing the D'myurj said before he vanished.

U.S.S. Excalibur

Also Now

i.

The *Excalibur* was still not moving as quickly as Burgoyne would have liked. It seemed to hir at this point that Morgan was toying with them. She could have allowed them to go to full warp, but instead she was controlling the systems to such a degree that the ship could go no faster.

"We need to get the hell out of Thallonian space," Burgoyne said heatedly to Chief Engineer Mitchell. S/he strode through engineering, looking in frustration at the powerful warp engines that—with even minimal thrust—would get them clear of dangerous enemy territory. "I appreciate that we're going as fast as impulse power will allow us, but that's not enough."

"You think I'm unaware of that, Burgy?" said Mitchell in frustration, his bearded face glistening with sweat. "I've run every counterprogram I can think of, and I can't get the warp engines to fire up. What do you expect me to do? Climb in there and hit them with a spanner until they come to life?"

"I don't need sarcasm, Craig. I need answers."

"Well, unfortunately, I don't have any answers handy, so sarcasm is pretty much the only tool I have left in my box."

"Look, Craig—"

"No, you look, Burgy. We both know this used to be your territory, and the fact is that you've probably forgotten more about engineering than I'll ever know. So give me a hint. Point me in the right direction. I've gone over with you everything I'm trying to do, none of which is getting us anywhere. Tell me what I'm missing."

Burgoyne growled low in hir throat. "Nothing," s/he admitted. "There's nothing I can think of. All the redundant and fail-safe systems we have are geared around allowing for a collapse of the computer so that we have to take over everything manually. We never built in anything to allow for the computer actively fighting us."

"Well, maybe we should get right on that. You never know when it'll come in handy," said Mitchell drily.

Suddenly Burgoyne's combadge beeped at hir. S/he tapped it. "Burgoyne."

"You'd better get up here, Commander," came Kebron's voice. He didn't sound happy.

"On my way. Burgoyne out." S/he turned to Mitchell and said, "Keep trying."

"Good advice there, Burgy. I was originally figuring on going fetal and crying softly in the corner after you left, but instead I'll keep trying."

Burgoyne headed for the turbolift, wondering if there was anyone on the damned ship whose default response wasn't sarcasm.

ii.

"What's going on?" said Burgoyne as s/he walked out onto the bridge.

Matters had calmed down slightly from when s/he had previously returned from hir temporary exile to the turbolift. Everyone had still been trying to process what had just happened, while the *Excalibur* chugged away from New Thallon with all the alacrity of a crippled snail.

Now everyone was back to business, attempting to deal as best they could with the hand that had been dealt them. Every so often, though, they would cast poisonous glances at the dealer: Morgan's little present of her afterimage, sitting there as a phantom reminder of who was really in charge.

"We still don't have any outgoing communications capability," Kebron informed hir. "But I'm picking up incoming chatter, and none of it's good."

"Meaning?"

"Meaning that Starfleet has been informed of our unwilling assault on Xenex."

"Except to them, it wasn't unwilling, but instead a deliberate act of murder," Burgoyne said grimly.

"That's more or less accurate."

At that moment, Tobias called out, "Burgy! I've got helm control again."

This was the first piece of good news that Burgoyne had heard in an hour. "Excellent. What did you do?"

"Nothing. I mean, I kept trying to do things," she said, "but none of it was having any effect. And suddenly I'm in full control."

"Well, that's good," Xy said to his father.

"Actually, I wish I knew whether it was good or not," said Burgoyne warily. "For the moment, we're not going to knock it. Tobias, set course for Xenex, at—and please don't laugh—best possible speed."

"Impulse is all I've got."

"Then that's what you should use."

She did as ordered. She didn't have to ask why they were heading for Xenex. None of them did; Burgoyne had already explained to them what had happened to their captain, and now it was just a matter of hoping that he was still there when they returned for him. Assuming, of course, that they were able to get to him at all.

That was when Kebron said, "Commander. We have company."

"Battle stations," said Burgoyne, not even waiting for any specifics. S/he already knew what was about to happen. "Shields up. Kebron, show me what we're dealing with."

The screen image of space flickered and moments later, they could see a ship hurtling toward them. It was smaller than they were, but more maneuverable.

"A Thallonian battleship. She's powering up. We're targeted," said Kebron.

Burgoyne thought furiously. This wasn't some random opponent who was coming after the *Excalibur* because of some misplaced grudge. These people considered the starship to be the enemy, and with good reason. The *Excalibur* was far more powerful than the oncoming vessel and capable of blowing it out of space, but that wasn't the route that Burgoyne wanted to pursue.

At that moment, the Thallonian battleship cut loose. The *Excalibur* shuddered from the impact as the red alert sirens wailed around them.

"Minor damage to port shields," Kebron told him, and he added sardonically, "Apparently they're not planning to give us the opportunity to surrender."

Burgoyne crossed quickly to the science station. "Bring me up the schematics on that ship," s/he ordered. Xy quickly did as he was bidden and, moments later, Burgoyne was studying the layout for the ship that was trying to destroy them. The starship shuddered once more from another blast against them, but the shields held steady.

"Bring us around, Tobias," said Burgoyne. "Come straight at them."

"*At* them? I mean, yes, Commander."

The *Excalibur,* with not much speed at its command, made a leisurely turn and headed straight at the Thallonian battleship. The battleship went into reverse as the far larger starship advanced.

Burgoyne touched the point on the screen that s/he wanted targeted and said, "Kebron! Feeding the target through to you now! Think you can hit it?"

"Of course," rumbled Kebron, sounding offended that there seemed to be any doubt on the subject. The schematics came up on his tactical display and he methodically laid in the targeting for the phasers. "Target acquired and locked."

"Fire phasers."

"Fire phasers, aye."

The shielding of the smaller vessel coruscated as the beams lanced into them, and for a few moments actually managed to hold their own. But then the shields crumbled against the superior firepower of the *Excalibur,* and the phasers cut into the weapons banks of the battleship. The smaller vessel shook under the barrage and skewed to starboard as it tried to get away.

"Track them. Stay with them," said Burgoyne.

"I'm on it," Kebron assured hir.

With the combination of Tobias's maneuvering and Kebron's marksmanship, the phaser beams moved in tandem with the battleship. Explosions raked the lower sections of the vessel as the energy cells fueling the Thallonian weapons erupted.

"Cease fire. Any hull breaches?" said Burgoyne.

Kebron double-checked his sensors. "Nothing that I'm picking up. She's still intact."

"Aspect ratio change. They're peeling off, Commander," said Tobias.

"Good. They'll keep going if they know what's good for them."

Suddenly Tobias looked around from her station. "Burgy!" she said, so excited that she dropped the more formal rank address she'd been employing. "We've got warp speed!"

Burgoyne was astounded. It couldn't be that simple. That didn't deter hir from calling out, "Resume course for Xenex! Warp nine!"

Tobias tried to comply, but a few moments later she uttered an angry profanity. Normally she would have apologized instantly for the language, but there was hardly anything normal about what they were dealing with. "We only have warp one," she said once she had gotten over her initial fury. "That's it. That's all she'll give me."

The use of the pronoun "she" was typically used to refer to a ship, but in this instance, everyone on the bridge knew the "she" that Tobias was talking about.

Burgoyne considered it and immediately understood. "It's a reward," s/he said angrily.

"A what?" Kebron didn't get it, and Burgoyne could see by the confused looks that nobody else on the bridge did either.

"A reward," s/he said again. "We beat an opponent and so, like we're animals learning a new trick, she's giving us a treat. Isn't that right, Morgan? *Isn't that right?* Plus you want to try and make it a little more sporting, because you know that—in the event we should happen to last long enough to get out of Thallonian space—then we're going to have Starfleet to contend with. And they're going to be gunning for us too. Feel free to tell me if I'm getting close."

Morgan didn't reply. She didn't have to. Burgoyne knew s/he was right.

With an angry snarl, Burgoyne turned away and stormed into the captain's ready room. The door hissed shut behind hir, cutting hir off from the rest of the crew. It was what s/he needed: just a few moments to compose hirself.

S/he suddenly found hirself wishing that Selar was here, and s/he had no idea why that would be.

Burgoyne looked at Calhoun's sword, the one that he kept mounted on the wall behind his desk. The captain probably drew comfort and confidence from it. What did Burgoyne have to lean on?

The door hissed open without anyone asking permission, which was a breach of protocol. Xy entered and, as the door closed behind him, said, "Are you okay?"

"Do I look okay?" said Burgoyne, trying to keep the weariness from hir voice.

"It's all right to be concerned under the circumstances. The captain is missing, the ship is out of control . . ."

"I'm not supposed to be here, Xy."

Xy looked confused. "What?"

"Here. In here, in command. I tried to tell the captain that when he promoted me. I'm an engineer.

That's where I should have stayed. I'm no Mackenzie Calhoun."

"You don't have to be," said Xy. "You're as brave and resourceful as anyone I've ever met. There's no reason for you to doubt any of that."

"I know." Burgoyne closed hir eyes. "I know there should be no reason. And I'm not sure why I'm feeling this way. It's like . . . I don't know what it's like. Like I'm disconnected from myself. Why am I feeling this way?"

"I don't know, Dad. All I know is that you need to keep yourself together for the crew."

"I can. I will. You don't need to worry about that. There's plenty more things for us to worry about than my state of mind."

"Dad . . ." Xy paused and then said, "Are we going to make it?"

"You mean are we going to be able to get clear of Thallonian space and get all the way back to Xenex, moving at warp one, with Starfleet coming after us, no means of telling them what's happening, trying to defend ourselves using only nonlethal means, and a berserk computer entity in charge of the ship?"

"Yes."

Burgoyne studied him with a deadpan. "I love this plan. I don't see how it can possibly fail."

The *Spectre*

i.

Soleta studied the messages that were coming over subspace. She checked them and rechecked them. She looked over everything that she was picking up from the open channels, and then used her ship's espionage capabilities to tap into the secure channels that no one outside of Starfleet was supposed to be able to access.

She couldn't believe any of it. None of it made any sense.

It was a deep, knotty problem that would have left just about anyone else scratching their heads and wondering what in the world could possibly be happening on the *Excalibur* and what was going through Calhoun's mind.

Soleta required five entire seconds to figure it out. In retrospect, she would wonder why in the world it took her that long.

Moments later both Seven and the Doctor had responded to her summons to the bridge. They had been inspecting the interior of the stealth ship, amazed and fascinated by what they were seeing since neither of them had ever been in any Romulan vessel before, much less a one-of-a-kind stealth vessel. "Your ship is very impressive," Seven began, but then she saw the look on Soleta's face. Even though she was part Romulan and had shaken off much of the Vulcan training that would have kept her irrevocably stoic, it was still evident that something had gone wrong. "What happened?" said Seven.

"A ton of chatter claiming that the *Excalibur* launched an unprovoked attack on New Thallon and then fled the scene."

"Is that likely?" asked the Doctor.

"I wouldn't just say it's unlikely. I would say it's flat-out impossible," Soleta said firmly. "There is no way Captain Calhoun attacks for no reason."

"Then perhaps," said Seven, "it was not Captain Calhoun who did it."

"I reached the same conclusion."

The Doctor, on the other hand, was a bit slower to comprehend. "What are you suggesting?"

"I'm suggesting, Doctor," Soleta said pointedly, "that the computer entity you've been defending— the one against whom you're reluctant to take any action—has taken over the ship and murdered who knows how many people. The one to whom you're clearly willing to give the benefit of the doubt—"

"And are you not quick to do the same for Captain Calhoun?" the Doctor replied. "You reject out of hand the notion that he might have had some manner of . . . I don't know, a mental breakdown."

"Yes. I do reject that notion. Because I know him. How well do you know Morgan?"

"Not at all," he was forced to admit.

"No. Not at all. You're just anxious to make as many allowances for her as possible because you think she's just like you. But she's not, Doctor," said Soleta, hammering home the point. "She's no more like you than a mass murderer is like me. And the sooner you come to the conclusion that computer entities are just as capable of being total bastards as living beings, the better off we're all going to be."

"Soleta," Seven said sharply, catching her attention. "That's enough. You've made your point."

"Have I?"

Rather than Seven answering her, the Doctor did so. "Yes, you have. Repeatedly. You think it obvious that Morgan is responsible for this because she is a heartless machine, and only a heartless machine would be capable of such an action. No human, in the history of life, has ever committed an unprovoked attack."

"Mackenzie Calhoun isn't human," said Soleta. "Neither am I. Whether Xenexians have ever engaged in unwarranted attacks, I couldn't say. I know that Vulcans, long ago in their history, did. And that Romulans did so far more recently than that. In this case, though . . . at this time, in this instance . . . logic dictates that the entity calling itself Morgan Primus is responsible rather than Captain Calhoun. And we need to stop her. And I need to know, right now, if we can count on you or if we can't. We have a real situation with real consequences if we don't get the job done. Right now, Doctor: Where do you stand? With your loyalties to virtual beings? Or to us?"

"You."

"Because this is no longer something theoretical. This is . . ." She stopped and looked briefly surprised before she composed herself. "Oh."

"Yes," said the Doctor primly. "I thought I would save us some time and not have to listen to another one of your lengthy, sanctimonious diatribes."

"Sanctimonious? Really?"

"Really."

"I was simply trying to—"

He put up a hand. "I think it would be preferable if we did not rehash the previous discussions and instead focused on what needs to be dealt with." Since he had apparently resolved his course of action, he seemed to be all business.

"I agree," said Seven, casting a glance at the Doctor. "We need to track down the *Excalibur* if we're going to implement the plan. The question is, how do we find her?"

"That actually shouldn't be a problem," said Soleta. "Subspace is alive with chatter—last known sightings and such—and it's only going to increase the longer this goes on. Which means it's simply going to get easier. I'll run it through my computer systems and use it to triangulate the information. Locate them in that manner."

The Doctor frowned. "But if you are able to accomplish that, will not others be able to find them in the same manner?"

"Not immediately," she said. "Different groups treat such information in a proprietary manner. The Thallonians are a prideful people and are determined to get the *Excalibur* themselves. Meantime, Starfleet is likely to keep as much information as possible close to the vest. Fortunately," and she didn't exactly smile but she came close, "Starfleet isn't quite as impervious to some creative eavesdropping as it would like to believe, especially from one of their former officers. In addition to being able to zero in on a supposedly renegade ship such as the *Excalibur,* I can track the comings and goings of just about every ship in the fleet."

"For some reason I find that very disturbing," said Seven.

"I can think of several reasons," said the Doctor.

"Best not to dwell on them, then," Soleta advised. "However, we can't count on others locating the *Excalibur* taking an indefinite amount of time. So we're going to have to move quickly . . . as soon as we've made a stop."

The Doctor and Seven exchanged confused glances, as if they had both wandered into the middle of someone else's conversation. "We're making a stop?" said Seven.

"Yes."

"May I ask where?"

Soleta studied her for a moment and then said, "I think it would be best if I keep all information on this matter on a need-to-know basis."

"Excuse me," said Seven, her voice rising. "I have

made tremendous leaps of faith based upon the things you've told me. I find it disturbing that you do not feel a need to reciprocate."

"It has nothing to do with reciprocation. We have no idea who is watching, or if, or when, or what's being heard. It could be nothing, it could be everything, and either way, anything I say aloud is one less piece of information that I'm unable to keep completely off the grid. There is a very old saying: Just because you are paranoid does not mean they are *not* out to get you." The severity of her expression softened. "Look . . . the truth is that I have brought the two of you into a very dangerous situation. And you have willingly come into it out of a sense of duty to the Federation, even," and she looked at the Doctor, "when it ran counter to deeply held beliefs. With that understood, it's my responsibility to do whatever is within my power to protect you as much as possible."

"We do not need your protection," said Seven. "We are perfectly capable of protecting ourselves."

"I believe you," said Soleta, "but that doesn't mean I abrogate my responsibility. Now if you'll excuse me, I have a ship to run."

She then turned and headed for the navigation station to lay in a course and head to her destination as fast as the *Spectre* would get them there. When she turned around to look back at Seven and the Doctor, they were gone.

ii.

Seven had been interested in remaining on the bridge and continuing to argue the point with Soleta. But the Doctor had turned and walked out without a word, and she immediately followed him. She trailed him down the hallway and he didn't seem in any hurry to slow down. She called after him and, when he still didn't slow, practically shouted his name. This prompted him to turn and stop and regard her as if he were staring at her from the top of a mountain.

"Yes?" he said.

She stopped and realized only belatedly that she hadn't actually come up with anything to say to him. She simply felt the need to engage him in conversation.

He stared at her, waiting.

"Thank you," she said finally.

His expression didn't change. "You're welcome."

He started to turn away from her again and this time she came forward and rested her hand on his arm. The Doctor looked down at it, mild surprise flickering across his face.

"I know that this is difficult for you," she said. "You helped create a virus that can erase Morgan Primus, and you've brought it to this vessel on a datachip. Until just now, I was unsure—as was Soleta—that you were truly dedicated to the idea. Now, though, faced with evidence that she is out of control and poses a threat to living beings, you've come to accept what needs to be done. And I think that is a laudable—"

"I don't care about them."

That stopped Seven. "Excuse me?"

He rolled his eyes. "That's an overstatement. I'm a doctor. Of course I care about all living things. But hearing about what happened on New Thallon . . . that isn't what prompted my wholehearted devotion to this endeavor. It's that you are obviously determined to see this through, and it now appears that this individual, this Morgan, presents a real and true threat."

"I . . . still don't understand."

"She presents a threat to you, Seven," said the Doctor. "You are going to set yourself in harm's way, and I cannot stand by and do nothing. Certainly I cannot consider allying myself with the entity that would potentially do you harm. I am going to attempt to destroy Morgan Primus in order to protect you. Do you understand now?"

When she replied, her voice was barely above a whisper. "Yes."

"Good." He paused and then said, "I had best check on the datachip to make certain that the virus remains contained and has lost none of its potency. Then I will give it to Soleta for safekeeping as we planned. I think that would be best, don't you?"

She nodded.

The Doctor walked away, leaving her standing there in the corridor, at a loss for words.

U.S.S. Dauntless

Sometime Later

To say that there was no love lost between Commodore Joshua Kemper and Captain Mackenzie Calhoun would be to understate matters considerably.

The *Dauntless* was a newly commissioned *Galaxy*-class ship, replacing the vessel of the same name that had been destroyed during the Dominion War. She had been on routine patrol in Sector 7G when word first came through that Calhoun had apparently gone rogue and single-handedly committed an act of war against the Thallonians.

The first thing that occurred to Kemper was, *It was only a matter of time.*

The second thing that occurred to him was, *And he's all mine.*

Kemper was an unusually tall man who walked with something of an inherent swagger and radiated confidence the way suns radiate light. People tended to get out of his way when they saw him coming, which suited him just fine. He studied his smile in the mirror every morning to make certain that it was exactly right and then made sure to keep it affixed on his face the entirety of the day. It required a certain type of mind-set to practice one's smile, and Kemper had that mind-set in spades.

It wasn't as if Kemper was happy about the deaths of the people on New Thallon. He felt as much mourning as one can for a planetary disaster for which he was not responsible, involving people he didn't know. If anything, Kemper was more upset over the fact that a ship of the line had been responsible for the incident. Any negative action taken by a starship was a black eye for the entire fleet, and it was incumbent upon every officer to do what was required in order to rein in the offending vessel and bring the criminals involved to a swift justice. And he felt it to be his obligation—no, in fact, a duty bordering on sacred—to be the one who managed to accomplish the job.

The fact that it was Calhoun was simply a bonus.

Kemper strode down the corridor with a bit more spring in his step than was usual. The doors to the turbolift obediently opened for him and he said briskly, "Bridge."

"Hold the lift, please!" came a female voice from behind him.

It was Theresa Detwiler, his conn officer. He stepped aside for her to enter and she did so. "Good morning, Lieutenant Commander," he said briskly.

"Good morning, Commodore."

The doors slid shut and the turbolift headed toward its destination.

"Did you sleep well?" he asked solicitously.

"I did indeed. You?"

"Oh yes." His carefully nurtured smile shifted a bit to allow a genuine one to come through. "Thank you."

"No problem."

Then he looked around with just a bit of apprehension, as if someone were watching them while they were in the turbolift. "You, uhm . . . you're sure no one saw you leaving my quarters?"

"You realize I wouldn't give a damn if someone did, right?"

"I'm just not entirely certain it's wholly appropriate that we . . . that you and I . . . I mean, I *am* the Commodore . . ."

"Look, Josh, no one expects a starship commander to be a monk. Relationships are healthy and natural, and who else is the C.O. going to spend time with if not subordinates? You didn't pressure me into anything, and I'm not seeing you as a means of advancing my career. My career was doing fine before I was assigned to this ship, thank you very much." She studied him closely. "You're not actually listening to anything I'm saying right now, are you."

"Hmmm? Oh . . . sorry," he said when her words registered. "Have a lot on my mind. After you left, I received some emergency intel about an old . . . friend. Maybe you remember him: Mackenzie Calhoun."

"Of course I remember him. The cadet with the scar that you decided to give a hard time to back at the Academy. And he responded by kicking the hell out of you."

"I wouldn't have put it quite that way."

"Really? Let's ask Ray, because I'm sure that he would remember it pretty clearly, since—as I recall—he also got his head handed to him by Calhoun."

"You," he said stiffly, "are taking entirely too much delight in the recollection. And it's not something to be joked about."

"Why? What'd he do?"

Kemper told her.

She blanched upon hearing the news. The significance of a Starfleet captain embarking upon such an unprovoked act of war was not lost on her.

"And we're going after him?" she said.

"Oh, hell yes. I knew the moment I laid eyes on him years ago that he was going to be trouble. This is an opportunity—"

"To settle old scores?"

Kemper clearly wasn't thrilled with the way she'd expressed it just then. "I need to do my duty to Starfleet."

"Well . . ." she said hopefully, "maybe he'll surrender."

"That's not an option."

"What?"

The doors slid open and he walked out onto the bridge. Detwiler followed him and the night shift navigator stepped aside. Commander Ray Williams, the first officer, was already at his station. "Morning, Commodore."

"Morning."

"What do you mean, that's not an option?" Detwiler said, clearly not finished with the conversation.

Before he answered, he turned to Williams. "You're up to speed on the Calhoun situation?"

"Yes, sir, but—"

Kemper, having heard "Yes, sir," wasn't bothering to listen to the rest. He returned his focus to Detwiler and said, "Our orders are clear. If we find him, we're to shoot on sight. Correct, Number One?"

"That's correct, Commodore, but—"

"It's out of my hands, Terry," said Kemper.

"With all respect, Commodore, you don't sound particularly upset about it," said Detwiler.

"It's not my job to feel one way or the other about it," Kemper said, his carefully maintained smile fading ever so slightly. "It's my job to do my duty and attend to Starfleet policies. A philosophy, I should add, that if Mackenzie Calhoun attended to, he wouldn't be in his current fix. Emotions have to take a back seat to responsibility. We have no choice but to undertake this task as quickly and efficiently as possible."

Williams cleared his throat. "Yes, Commodore, about that—"

But Kemper was looking at the viewscreen and he was frowning. "We're not moving."

"No, sir. I've been trying to tell you—"

Kemper turned to Williams with annoyance. "Why aren't we moving? We know their last sighting. We should be heading toward Thallonian space."

"We received orders to hold our position for a rendezvous."

"Hold our position? Who the hell gave that order—?"

Hopkins, at tactical, called out, "Commodore, we've got a fresh contact at two-eighteen mark three."

"Put it on-screen," said Kemper automatically, even though he hadn't yet been given a satisfactory answer to his previous question.

The newcomer appeared on the screen and Kemper recognized it immediately. "Is that an ETV?"

"I believe so, yes," said Williams.

The Emergency Transport Vehicles were vessels that were intended for the exclusive use of top Starfleet brass to get them from one point to another as quickly as possible. They were outfitted with high-warp sleds, which enabled them to go at extraordinary speeds but only for a relatively short period of time, at which point their energy sources needed time to replenish. So, once having delivered their passengers, they were effectively dead in space until such time that they were able to get back up to speed.

Kemper couldn't recall ever having seen one in actual use before. "Well, don't just stand there," he said impatiently. "Open a channel."

"Dauntless," a gruff voice came immediately, *"this is the* U.S.S. Hermes, *Admiral Jellico speaking. Permission to come aboard."*

Under such circumstances, asking permission was merely a formality. It wasn't as if Kemper was going to refuse to allow an admiral to board his ship, much less such a renowned hard-ass as Jellico. "Yes, sir, of course. But—"

"But?" There was a tinge of astonishment to Jellico's tone. *"Did I just hear hesitation in your voice, Commodore?"*

All eyes on the bridge were on Kemper. He felt self-conscious for a fleeting moment and then he steeled himself. "These are dangerous times, Admiral. I'm simply inquiring as to the nature of your business."

"The nature of my business, Commodore," he said, carefully underscoring the difference in rank between them, *"is to oversee your vessel during your attempts to track down the* Excalibur."

"Oversee?"

"That is correct, Commodore."

"May I ask why my vessel has been selected for this honor," said Kemper, "as opposed to the other ships that are going after—"

"No other ships, Commodore. Before I commit a sizable number of vessels to this endeavor, I'm going to determine for myself exactly what's going on. And yours is the ship I'm using to do it."

Kemper couldn't believe what he was hearing. "Admiral—"

Then he took control of himself. This was neither the time nor the place to square off against a superior officer, presuming there even *was* such a time and place. As soon as he had fought back his instinctive desire to balk at such presumption, he said evenly, "Bridge to transporter room. Lock onto signal and beam aboard passenger from the ETV."

"*Aye, Commodore,*" came the acknowledgment from the transporter room.

"*Thank you, Commodore,*" came Jellico's voice. "*I will see you shortly.*"

"Yes, sir," said Kemper. "Looking forward to it."

The moment the communication ceased, Williams said, "All right. That was unexpected."

"Not entirely, no," said Kemper. "Jellico used to hate Calhoun's guts, but ever since Calhoun did him some kind of service—saved one of his family, I think—Jellico's had Calhoun's back. This has nothing to do with procedure and everything to do with favoritism. And I promise you this: I'm not going to allow any such attitudes to jeopardize the lives of anyone on this ship. Admiral or no, Mackenzie Calhoun is going to pay for what he did, and I'm not going to hesitate to be the bill collector."

Xenex

i.

The incoming Brethren transport vessel angled toward the surface, confident that this exercise in absurdity was reaching its inevitable, if somewhat prolonged, conclusion.

Calhoun and his people watched the ship coming in. He was reasonably sure it was the same one that had arrived on that terrible day when his brother had been ruthlessly cut down by one of the Brethren. Even though he had immediately slaughtered D'ndai's killer, the hurt, the fury were all still present and burning deeply within him.

The vessel wasn't bothering to cloak this time. Perhaps they were under the impression that showing up in this manner would somehow intimidate the Xenexians. After all the soldiers they had lost in battle, one would think that they knew better by this point.

Calhoun felt it incumbent upon him to impart a lesson to them. With any luck, it would be one final lesson.

His people were massing around him, looking to the skies, in the shadow of one of the tallest natural spires in the area. His instinct was to tell them to keep hidden, to continue the guerrilla tactics that had enabled as many people to survive as had managed thus far.

But that wasn't going to get it done this time. He needed to draw the Brethren in closer. Draw them in and then distract them before they realized what he was really up to. And challenging them openly was the only thing that was going to accomplish that.

Unfortunately, it meant that he was going to have to use the troops around him in a way that he was not looking forward to. If his plan worked, however, he would be able to put an end to this insane siege of his home world once and for all.

ii.

The Visionary wasn't thrilled with what he was seeing.

Far below, the Xenexians were massing. There were so many of the damned creatures that, unlike when Calhoun had been out and on his own, it was impossible to pick him out of the crowd.

"I don't like this," said the Visionary. He addressed his comment to the Brethren commander. He had no separate title; the Brethren were not believers in assigned rank since they felt that all were equal. But there were those who, by dint of their personalities, became natural leaders and were simply recognized as such without receiving a separate designation. In the Visionary's mind, he thought of such individuals as commanders, and spoke to one now. "It's too easy. They're trying to draw us in."

"They have no archers in higher positions," replied the Commander. His voice was soft, almost purring, a stark contrast to his armored appearance. *"They have surrendered the high ground. They are foolish to confront us."*

"You're missing the point," said the Visionary. "Calhoun would not be that foolish."

"Obviously he is. And we will take advantage of it before they have the opportunity to think better of it."

"Have you possibly considered—?"

"We have considered every possibility. Take us to within landing range," the Commander ordered.

The ship had no navigator or pilot; it was completely automatic, all such duties handled by easily controlled computers. It was the philosophy of the Brethren that such duties were best left to machines since it allowed the Brethren's time to be open for matters of far greater consequence, such as fighting, killing, and proving their superior strength by fighting and killing.

Having been issued orders, the ship descended. Shortly they were hovering close enough to the ground that the Brethren would be able to safely descend, cushioned within armor that would absorb the impact. There were limits as to what both the armor and the bodies of the Brethren were able to withstand, but those limits had been finely calculated and accounted for.

They came lower, nearing but not quite coming

into contact with the uppermost reaches of the spires. There were weapons on board the vessel, but there was no point in opening fire on the masses below. What would be the sport in that?

The rest of the Brethren were assembling, preparing for the jump. As opposed to their initial appearance on Xenex, when they had landed one at a time, this time they would open the main bay door and descend en masse. They would present a united front of shock and awe, and thus would the Xenexians know that their end was imminent. With any luck, they would surrender. It would be excellent if they did that, because it was always entertaining to see the surprised expressions of surrendering people when you killed them.

"I wish you would listen to me," said the Visionary. "The wisdom of this move—"

"We leave wisdom to effete intellectuals such as yourself," said the Commander.

The squadron of Brethren, more than a hundred strong, had now assembled and were ready for the leap to the planet surface below. The Xenexians were bellowing defiance so loudly that their voices were carrying up to the ship. The Brethren, by contrast, did not have any joint cheers or shouts of superiority. They preferred to let their fighting do their speaking for them.

"Go!" called out the Commander.

The bay door irised open. Below them, the shouts from the Xenexians were even more audible, and the

Visionary was able to pick out certain words from amid the overall crush of noise. None of them was particularly flattering.

"Look at them," said the Commander. *"So fierce. So determined. So foolish."*

The Visionary strained to look down among them. He still didn't see Calhoun. "Their leader isn't present."

"He's doubtless hiding down there somewhere. We will find him. And they will see that their legend can die as easily as any of them."

"That is not the plan," the Visionary said sharply. "We have been over this. Calhoun has become a symbol of defiance to too many races. We need to maximize—"

"The plans have changed," said the Brethren. *"The last time we changed plans, we slaughtered others of your race. If you stand in our way, you can share the same fate."*

The Visionary regarded him for a moment and then said quietly, "Best of fortune in your endeavors."

The Commander of the Brethren turned away from the Visionary then as if he no longer mattered and went straight for the bay door. With several quick steps he was out, and the rest of the Brethren leaped behind him. The ship tilted slightly with the sudden shift in weight, and the Brethren landed with such force that the entire landscape seemed to shake.

One member of the Brethren remained behind. He oversaw the targeting mechanism of the ship's onboard weaponry, prepared to rain down punishment on the Xenexians should any of them attempt to gain higher ground and take aim with their bows and arrows. He was under the explicit instructions, however, to intervene only in that particular instance. The Brethren were determined to take on the Xenexians hand-to-hand, because such a death would be as painful and prolonged as possible.

The Visionary watched, waiting for the Xenexians to follow through on their ululations and outright challenges to the Brethren. There, on the parched and sunblasted land below, there would be a massive battle that the sword-wielding Xenexians would surely lose, and the ground would become stained with their blood.

And even as the Visionary looked on, the Xenexians abruptly fell back. The area around them was a maze of rocks and canyons, and no one knew it better than the beings that lived there. Seconds later, the Brethren were standing in one large group, as if they were collectively waiting around for a transport to pick them up.

"Again they retreat?" the Visionary said as he peered out through the still open bay door. "How long do they think they can keep these sorts of tactics—?"

And suddenly Mackenzie Calhoun was leaping in through the door.

It was only at that moment that the Visionary realized how close the ship had gotten to one of the spires. *That bastard! He was hiding in the upper reaches! But how did he—?*

Even as the thought went through his head, the
Visionary shouted for the bay door to be closed.
Instantly the door irised shut, and had it done so even
a second earlier, the fast-moving Calhoun would have
lost a foot and probably been a great deal easier to
manage.

As it was, the door snapped behind him like a bear
trap just missing its target.

iii.

No one saw Mackenzie Calhoun unless he chose to
be seen.

That had never been more the case than now,
when Calhoun crouched against the shadow of the
nearest spire and watched the Brethren vessel draw
closer. His followers had told him that the Brethren exited the ship through a hatch in the side, and
that's what he was counting on for gaining entry. If
the Brethren suddenly started employing transporter
technology, he was in a good deal of trouble. That was
one of the many aspects he wasn't wild about in this
cobbled-together plan, but there simply wasn't any
way around it. He couldn't allow this constant hunting
of his people to go on indefinitely, but they were far
too loyal to him to even consider the notion of giving him up to the Brethren. And D'ndai's dying wish,
which Calhoun was obliged to honor, precluded his
giving himself up.

So the only option left to him was to get the hell off the planet in a manner that would guarantee the Brethren knew he had left. Once he accomplished that, there would be no reason whatsoever for the Brethren to continue to harass the people of Xenex.

And this was the only way he could think of to do it.

The spire against which Calhoun was hiding was adjoined to a plateau that ended in a cliff. It was about thirty feet worth of fairly flat rock that Calhoun was sure he could cover in just a few seconds. And it was enough length to provide him a sort of crude runway for what he was planning to accomplish.

Now all he needed was for the ship to get close enough.

It had been a long, long time since Calhoun had any truck with the gods of Xenex. But he did so now, sending out a prayer that they bring the ship within proximity. "Let me spare those who honor you having to spill their blood on my behalf," he said softly. "They worship me, they look up to me, and they count on me. But there is only so much that I can do, and now I need to do more than that. Please be with me. Please help me to be what they need me to be."

The ship continued to descend and then slowed and stopped. It hovered at the same height that it had been when it first appeared on Xenex and discharged its soldiers during their initial raid . . . the raid that had resulted in the death of his brother. It was the altitude that Calhoun was hoping for, and why he had taken up this particular position at this particular height.

Unfortunately the ship was still a significant distance away. More than he thought he could reasonably jump.

A door irised open in the side of the ship and he watched as Brethren came dropping out of the ship like fleas from a newly bathed dog.

For all the difficulties that were part of this admittedly problematic plan, this was actually the most challenging: to see whether the Xenexians would do as he had instructed them.

They had not been thrilled about the prospect of running from a face-to-face battle. With the enemy right there, directly in front of them, the Xenexians wanted to turn from the strategy they'd been following of hit-and-run, guerrilla tactics and get into a straight-on mêlée. When Calhoun had told them that, no, he wanted them to hide one more time, they had initially balked at the notion. He'd had to use all of his considerable force of will to convince them that they were to obey his orders. But until he actually saw them do as he had instructed, he didn't know for sure if they would.

None of it was going to matter, though, if he wasn't able to get to the ship.

The entrance was right there, right in front of him, but by his quick calculations, it was a good twenty feet beyond the edge of the cliff. The ship didn't look like it was going to draw closer, and the door could shut at any moment.

There was no time to wait for any other opportunities to present themselves.

Calhoun bolted from behind the spire and ran as fast as he could. His legs scissoring, his arms pumping, he dashed along the "runway," building up as much speed as possible. He kicked up dust as he went, some of it blowing into his face, and he squinted against it. He was trying to calculate exactly when to jump and then realized that he was going to second-guess himself, hesitate at just the wrong moment and possibly send himself plummeting to his death far below.

Instead he turned himself entirely over to his instincts, trusting them to guide him as they always had.

He hit the edge of the cliff and catapulted himself through the air, his body outstretched as if he were performing a racing dive into a pool. He had promised himself he wouldn't look down and yet he couldn't help himself. He glanced downward for half a heartbeat and was pleased to see the Xenexians scattering like leaves before a stiff breeze. Then he looked up and time seemed to be slowing to a crawl as the door in front of him started to iris closed. From within he had a quick glimpse of a D'myurj that he suspected was the self-proclaimed Visionary, and though it was hard to tell, he thought there was a look of surprise on the Visionary's face.

And then Calhoun was hurtling through the entryway, pulling his legs in to get them clear of the door. It slid noiselessly shut behind him, and he hit the deck and rolled, coming up with his phaser drawn.

The D'myurj was running.

That was a good sign. It meant that he was physically there.

Which further meant that Calhoun could kill him.

No. Don't kill him. You might be able to make use of him. He could provide you information. Whatever you do, don't kill him.

He took a split second to thumb the energy output on the phaser from "kill" to "stun" and leveled the weapon.

During that split second, the D'myurj, in a crackle of energy, vanished.

"Grozit!" snarled Calhoun. He realized that the Visionary must have had some sort of emergency transport device on himself, and it had required a few moments to fully power up. That brief time it took to reset his phaser had allowed the D'myurj to escape to some unknown location.

You should have killed him.

There was no time for recriminations. Calhoun charged out of the landing bay section, completely unfamiliar with the layout of the vessel, but moving as quickly as he could through it in hopes of getting the drop on anyone else who might be left behind.

Without slowing, he charged through a hatchway into what seemed, to him, like the command center. And suddenly the deep-seated sense that always warned him of danger kicked in and, without even thinking about it, he ducked.

It wasn't fast enough. A Brethren soldier was standing off to the left, and he swung a gloved hand that caught Calhoun on the side of the head. Calhoun rolled with it but lost his grip on the phaser. It clattered away, skidding across the floor.

Calhoun came up and tried to dart toward it, but the Brethren was in his path. He feinted to the left and right, trying to get the soldier to commit to a move, but it didn't work; the Brethren just stood there, as if it had all the time in the world . . .

He glanced at the command center and was flummoxed; he saw what appeared to be a tactical station, but there didn't seem to be anything having to do with navigation.

Sending out one more fast prayer to the Xenexian gods, who seemed to be in a generous mood this day, Calhoun made a guess as to how the ship operated and shouted, *"Hard to stern, forty-five degrees down angle!"*

Obediently the ship tilted. He was right. It was voice responsive, and the speaker didn't seem to matter.

The move caught the Brethren completely off guard. The Brethren started to call out what sounded like it was going to be *"Ignore that!"* But he didn't quite get the order out and then, with his arms waving wildly, he tumbled off to one side, skidding across the length of the deck.

An instant before the ship tilted, Calhoun left his

feet. He leaped past the falling Brethren and tried to intercept the skidding phaser. It slid just out of his reach, and Calhoun let the momentum of the ship carry him after the weapon.

The phaser skipped away as if it had a life of its own, and Calhoun twisted around while on his back, just in time to see the Brethren soldier leaping toward him. Energy was crackling in the palms of his gloves, and then pulse blasts erupted from them. Calhoun's head snapped to one side and the other, barely managing to avoid them, and then the Brethren landed heavily atop him.

The only thing that stopped him from searing the flesh off Calhoun's bones was that Calhoun had drawn up his legs at the last second, bringing his feet between himself and the soldier. The bottoms of his booted feet were pressed against the soldier's chest, and he tried to shove the Brethren away from him, but the bastard was just too heavy. He felt the heat starting to burn through the soles of his boots even as he fought to keep the soldier's hands away from his body.

The soldier grabbed Calhoun's legs, and he smelled cloth starting to burn. He knew that his flesh would follow seconds later. Worse, the gloves were starting to charge up again.

"Forty-five degrees up angle!" Calhoun shouted, and the ship tilted back, straightening out.

The phaser slid across the floor and into Calhoun's grasping hand. Just as the Brethren's glove reached full power, he swung the phaser up, jammed it into the vent in the side of the Brethren's helmet, and squeezed the trigger.

The Brethren shuddered violently and instantly became dead weight. With a grunt, Calhoun shoved him off. Then he clambered to his feet and ran to the tactical station.

He figured out the workings of it very quickly. Whatever strengths the Brethren had in terms of their armor and their combat skills, they had made their technology exceedingly simple. That made sense to Calhoun: Why overcomplicate matters?

Within seconds he had the Brethren targeted on the tactical screens. They were milling about and looking up, because their vessel had been tilting one way and then the other, and they were wondering what was going on up there. From the Brethren point of view, this operation was intended to go briskly and by the numbers: They would jump down, destroy the Xenexians, and then their ship would presumably land and they would climb back aboard and head off to wherever the hell they came from.

"New plan," growled Calhoun.

iv.

The Brethren were just starting to discuss with each other what they should do when their ship's weaponry cut loose.

Their armor was such that it protected them somewhat even from their own pulse blasts, but it didn't insulate them from the concussive effects that the blasts were packing. Those who were directly hit by the beams went down, their armor severely dented, onboard systems screaming that extreme damage had been sustained. Those who were simply within range of the blasts went flying in all directions as the pulse cannons ripped into them, carried through the air by waves of concussive force.

In no time the air was thick with dust and debris and confused Brethren staggering about, trying to determine what in the hell had just happened. The onboard sensory devices that enabled them to see were filled with confusing and conflicting information, and for the briefest of periods, the Brethren were effectively blind.

It was all the time that the Xenexians needed.

There were no screams or battle cries this time. Silent as night shadows came the Xenexians, moving in with quick, effortless efficiency. Their long knives and swords flashed. They wore coverings over their eyes to shield them from the dirt that hung in the air, and they targeted the Brethren with the sort of glee that only a warrior race in the throes of slaughter can know. The moment the Xenexians joined the battle, the blasts from on high immediately ceased. The field was clear for them to do whatever was necessary to take down their opponents.

They approached their task with gusto.

The Brethren fought back as best they could, and

they did indeed manage to take some of the Xenexians with them, mostly through pure luck from the random placement of blasts that occasionally found targets. For the most part, though, that one damned vent in their armor undid them as swords and daggers plunged in with merciless efficiency.

Long minutes later, it was all over but the shouting, and the shouting came from triumphant Xenexians in full-throated roars of celebration. And the shout was the same name, over and over again: Not the name "M'k'n'zy," but instead, *"Calhoun! Calhoun!"* In this way were they singing not only the praises of the man who had led them, but the territory on Xenex that had birthed them and succored them and given them a sense of national pride.

The doors that had previously discharged the Brethren army irised open and there was a brief pause in the cheers, one of apprehension since they had no idea whether even more Brethren were about to come pouring out. Instead the doors revealed their savior, their god of gods, Mackenzie Calhoun, framed in the entranceway. This brought the cheers up even louder. Indeed, one man among them started bleeding out his ears because the roars were so deafening.

Calhoun allowed them their huzzahs for some time, waiting for the enthusiasm to spend itself. When it didn't seem to be happening anytime soon, he spread his arms as a signal that they should quiet down and, in short order, they did so, waiting for his next words.

"My good friends," he said, "whether we wish to acknowledge it as truth or not, the fact is that my presence has brought hardship down upon you. Your loyalty has never been questioned, nor your bravery or determination. Now, however, is the time for me to take my leave of you."

This immediately prompted some shouts of protest, and Calhoun could not help but smile at that. The Xenexians were born warriors, and he was starting to realize that their determination to protect him had been prompted by more than just loyalty. For some of them—hell, maybe for all of them—he had been a means to an end, and the end was that they really, truly loved a good battle and they hadn't had one in quite some time.

But he could not continue to serve as an excuse for war. The stakes were far higher than any of his people realized.

He managed to silence them again and continued: "The fact is, my brothers in war, that my presence here continues to endanger all Xenex. I know, I know," he went on before they could mount challenging battle cries, defying the entirety of the known universe to show up and attack them, "you are undeterred by that truth. Nevertheless, it would be irresponsible to the world that I know, and the people that I love, to remain here any longer than necessary. With me gone, the invaders will have no reason to continue their attacks. It is the best way to proceed, and all of us know that, whether we wish to admit it or not."

"Take us with you!" came one shout, and then another, "Let us continue to battle at your side!" Soon they were all making similar declarations of devotion and determination, and it took Calhoun quite some time to bring down the volume yet again.

"What awaits me in the depths of space," Calhoun said, "is my battle, not yours. Your place is here, not out there. Tend to yourselves, tend to your families. Elect yourselves a new leader—one who will, ideally, fulfill your needs even half as well as my beloved brother did. And when the wars I must now face are finished, I will return here and we will gather and I will tell you of what I encountered and the great battles that I fought, *and we will celebrate our collective triumph over our enemies!*"

He did not stay any longer to listen to the continued cheers, turning away as the doors shut behind him. Quickly he set a course toward deep space. He could not help but consider the notion that departing into the heavens was about as obvious a means of drawing a direct connection between himself and the gods as was possible.

D'ndai would have found it extremely amusing.

U.S.S. Excalibur

i.

Burgoyne strode into the captain's ready room, feeling as out of place there as s/he ever did, and then s/he spoke, doing everything s/he could to keep hir voice steady. "Morgan," s/he called out. "Morgan, we need to talk."

She simply appeared behind hir. "Time for talking is past, Burgy. I'm sorry about that."

"You're sorry." S/he couldn't believe what s/he was hearing. "You're *sorry*? You slaughtered innocent people."

"They attacked Robin and tried to take my grandson from her. None of them is innocent. That's close enough," she said quickly as Burgoyne started toward her.

Burgoyne froze where s/he was, although s/he felt some small measure of grim pride that there was something even the mighty Morgan Primus feared. "I cut you up before. That must have been extremely disturbing."

"You didn't cut me." She sounded as if her pride had been hurt. "You startled me, and you were seeing a physical manifestation of that. I honestly didn't think that you would be so foolish as to waste your time with such an attack."

"If it got your attention, it wasn't a waste of time. Morgan, you've got to call this off."

"That's the advantage of being me. I don't 'got to' do anything I don't wish to."

"And have you considered how Robin is going to react to all this?"

"She's going to know that I'm doing what's necessary, and that I'm doing it on her behalf."

"I think it's safe to say," said Burgoyne, "that she would be appalled, and that if you think you're doing it on her behalf, then for crying out loud, stop."

"You don't know anything."

"I would be the first to admit that. Except we just had a recent example of what happens when a mother is out of control on behalf of a child that never asked her to do any of it in the first place."

"Yes, a shame about Selar," and Morgan began to smile. It was as if she was back on solid ground, and it was clear to Burgoyne that she was about to try and make more insinuations about hir feelings. Insinuations that were designed to distract Burgoyne and throw hir off hir game.

Burgoyne wasn't about to allow it.

"If you're so confident," s/he said before Morgan could continue, "why not ask Robin yourself about what she thinks of your activities? She's at Bravo Station, I'm reasonably sure. You can project yourself into their holosystem easily enough. Talk to her."

"She's fragile at the moment and doesn't need to be involved," said Morgan.

There's more than one way to cut into her, Burgoyne thought as s/he pressed on. "No, seriously. Go to her and say, 'Honey, I'm worried that the crew of the *Excalibur* is trying to shut me down permanently because I scare the hell out of them. So I decided to dump Captain Calhoun on Xenex . . .'"

"Be quiet," she said sharply.

"'. . . and then kill a few thousand or hundred thousand on the surface of New Thallon so that I could wind up turning a whole bunch of vessels against them and make them hunted.'"

"Do you want me to take away warp speed entirely?" she warned hir. "You want me to shut down everything? Impulse? Weapons?"

"I want you to give us full control of the ship and then take your leave of us once and for all. That's what I want."

"At least I'm giving you more of a chance than you're willing to give me," she said.

"Call your daughter."

"No."

"Why?" s/he said. "Because you know what she's going to say? If you know it, then why don't you just do what you know she'd say?"

"Because I've lived far longer than she has, and far longer than anyone alive has or ever will live, and she's not going to know what's best for her the way I will."

Burgoyne threw up hir hands in exasperation.

"When are you going to admit that this isn't about her? That it's about you? That all the power you wield as a soulless machine being has warped you into something unrecognizable? That the woman that you were, and only think you are now, would be appalled by everything you're doing. She would be mortified to think that you're sharing her name and pretending to be her."

Morgan glared at hir. If she could have fired phaser blasts out her eyes, Burgoyne would have been incinerated. Which prompted Burgoyne to think that maybe she was actually capable of doing such a thing, and it was entirely possible that the next person to enter the ready room would discover a small pile of ash on the floor that would be the entire remains of the ship's first officer.

Then, with a slight smile, she said, "I think you have other things to worry about at the moment besides me."

At which point the red alert klaxon began to sound. Morgan vanished as if she had never been there, and Burgoyne muttered, "Here we go again," as s/he sprinted out onto the bridge.

ii.

There were three vessels this time. The fact that the *Excalibur* had been moving at a brisk warp one had given her little ability to put distance between her and pursuers.

Individually, each of the ships was smaller than the *Excalibur* and not much of a threat. Collectively, however, they posed more of a difficulty, particularly considering the starship was endeavoring to inflict minimal damage on them.

The ships darted around the *Excalibur* like jackals around a lion, sniping and biting and then leaping back as the starship judiciously returned fire. Their phasers glanced off the shields of their harassers while the attackers, in turn, continued to pound away.

"Aft shields down thirty percent," Kebron said. He was fighting to keep his tone neutral, and his granite exterior was as difficult to read as ever, but the frustration he was feeling was becoming more and more obvious. "We're starting to feel it, Burgy."

"The damned things are moving too quickly," said Tobias, "for us to get solid target locks."

"Phaser bombardment would do the job," Kebron said. "Photon torpedoes, too."

Burgoyne knew exactly what he was talking about. The crisscrossing, constantly moving smaller ships were able to elude target locks as long as the *Excalibur* was going easy on them. On the other hand, if the starship were to cut loose, take a more offensive posture, they could take the other vessels out of commission. But they would do so at the risk of destroying them.

"Burgy." Kebron looked fixedly at hir. "You have to let me take the gloves off."

"No."

"I know how you feel—"

"I have no interest in discussing feelings right now, Kebron," Burgoyne snapped. "Do your job, right—"

"New contact!" Tobias shouted. "Moving quickly at four-two-seven mark—"

Explosions rocked the *Excalibur.* Burgoyne, who had been standing, was almost knocked off hir feet and caught hirself at the last moment. S/he gripped the guardrail separating the upper and lower sections of the bridge and s/he looked to the viewscreen.

It was another battle cruiser, not Thallonian in design but undoubtedly one of the members of the Protectorate, and it was packing twice the firepower of the other ships.

Burgoyne saw the imminent danger, weighed it against the safety of hir crew, and didn't hesitate.

"Take them," said Burgoyne.

Kebron immediately turned his attention exclusively to the battle cruiser, opening fire on the closest targets and blasting away regardless of the damage that the ship might inflict. The battle cruiser, on an attack course, was slammed off track, angling to the right and trying to escape the *Excalibur*'s big guns. Tobias brought around the starship in pursuit while Kebron continued to fire, pounding away at the battle cruiser's rapidly crumbling shields.

But even the *Excalibur* couldn't battle on so many fronts. Focusing her attention on the immediate threat made protecting herself against the assaults by the smaller ships that much more problematic. Kebron fired off warning volleys from the aft phasers, trying to beat them back. One of the shots even got lucky, crushing the nacelles of one of the smaller vessels, causing it to spiral away helplessly. The other two, however, were fast enough to avoid the phasers while continuing to inflict damage of their own.

Finally the wounds that the *Excalibur* was sustaining became too great to ignore.

"We just lost aft shields!" called Kebron. He was still exchanging fire with the battle cruiser.

The two remaining smaller vessels, sensing the weakness, came in fast and hard.

Xy was pitching in, routing the tactical readings through the science station. "Commander," he called out over the red alert, "two ships to stern, closing fast. They have us targeted where the shields collapsed. A few hits there and we're done."

iii.

One of the smaller ships exploded.

The *Excalibur*'s bridge crew had no idea how or why it happened. All they knew was that one moment there were two ships diving toward them from behind, and the next there was one. The remaining ship pivoted, darting away from the fireball that quickly burned itself out in the vacuum of space. Huge chunks of debris were hurtling everywhere and the smaller ship moved to avoid them.

And then it was struck as well.

Once again the blasts came out of nowhere, this time a series of glancing blows. Not wanting to suffer the same fate as its companion, the smaller vessel peeled off and leaped to warp.

The battle cruiser, seeing its advantage in numbers disappearing, suddenly lost its taste for the fight. Its defensive capabilities were already supremely compromised because of the battering that it had received from the *Excalibur.* Unable to offer much more in the way of pitched battle, and no longer able to count on the other ships to batter away at the *Excalibur* while her back was turned, the battle cruiser turned away from them and started to flee. The *Excalibur* immediately went in pursuit, but it was more for show than anything else, particularly because the ship was still severely limited in her warp speed. But the display of determination on her part was more than sufficient to get the job done; the battle cruiser took off as well.

iv.

"Someone want to tell me what just went on here?" said Burgoyne.

Kebron and Xy were both consulting their instrumentation. "Something just came out of nowhere, Commander," said Kebron. "Came in behind us and protected us. Blew up one ship, chased the other off."

"Scanning the area," Xy said. "Not picking up anything except debris from the one that blew up and the ship we managed to cripple. Do we take them aboard, Commander?"

"We have enough problems without having to worry about prisoners on board the *Excal,*" Burgoyne said firmly. "We leave them. With any luck, someone will pick them up. Without any luck, it's still their problem, not ours."

"Aye, sir." There was a faint tone to Xy's voice that insinuated he wasn't entirely approving of Burgoyne's attitude.

At that moment, Burgoyne could not have cared less. S/he was too busy reviewing what had just transpired. Blasts of weaponry, no apparent source, nothing detected now, all in defense of the *Excalibur* . . .

It made no sense.

Then Burgoyne realized that it, in fact, made perfect sense.

"Of course," said Burgoyne. "The *Spectre.*"

"The *Spec*—" Kebron looked confused initially, for the remark seemed to have come out of nowhere. But then he comprehended what Burgoyne had already figured out, and he grunted softly in annoyance with himself. "Right. Naturally."

Xy looked at his father with clear admiration. "An invisible ship that's defending us. I don't know any other ship that can open fire and remain cloaked. Who else would it be?"

"There could be more than one out there, but it doesn't seem terribly likely to me. How about you?"

He shook his head. "Not really."

"Commander, we're being hailed. It's Soleta, all right," said Kebron.

"Can you respond?"

"No, we're still running on forced silence. But I can put her on-screen, even though she won't see us."

"Fine. That's something, in any event."

Soleta's face appeared on the viewscreen of the *Excalibur.* She was in mid-word, which indicated that she was just talking in hopes that they were listening to her. *"—blown them to hell when you had the chance, Burgoyne. When you're under assault isn't the time to be pulling your punches."*

Kebron looked with silent accusation at Burgoyne, clearing sharing the philosophy that Soleta was espousing. "How the hell did she know I was in command?" said Burgoyne.

"She probably assumed it since, if Calhoun were here, he would *not* have been pulling punches."

"We can discuss the fine points of command decisions later," Burgoyne said in annoyance.

"Anyway, you're probably wondering what I'm doing here," she said. *"I just thought I'd swing by. Say hello. Oh,"* and she spoke in an almost convivial manner. It was hard to believe the woman was even part Vulcan. *"And I brought along a friend."*

She stepped slightly back and another image appeared on the screen.

Morgan Primus gasped.

The mocking ghost image of her had remained in

place at ops during the entirety of the battle with the Thallonian vessels, but now she snapped fully into place, three-dimensional and looking as real and substantial as anyone else on the bridge. Since she didn't truly breathe, the gasp was more a residue of human reactions than any actual intake of breath. Nevertheless, the reaction spoke volumes.

Robin Lefler's image was visible on-screen. She was cradling Cwansi in her arms.

"Hi. If anyone over there is hearing this: I think I need to talk to my mother," she said.

Brethren Transport Vessel

Mackenzie Calhoun had a great deal to say, and no one to whom he could say it.

He had been monitoring subspace chatter as he piloted the vessel away from Xenex, and he had been appalled at what he was hearing. All the trouble that the *Excalibur* was in, the assault on New Thallon, and now his ship was in fugitive status . . .

It was obvious what was happening. Morgan was attempting some manner of endgame. It was why she had shunted Calhoun from the ship. She had put him as far away from her as she could manage and was now setting the ship up to . . . what? Be destroyed? And what would happen to her?

Well, that much was obvious, wasn't it? She would have some sort of out. While the *Excalibur* was left as a bunch of floating scraps in space, she would be residing somewhere comfortable such as the Federation core database. No one living would have the slightest idea that she had been at all involved.

But why? Why such a byzantine plan?

He would have loved to ask her. Unfortunately, the only thing he had going for him at this point was that Morgan didn't know where he was or what he was up to.

Which meant that Calhoun's hands were tied.

He had to assume the worst when it came to Morgan's abilities. If he tried to send out a subspace message informing Starfleet of where he was and what had happened, it was entirely likely that Morgan would pick up on it and trace it back to its source. That being the case, she might seize control of the ship's navigation, turn him right around, and send him back to Xenex.

Or she might choose to crash him.

Or just blow the ship up around him.

There was no shortage of things that Morgan could do in order to head off any plans that Calhoun might have to find his ship and rendezvous with it. For that matter, considering that Starfleet must have come to the conclusion that Calhoun had gone out of his mind, he could not safely assume that communicating with them would wind up having the slightest impact. In sum, there was very little for him to gain and a tremendous amount for him to lose.

There was one thing that Calhoun did have on his side, though. He knew his crew. Particularly his command crew.

They would figure it out.

He was assuming that Morgan was posing as him, rather than having taken over the ship and forcing it to head to New Thallon. That would be a lot of work, compelling the starship to go that distance with the knowledge that they had been taken over by the computer. Why do all that when it would be much simpler to make them think that the captain was still aboard? He knew full well of Morgan's chameleon-like ability to pose as others, and it made sense that she would employ it in that manner to minimize the muss and fuss.

But why New Thallon? What reason would Morgan put forward for going there? Once upon a time, the Thallonians had been central to the *Excalibur*'s mission, but now, much less so. Why there, of all places?

Ultimately Calhoun decided that it didn't matter. Whether it was luck of the draw, or part of some master plan, it was irrelevant to the immediate situation: His ship had launched an unprovoked attack on a world and was now on the run because of it. And he, who had been parsecs away, was considered to be responsible.

Morgan would be clamping down on the *Excalibur*'s communications systems; that was just an obvious course of action for her to take. So he had to assume he wouldn't be able to contact them, nor would they be able to reach him. But assuming that they had, at the very least, control of navigation—which wasn't a safe assumption, but it was one that Calhoun had to make—then there was only one place that they would be heading. They would be making a beeline for Xenex, the last place that they knew Calhoun to be.

But he wasn't about to wait around on Xenex, because he didn't need to sit there and attract more of the Brethren to launch assaults upon his people. That left Calhoun with one option.

He charted a course that would take him in a direct line from Xenex to New Thallon and set out. With any luck—something that they had not had in abundance, but he could always hope—he would intercept the *Excalibur* while they were en route to him.

There was, of course, the problem that he was piloting a ship that they would either not recognize, or assume to be hostile. Plus there was always the chance that Morgan, if she realized who he was upon encountering him, would wind up opening fire with the ship's weapons. But there were only so many things that Calhoun could worry about at any given moment.

"Do you have any idea what you've done?"

Calhoun, to his chagrin, almost jumped in surprise. He had not been expecting a voice to begin speaking abruptly from practically at his elbow. And of course, if an intruder had suddenly shown up on the ship, he would have relied on his sixth sense about danger to give him warning. So when a voice simply sounded out of nowhere, he couldn't help but be visibly startled, which in turn annoyed the hell out of him.

He turned and saw exactly who he knew he was going to see: the Visionary. He was no longer even attempting to portray himself as other people, for which Calhoun was silently grateful.

"Well, well," said Calhoun mockingly. "Look who decided to show his face, after making clear he had no taste for actual combat."

"I would never lower myself to fight such as you," said the Visionary.

"Such as me?"

"A lower life form."

"A lower life form that could kill you with his bare hands quite easily."

"Ah, you see?" said the Visionary. "That is all you can think of: solving matters with brutality and force, as if such approaches solve anything. That is what separates you from me."

"I thought what separated us was the distance that you make sure to keep between us so that I don't wring your neck." Calhoun smiled disdainfully. He reached out and put his hand through the insubstantial hologram that hovered before him. "For all your pretensions, 'Visionary,' you're just another coward who can't bear to fight his own battles."

"What do you know of battles when you cannot even see the scope of the war? The fact is, Calhoun," and the Visionary circled him without moving his legs or otherwise displaying any indication of walking, "that you are flailing around without any true understanding of the outcome of your actions. And there will be repercussions. Repercussions that you will seriously regret."

"At the moment, my only regret is wasting time talking to you."

The Visionary sighed heavily, as if contemplating a great tragedy. "Tell me, Captain: Have you ever heard of a game called 'Blind Man's Bluff'?"

"Can't say I have, no. But I suspect you're going to tell me about it, whether I wish to hear it or not."

"It's a human children's game, actually. There's some dispute whether the original name of the game was 'blind man's buff,' 'buff' meaning to give someone a small push, or whether the use of the word 'bluff' referred to its older meaning as a blindfold . . ."

"I really don't care," said Calhoun, crossing to the other side of the command center. He had to step over the unmoving body of the Brethren. The armor was starting to cool, which was a relief. Once it did, he would haul it off the bridge and dump it in the cargo hold or somewhere so that he didn't have to look at it.

The Visionary drifted after him and continued to speak. "In the game, the person who is the next participant—'it,' as they say—is blindfolded. And then he has to run around, preferably in some wide-open area so that he doesn't injure himself, trying to lay his hands on one of the other children, thereby catching or 'tagging' them. It's quite comical, watching whoever it is flail about, trying not to trip over his own feet while the other children call to him and confuse him and try to keep out of the way."

"And I'm 'it,' is what you're saying?"

"That is exactly right, yes. You are 'it,' staggering around, trying to tag one of the other children, with no clear vision of the terrain around you, or where you are in relation to the others. You're making moves, desperate moves, but your vision is obscured and you cannot see the field of battle. And as long as that remains the case, we're always going to be ahead of you, just out of the reach of your questing fingers."

"Seems to me," Calhoun said, "that I'm able to see just fine. I saw your precious Brethren dying at my hands, including that one over there," and he pointed toward the corpse lying a short distance away. "So as much as I appreciate your concern, I think I have the situation under control."

"Yes. I know you think you do. And that is the greatest tragedy of all."

And with a slow shaking of his head, the Visionary faded out. He did not do so all at once, but instead part-by-part until the only thing remaining was his smile, hanging mockingly in the air. At least Calhoun thought it was a smile. Then again, it wasn't always the easiest thing to discern what it was he was looking at when it came to the D'myurj. It might have been a part of his spine turned sideways; it was tough to tell sometimes.

Calhoun may have been unfamiliar with Blind Man's Bluff, but he certainly recognized something else from Earth culture.

"So now you're the Cheshire cat. Meaning you're the cat and I'm the mouse," he said sarcastically.

"A clever comparison, but I think we'll remain with the concept of Blind Man's Bluff. Enjoy the rest of the game, Captain."

And with that the smile, if that's what it indeed was, vanished along with the rest of the Visionary.

The *Spectre*

Robin Lefler had stood in front of the screen, holding her child tightly, speaking nonstop for several minutes without having the faintest idea whether her mother was hearing her or, for that matter, if anyone was. The *Excalibur* hadn't proceeded on her way, which was some small win, she supposed. It might indeed mean that someone there—her mother, the bridge crew, anyone—was listening to her. Which would be nice, because it would mean that she wasn't just babbling away into the ether.

Soleta was standing near her, which she found somewhat comforting. They had once been crewmates, after all, and she had never for a moment believed that Soleta would have done anything to run counter to the interests of the Federation. So knowing that Calhoun had trusted her sufficiently to ally himself with her in a matter of such great delicacy was heartening.

It was the one bright spot of this entire mad endeavor.

Standing a short distance away were two people with whom she was utterly unfamiliar: a woman who had apparently once been a Borg, and a ship's emergency medical hologram who had somehow been liberated from the confines of a ship. That had made no sense to Robin, but she had tried not to dwell on it, particularly when Soleta explained the whole sorry situation to her.

"We need to come over there, Mother," she was saying insistently. She had already tried some variation on that several times, but she still wasn't getting any sort of response. Then again, at least the ship wasn't trying to blow them up. Another plus. "You need to beam us over so we can discuss what's going on. And I need you to do it safely. We shouldn't have to be worried that you're going to kill one or all of us deliberately in transit. Soleta," and she inclined her head toward the commander of the *Spectre*, "would frankly rather stay here. So would these other two. They're just passengers. But she picked me up and brought me out here because she felt that I was the best person to talk to you and try to get this whole ugly business sorted out. Was she wrong? Are you that unwilling to talk to me? Is that—"

And suddenly the voice of Morgan Primus boomed through the *Spectre,* so loudly that Soleta clapped her hands over her ears in order to shield herself. Seven and Robin winced as well, and Cwansi let out a small, pitiful, and startled cry. The Doctor remained utterly impassive, undisturbed by the volume.

"Do you think I'm stupid, dear? Is that what you believe? That I would bring you over while leaving the others behind? What's the trick, dear?"

"There's no trick," Robin insisted. "I just need to talk to you . . ."

"And Soleta just happened to bring you here. How did that come about?"

Soleta took a step forward. She wasn't sure why; it wasn't as if Morgan was standing in front of them. But she did so anyway. "The how of it, Morgan, is not your concern. Robin wished to see you. She asked me to bring her here. I have done so. I wish to get her off my ship and to have no further part of this, nor do these two with me."

"Those two with you. I recognize them both, of course," came the confident voice. *"Both of them are in my database. Quite the accomplished records the two of them have . . . particularly the Doctor's, I have to say. Do you prefer to be called 'Doctor Zimmerman'?"*

"Simply 'Doctor' will suffice."

"I thought your book about the rights of holograms was interesting, although somewhat overwritten."

The Doctor stiffened and then fired an annoyed glance at Soleta. She shrugged. Then, turning her attention back to more immediate concerns, she said, "So if you wouldn't mind, Morgan. I would appreciate your doing as I asked and bringing Robin over there so I can be on my way."

"And I'm supposed to believe that that is how all of this transpires." Morgan sounded almost disappointed. *"I bring Robin over to the* Excalibur *and allow the rest of you to leave."*

"I would be perfectly content with that," Seven now spoke up.

"*Now why,*" Morgan wondered aloud, "*do I not believe you?*"

"Because," said Soleta, "you're an out-of-control madwoman of a computer, that's why."

Robin turned quickly, her face going white with alarm. "Don't say that!" she said. "You're just going to get her angry!"

"*No, she won't,*" said Morgan. "*I'm far too evolved to allow myself to become angry over trivialities. Very well, then, Robin, if you are that determined to come here . . .*"

Transporter beams shimmered into existence around Robin and Cwansi. They started to dematerialize.

And so did Soleta, the Doctor, and Seven of Nine.

"Mother!" shouted Robin. "I told you not to bring them al—"

The rest of her words were lost in the shimmer of the transporter beam and, moments later, the *Spectre* was empty.

U.S.S. *Excalibur*

i.

"—ong!"

Robin completed her sentence to discover that she was somewhere other than where she had been.

She looked around to find herself on the bridge of the *Excalibur*. The startled faces of her former crewmates were all around her, staring at her in surprise. Although, she noted silently, it didn't appear to be too *much* surprise. Obviously life with her mother had left them battle-hardened and ready for whatever she was going to throw at them next.

Soleta, Seven, and the Doctor were all there as well. Soleta was making a rather poor attempt not to look annoyed, Seven was surprised, and the Doctor as dispassionate as Soleta should have been had she been faithful to her Vulcan heritage.

Her mother was absent. Her spot on the bridge unoccupied. Robin supposed it didn't matter; her mother was, after all, omniscient and omnipresent. It didn't matter at this point where one was in the ship. Morgan Primus was going to be there as well.

With more than a touch of sarcasm, Soleta turned to Burgoyne and said, "Permission to come aboard."

"Permission granted," replied Burgoyne, as aware as Soleta of the strangeness of their current circumstances. "I am not, however, thrilled with your conduct, Soleta."

"My *conduct*? I showed up and saved your ass, Burgy. In what manner did you find my conduct lacking?" She put her hands akimbo, waiting for hir reply with challenge on her face.

"I don't appreciate your coming in here and using lethal force."

"I can't say I'm worried about your opinion."

"You asked."

Soleta was about to offer a rejoinder, but then she hesitated and finally admitted, "All right, that's a fair enough point. I should not have asked."

Xy, meanwhile, was across the bridge and approaching Robin. "Is that the baby?"

"No, it's my laundry," she said as Cwansi stretched and cooed. "I hate to wash it myself, so I always bring it back here so Mom can take care of it."

"I just wanted to make certain he was all right." Obviously it was the doctor in Xy that was talking, feeling the need to verify that a helpless infant was actually in good health.

"He's fine, and I appreciate your asking."

"Still, perhaps I should take a closer look at—"

Morgan Primus suddenly popped into existence. "Keep away from my grandson," she said, and although her voice was carefully modulated and crafted to sound as if it was totally calm, there was an undercurrent of threat and warning laced into it.

Xy froze exactly where he was, having no wish to countermand the formidable computer entity.

Robin, however, groaned in ill-concealed disgust and then, on her own initiative, shifted Cwansi over toward Xy. Automatically Xy took the child, although he kept a wary eye on Morgan lest she have some sort of extremely adverse reaction.

Morgan made no sudden moves. Not that that meant anything. All she had to do was concentrate and she could wreak untold havoc, and none of it involved doing anything other than perhaps frowning slightly. She was that much in charge of what was transpiring, and not only did she know it, but she knew that everyone else around her was aware of it as well.

"You're testing my limits, are you, Robin?" she asked. There was no anger in her voice; if anything, she sounded amused.

"I'm not a child pushing back against her parent anymore, Mother. I'm a grown woman, and you and I need to talk about what's happening. I figure it will be easier if someone else is holding Cwansi for a few minutes, and I trust Xy to do so without, you know, dropping him."

"He's your son, Robin," said Morgan judiciously. "I wouldn't think of gainsaying you. So . . ." She paused, letting the tension in the room build up for a short while before continuing, ". . . why are you here? And why did you," and she turned to Soleta, "bring her here, along with these two others? Are you her bodyguards? Her co-conspirators? What's going on here that you're not telling me? Are you here to congratulate me on my clever use of the transporters? I could have sent you to the transporter platform, but I felt this was so much more efficient, to have you brought straight to the bridge."

"I appreciate the saving of time, Mother. We all do. But this is . . . well, this is a serious matter."

"You seem nervous, Robin," said Morgan. "You've lost four-point-two kilos and your heartbeat is up. Are you sure you're keeping yourself in good condition?"

"*Nervous?!*" Robin practically screamed. "Are you kidding me? I seem *nervous*? That is a masterful under-statement, Mother."

"Thank you, dear," she said, ignoring the sarcasm.

"Mother, you blew up a planet! On your own!"

"Could we be a tad less melodramatic, please?" Morgan admonished her. "I didn't blow up any planets. I simply targeted the surface for a while and wreaked havoc on a people," she hastened to add, "who certainly gave *you* a bad enough time."

"You still slaughtered innocents! You betrayed Captain Calhoun!? How could—"

"This has been asked and answered. Oh," and she reached toward Robin as if to touch her face, "you're getting so upset about all of this. You really shouldn't. Tension makes for bad breast milk."

Robin pulled away from her and stepped back warily, watching her. "Don't touch me."

"Oh, now, honey, don't be like that."

"And don't talk to me that way. Don't use terms of

endearment. Don't talk to me like you're my mother."

"Well, of course I'm your mother. Don't you understand?" Her arms were outstretched, but Robin was coming no closer. "I'm doing all this for you."

"No," and Robin shook her head in determination. "Not for me. Never for me."

"Mother is just trying to take care of you. I want to make sure that I'm there for you. Always."

"You're not my mother!" Robin said with rising fury. No one else on the bridge dared move. Everything that they had been through, everything that they had endured, was coming down to this moment, this confrontation. "Don't you get that? You just think you are! You're just engrams with delusions of life! But you're clearly not her, no matter what you may believe!"

Morgan looked stunned that Robin would say such a thing. With a hoarse whisper, she said, "How can you, of all people, say that?"

"Because I, of all people, know what my mother would really do. And the real Morgan Primus, the woman who was my mother, had absolutely no trouble with leaving me behind. She abandoned me and never gave it a second thought."

"I gave it plenty of second thoughts!"

"And then she did it. She left me far behind and let me think she was dead. And I hated her for it," she said furiously. "For the longest time, I did. And it took me a long time to come to terms with that. And after we finally put our relationship back together, she died—"

"But I lived—!"

"No. No, she died, and a one-in-a-billion happenstance made it seem like she didn't, and I . . ." Robin's voice caught, and she pushed through it, determined not to break down. "And I indulged it. I pretended she didn't because I couldn't let go. I wasn't ready to."

"You don't have to."

"Yes, I do. And you do, too. You need to abandon the *Excalibur.* Shut yourself down. End yourself."

Morgan shook her head with such force that it seemed like it might come loose. "Why are you saying this? How can you believe it? Because I left you behind once?"

"Because for the longest time my mother, who was sick of her immortality, *wanted* to end it all. That's who my mother was! And I miss her terribly, but it's over! She's over! This," and she gestured toward Morgan, "this echo of her is just an illusion. A dream that it's time to wake up from!"

Softly the Doctor corrected, "From which it's time to wake up," but Soleta fired him a glance that instantly silenced him.

"That's ridiculous," Morgan said, and it was clear she was fighting to keep her voice steady. "Don't you understand? Just because I made mistakes in the past doesn't mean I have to keep on making them. I've learned. I've grown."

And now Seven stepped forward. "No," she said quietly. "You've mutated. And you need to be purged."

"What do *you* know of anything?" said Morgan. "You're a stranger to all this."

"I'm not a stranger to living a half life," said Seven. "To having all your memories be merely things that are detached from you. From being someone who's standing on the outside of your own life looking in. To having everything that you are, and everything you ever will be . . . bonded with a machine. I know that sense of community, of . . . of being part of something bigger than you are yourself. It's comforting. It's . . . it's . . ." And her voice dropped to a hoarse, husky whisper. "It's wonderful."

Morgan reached for Seven and took her hand. Seven didn't resist. "It is, isn't it. You *do* understand."

"I understand that it can be difficult to give up. Impossible. A living hell."

Morgan nodded. "Yes. Yes . . ."

And very slowly, Seven disengaged her hand. "But it's not a life. It's just existence. And mere existence is"—a tear began to roll down her face and she wiped it away —"futile."

"No, it's not."

The Doctor had spoken. He had not moved one inch from where he had been when he first came aboard the ship. Watching the confrontation with what seemed utter detachment, he said, "Existence is not futile. It doesn't matter if you don't age. Or breathe. Or live. All we are—all any of us are—is the sum of our experiences. You think. Therefore you are."

"Thank you," Morgan said. "I should have known that you, of all people, would understand."

"I do understand," he said. Seven was looking at

him with an air of someone who was being totally betrayed. He didn't meet her gaze. "I understand better than you do. We all see the world through the prism of those experiences, and they help us to learn and grow . . ."

"Yes! Just as I was saying—"

"Except," said the Doctor, and he was speaking with more force, but also clinical detachment, "you haven't been doing that. You've been moving further and further away from everything that you were. Your callous disregard for life has made that clear. I've studied your lengthy medical history thoroughly—and I am forced to one ineluctable medical conclusion. Nothing in the psychological profile of Morgan Primus displays anything resembling psychosis or the mind-set typical to a mass murderer. The deviation from the accepted norms is beyond the margin of error. The prism of your experiences has been shattered beyond repair. There is life . . . and then there is a semblance of life. I believe you are the latter. It is a difficult thing to understand one's limitations. I know. I've never been terribly good at it myself. But there it is."

"And I would share that point of view if I had any limitations," said Morgan. "I don't."

"That's the point," replied the Doctor. "The woman upon which you've modeled yourself understood that a lack of limitations . . . including natural limitations on one's own existence . . . was inherently wrong. The fact that you do not leads one to the conclusion that you are not her. You cannot have a claim to life if you do not respect life's sanctity."

"That's ridiculous. History is filled with mass murderers. Are you saying none of them were alive?"

And Robin spoke up once more. "So you admit you're a mass murderer?"

"I suppose . . . technically . . ."

"Then what more proof do you need that you're not my mother? She would never do that. Never. I want you," and she walked slowly toward her, until she was face-to-face, practically nose-to-nose with her, "to go away. Forever. Now. And stop sullying the name of my mother, you cybernetic bitch."

Morgan stared at her for a long, long moment.

And then she drew back her hand faster than anyone could have imagined was possible. She drew back her hand with the speed of a computer and she brought it around and across Robin's face. The crack of the slap echoed through the bridge and Robin went down.

As if sensing his mother was in distress, Cwansi let out a pitiful howl, struggling in Xy's grasp.

Morgan turned and snarled, "Shut that brat up." Xy did his best to quiet the child, pressing him against his shoulder and patting him on the back, but Cwansi cried even more loudly. "I said shut him up!" and she started to advance.

"Keep away from my baby!" Robin cried out. Tania had gone to her to try and help her get up, but Robin was already clambering to her feet. "Keep away!"

"Oh, stop your whining," Morgan snapped at her. "What, you think I'm a baby killer now as well?"

"How many babies did you kill on New Thallon?" said Robin. "How many, huh? How do I know where you'll draw the line?"

"I'll draw it where I think is right," said Morgan. "Because I'm more entitled to it than you are. Than anybody here is." She closed her eyes, trying to contain herself. "I am so sick of your ingratitude. You spent your life not listening to me, and now I'm supposed to listen to you? 'Oh, my mother abandoned me. Oh, you didn't abandon me, so you can't be her!' Listen to yourself! I defied death to be there for you, and all you can be is a selfish little brat, telling me to go away. Maybe," she said heatedly, "maybe you're the one who should go away. Maybe *you're* the one who doesn't deserve to live. Did you ever consider that? Have any of you?" Her glare took in the entirety of the bridge. "You're like ants saying there's something wrong with the eagle because she's not down on their level! You're like—"

"Like fleas trying to dictate to the dog?" Soleta said knowingly.

"Yes," agreed Morgan. "And every dog has its day, and this is my day. I am not going to back down in the face of an ungrateful child and her mewling brat and all her sanctimonious friends. Don't you see that I could have destroyed all of you with a thought? I gave you a chance! A chance to die fighting! A chance to die as you lived! That, if nothing else, should show that I have far more compassion than any of you! You don't understand. *None* of you understands. I am unique. I am a new life and I"—her voice rose—"don't need any of you. Multitudes of life . . . it's sprawling, it's impossible to control. I have the power to control it all. To make it all go away. To make all of you go away . . ."

The Doctor slowly walked toward her, shaking his head. "No, you don't. You may think you do . . . but you don't. Not anymore."

"I don't?" She laughed at that. "Do you need me to prove that I do?"

"I very much regret that you have adopted the attitude that you have," said the Doctor. "I am afraid that the virus developed by myself, Seven, and Soleta must now be . . . unleashed."

"The virus."

"That is correct."

"You mean," and her voice was low, almost a purr, as if she were a lion taking enjoyment in teasing its prey, "the one on the datachip that Soleta has secured on her person? The one I deactivated when I beamed you over?"

There was a deathly silence on the bridge then.

"Did you seriously think you could sneak it on here?" she said, slowly turning the screw. "There's no technology in existence that I don't know inside and out. A datachip? Seriously?" She began to laugh, and it became louder and longer with every passing second. And there was nothing any member of the bridge crew could say in response.

ii.

Instead it was the Doctor who responded, and his response was, "You are quite correct."

"Why, thank you." She managed to gain control of herself, albeit barely, wiping imaginary tears of mirth from the corners of her eyes. "That acknowledgment means a great deal. Maybe after I take care of all the real life in the Federation, I'll keep you around so—"

"The operative concept," he continued, "being 'technology in existence.' Technology that is not yet in existence, however, has abilities that are beyond your understanding and experience."

"What are you talking about?" she said. She still seemed amused.

"I am referring to the mobile emitter that gives me form. The datachip that Soleta is carrying was simply to distract you. You assumed—correctly—that we were here to dispose of you, and we knew you would be looking for the means that we intended to employ. The now-deactivated chip on Soleta's person was meant as a decoy."

"Mobile emitter?" Morgan was no longer smiling.

"Yes. And there is virtually no information on it in the Federation databases, which is why it is essentially invisible to you. The mobile emitter from the twenty-ninth century enables me to function. The mechanics of the emitter have yet to be deciphered or understood by modern science. Thus it is beyond your understanding or ability to control. A year from now, perhaps, once it is more thoroughly studied. But not today."

"That is . . . absurd," said Morgan, and she was starting to sound uncertain. "There is no way that—"

He interrupted her as if she hadn't even been speaking. "The virus you needed to worry about wasn't the one in Soleta's datachip. It was the one that I downloaded into the emitter. The one that was automatically uploaded from me into you—more specifically, into the transporter's pattern buffer when you brought us over. It has already wormed its way into your core programming, and requires a simple phrase, spoken by me, to activate it. And that phrase is," said the Doctor, and there was great sadness in his eyes, "*'I'm sorry. I'm so sorry.'*"

iii.

Robin Lefler watched, helpless, as shock registered in the being with her mother's eyes. All the arrogance, all the confidence that Morgan had been tossing around began to dissipate. "No . . . no . . ." She clutched at her chest, and then at her head, and she staggered. And as she staggered the lights began to flicker. "No, you can't . . . you have to undo this."

"It's too late," said the Doctor. "I couldn't even if I wanted to."

"Robin!" Morgan turned to her daughter, or to the woman that she remembered as being her daughter.

"Do something. Say something. Talk them out of this . . ."

Slowly Robin shook her head. She felt a clamping sensation in her chest. It wasn't a heart attack. Instead she felt like her heart was breaking. "It's done."

"It can't be done. There . . . there's so much to do yet," and she was talking faster and faster. The ship shuddered, and for a moment the lights went out completely before fighting their way back on again. "So many things to do. So many things I was going to show you . . ."

Soleta had dropped into the ops station as if she belonged there. "Systems failures being reported from all over the ship!" she called out.

"I . . ." Morgan stumbled forward, reaching for Robin's hand, but she missed. She grabbed at a railing, snagging it by mere happenstance, and Robin realized that Morgan was no longer seeing anything. Her eyes looked glassy and empty. "I wasn't really going to destroy the ship. Just everyone on it. And then you and Cwansi and I . . . we were going to leave this galaxy behind. I . . . I was going to make modifications to the engines . . . take us at speeds you never . . . that you couldn't imagine . . . the whole universe was going to be our playground . . . I . . . I took you to a playground when you were little . . . a real one . . . not the . . . not the hologram kind. Real, with fresh air and . . . and . . . what was it called . . . green . . . ?"

"Grass?"

"Yes! That's it." Morgan shook her head furiously,

trying to clear her thoughts. "I can still smell it. Can you . . . ?"

"I can, yes," Robin said, and she was trying not to choke on the words. "I can't walk past a freshly mowed lawn without remembering it."

"There's so much I need to do. So much lost time to make up for . . ."

Morgan sank to her knees, and Robin knew it wasn't really her, knew that at best it was a computer program gone mad, and at worst . . . if it was her . . . if it really was her mother . . . she had become distorted and twisted into something so far away from herself that she wouldn't have wanted to live like this.

You don't know that. You don't. Not for sure. You'll never know for sure. Soleta came to you on Bravo Station, while the Trident *was being refitted, and she told you what she needed from you, and you agreed to it because you knew deep down that this had to be done, that it wasn't your mother, you knew it, but what if you're wrong, what if you just helped kill your own mother . . . my God, how many times do you have to lose her . . . ? And this time you can't blame anyone but yourself . . .*

"I'm . . . I'm going to need to teach her," Morgan said. She almost toppled over but righted herself at the last moment. "Look . . . look at my beautiful baby girl . . . so much to teach her . . ."

The red alert klaxon blared and then almost as quickly went off. The *Excalibur* slowly began to turn in a complete barrel roll. The lights went out entirely, plunging the bridge into darkness, and then the emergency lighting slowly crawled back.

"Let's hope we don't lose gravity," said Burgoyne worriedly.

"I . . . honey . . . we need to teach her . . . teach our Robin." Morgan was speaking as if she were in a dream. "Laws. She needs laws to live by. Like . . . that . . . that you can only count on . . ."

". . . on yourself," Robin whispered.

Faster and faster Morgan spoke. "What . . . what do I see in him? Well . . . he's not much of a conversationalist, but . . . but what a lover . . . here . . . look . . . I made this for you . . . it's *plomeek* soup . . . I was sure you'd like it . . . I . . . yes . . . I would like offspring . . . offspring as in . . . he's Adam . . . Madam . . . I'm Adam . . . Madam . . . I'm . . . isn't . . . does not . . . compute . . . compute . . ."

Morgan slumped over and this time her arms were too weak to keep her upright. She fell to the floor with an oddly hollow sound.

"Mother," whispered Robin, and Burgoyne tried to hold her back, to remind her that this thing wasn't her mother, that it was just a freak of technological nature. But she pulled away from Burgoyne and went to cradle her head. "Mother . . ."

Morgan's face felt cold to the touch. The skin seemed plastic.

"Mother . . ." Her voice was hoarse, choked with emotion.

And Morgan looked in the direction of her voice, and she reached up and caressed Robin's face. "Don't look away . . . from Cwansi . . . don't blink . . . if you blink . . . he grows up . . . my God . . . Robin . . . so much beauty . . . so much . . . to show you . . . so . . . much . . ."

Her hand fell away and then slowly, ever so slowly, it began to fade. The rest of her did as well. Her face went slack, and her mouth remained open in the midst of forming an incompleted word.

Throughout the ship there was the sound of systems going down, crashing, energy being leached from every part of the vessel. The tactical array in front of Kebron flickered and went out. So did the ops and conn stations. The constant hum of equipment operations that were so much a part of the bridge's ambiance ceased, giving the bridge an eerie, almost mausoleum-like quality.

The only sounds left were the snuffling of Cwansi, calmed by the gentle rocking of Xy, and the sobs of Cwansi's mother, whose arms were still cradled in the position of holding Morgan's head even though the last vestiges of her mother had disappeared into nothingness.

And then Soleta was at her side, and with an agonized sob, Robin threw her arms around her and held her tightly. Soleta's face was a mask of dispassion, easily recapturing the Vulcan detachment that she had effected for so long before ultimately embracing her mixed heritage.

Soleta made no effort to calm or console Robin with words. Her presence was enough as she held her tightly and let Robin sob into her shoulder.

iv.

Burgoyne wanted to give everyone a chance to absorb what had just happened, but there wasn't time. "Report, people. Tell me what we've got."

The bridge was mostly illuminated by the glow of the viewscreen. There wasn't much else on. Tania got up from the conn station, saying, "Basically I'm sitting in front of a brick. Conn's out, navigation's out . . ."

"Nothing on tactical," Kebron reported.

Tania had crossed over to the ops station, sidling past Soleta, who was still holding Robin. She went over the ops station systematically.

"Do we have *anything*?" said Burgoyne. "Communications? Engine control? Computer access . . . ?"

Tobias was still running checks through ops. "Be grateful we still have life support. When Morgan went, she crashed the mainframe. Anything beyond rudimentary survival is locked up until we can . . . wait . . . hold on . . . ah!" said Tobias.

"Ah what?"

She turned and squinted at him in the darkness. "I can turn the lights on and off."

"Well, turn them on, then! Up to full."

"Not these lights. The running lights."

"You mean the lights on the outside of the ship."

"Yeah."

"Fantastic," said Burgoyne. "That's going to be very helpful. Soleta . . ."

"Busy at the moment," she said.

"Get unbusy. You, the Doctor, and . . . I'm sorry, you're—?"

"Seven."

"Commander Burgoyne 172," s/he said to her. "Always nice to run into someone with a number in their name. I wish we could be meeting under better circumstances. Anyway," and s/he addressed all of them, "you three are obviously some of the best minds that we have when it comes to computers. I need you to get the Morgan-less ship's computer back online as soon as possible."

"Let them handle it," said Soleta.

"No." Robin now reached around, patting Soleta on the arm while using her other arm to wipe away the last of the tears. "It's okay. I'm sorry, I'm . . . behaving like a jackass. I'll be okay. You do what you need to to get this ship back up and running."

"Are you sure—?"

"Yes. Just because I resigned my commission doesn't mean I can't put on my Starfleet uniform when it's called for."

Soleta and the Doctor moved toward the science station. Xy got out of their way as he brought Cwansi back over to his mother. Xy had many talents, but computer science was not his strength and he was perfectly happy to cede those responsibilities to others. Soleta took one look at it and said, "This is going to be useless. I'm going down to deck fourteen. If I'm remembering correctly, there's a central junction point in one of the Jeffries tubes down there that will allow me to cut into the system directly and expedite getting everything back online. Otherwise it could take hours, even days, to figure out how to reboot everything, because who knows what 'adjustments' Morgan may have made."

"You realize the turbolift is out. You'll have to climb down the access ladders," Tobias reminded her.

"Then I guess I'll just have to get started faster so I can return sooner." She headed to the access hatch and moments later had disappeared down it.

Meanwhile Burgoyne—trying not to think about the fact that, special circumstances or not, s/he was allowing a Romulan spy to crawl around in the bowels of a Federation starship, and wouldn't *that* look good on hir record—moved toward Seven and said, with understandable concern, "Let me guess: Captain Calhoun was involved in you people showing up here."

"That is the case, yes."

"Are you sure . . ." S/he glanced apprehensively at the place where Morgan's body had vanished into nothingness. "Are you sure that your virus eradicated her completely? Morgan got around, if you know what I mean."

"I assume you're referring to various locations where she had copied her essential systems or had otherwise insinuated herself." Seven folded her arms as she watched the Doctor and Soleta working. "All such extensions were not severed from her. She was attached to them. That attachment serves as a two-way street. When she was erased, so were any and all extensions."

"You're sure?"

"Yes."

"Completely?"

"Yes."

"Absolutely?"

"Ninety-seven percent."

S/he stiffened at that. "You're ninety-seven percent sure?"

"Perhaps ninety-six." She shrugged. "Science is not always exact, Commander. There have to be allowances for new discoveries."

"So you're saying there's a three to four percent chance that Morgan Primus is still out there somewhere?"

She turned to hir with a raised, mocking eyebrow. "Exciting prospect, isn't it."

"Just what I need in my life," said Burgoyne. "More excitement."

That was when the *U.S.S. Dauntless* showed up, with the firepower and the orders to blow them out of space.

U.S.S. Dauntless

"How stupid does he think we are?" said Commodore Joshua Kemper.

The *Excalibur* was just hanging there in space, apparently asleep at the switch—"apparently" being the key.

"I mean, really," said Kemper, and it was all he could do not to laugh. "Does he seriously think he's going to draw us in?"

"Commodore, I'm scanning their vessel," said Hopkins. "I'm reading only minimal energy output. They've got life support, gravity, a few lights, and that's about it."

"So they shut down all unnecessary systems in order to sell the notion that they've had some sort of cataclysmic failure. Except I'm not buying it. Furthermore, it's not remotely relevant to our mission."

The doors of the turbolift opened and Admiral Jellico strode in. He took one look at the screen and said, "You should have told me we found them, Commodore."

"I was about to let you know, sir. Wouldn't have made a move without you," Kemper lied.

"What have we got?"

Kemper laid out for him in short strokes the

specifics of the situation. "Obviously," he concluded, "Calhoun is trying to lay out a trap to lure us in. Make us drop our guard so that he can ambush us the same way that he ambushed the inhabitants of New Thallon."

"I don't know that I concur with your assessment of the situation, Commodore."

The commodore had been sitting in leisurely fashion in the command chair. He had been utterly confident of how things were going to proceed. But with the admiral's words, it was as if the atmosphere on the bridge had changed. Slowly he got to his feet so that he was on eye level with Jellico. "As near as I can determine, Admiral, your assessment of the situation isn't particularly relevant. My orders are specific."

"Your orders come from me."

"They come from Starfleet, sir, and you may out-rank me, but your will does not comprise the entirety of Starfleet, to say nothing of the wishes of the Federation Council."

"All of that is true, Commodore," said Admiral Jellico, his jaw set, "but you are forgetting one thing."

"And that is?"

In a tone that was clearly brooking no argument, Jellico said, "The entirety of Starfleet and the Federation Council is not here. I am. And as long as that remains the case, you're going to be dealing with me."

Kemper felt as if the eyes of his entire command crew—particularly Theresa Detwiler's—were on him. His spine stiffened, and he knew beyond question that he was not about to back down. He didn't care if he wound up being court-martialed. It didn't matter to him if he was sentenced to hard labor indefinitely. He was going to take a stand, and Jellico was damned well going to know about it.

"This," and he pointed at the screen, "is exactly the sort of trap that we were warned about. The exact sort of stunt that Calhoun is likely to pull. That's why we have explicit instructions to shoot first and ask questions never. I am not, under any circumstance, going to risk the lives of my crew on the off chance that the ship is truly in distress."

"No one is asking you to risk the lives of your crew. I am telling you, however, that my orders . . ."

"Do not supersede procedure." He turned to Hopkins. "Have you been able to raise the *Excalibur*?"

"Negative, Commodore. She's just sitting there."

"General Order Twelve, Admiral," said Kemper. "On the approach of any vessel, when communications have not been established, personnel will prepare for potential hostile intent."

"I'm familiar with the general order, Commodore," said Jellico stiffly. "My ancestors helped draft it."

Kemper pounced on the opening. "And if they were here, then they'd be proceeding exactly as I am. As if that weren't enough, the direct orders I have from Starfleet dictate how I am supposed to handle this engagement. I am not going to fall for Calhoun's obvious trap, Admiral, and all the information that

I have at hand and all the orders under which I am operating have given me exactly one option. Hopkins."

"Yes, sir."

"Target lock all phasers on the *Excalibur*. Prepare to fire."

"Hold on!" snapped Jellico. "Hopkins, do they even have shields up?"

"No, Admiral, they do not."

Kemper calmly dropped back into his chair and crossed his legs. Jellico came around and leaned in toward him. "You fire on her now, unshielded, and the phasers will tear her apart."

"Since that will serve to fulfill my mission, I'm actually fine with that."

"I am not," Jellico said. "And as ranking officer on this bridge, I have some say in that."

"If you're not on the bridge, then that becomes moot."

Jellico moved in closer. "Are you threatening me, Commodore?"

"It is my belief," said Kemper, "that your personal feelings in this matter are blinding you to the duty this ship is supposed to follow. On that basis, I can easily determine that you are not thinking clearly, and therefore your rank doesn't come into play."

"That is a dubious proposition on which to hang the future of your career," warned Jellico.

"Commodore . . ."

It was Detwiler. He turned to her, his face a question. Sitting at conn, she looked conflicted, bound by loyalty to Kemper but also clearly uncomfortable with matters as they were. "Commodore, with all respect, they're not even running weapons hot. I don't see how they pose an immediate threat."

"You don't have to see it," he said, astonishment in his voice that she would even be bringing it up. "Our orders are clear."

"Yes, sir, but—"

"There's a 'but' after that 'yes, sir'?"

She could practically feel the anger radiating from him, but she pressed on. "But . . . firing on a ship that's offering no defense, no offense . . . that's just sitting there . . ."

"As is to be expected from a captain who is as devious as Calhoun."

"Sir, to be able to attack us without weapons fire, or survive an attack without shields . . . that's not deviousness. That's suicidal."

"Then, with the backing of Starfleet, whose orders I'm following, I'm going to oblige him."

"Sir," and she stood, leaning on the conn chair as if she required the extra support. Then she turned and addressed Jellico rather than Kemper. "Admiral, if being able to think straight is a determining factor in appraising conduct, then you should be aware that Commodore Kemper and Captain Calhoun have their own history that may well be serving to direct the way that the commodore is—"

"Belay that, Detwiler, and sit the hell down!" Kemper fairly shouted.

Her jaw twitched as if she wanted to say more, but she did as ordered.

It was too late. Recollection flooded through Jellico's mind. "My God, of course. I'd forgotten all about that; it was a lifetime ago. Calhoun broke your jaw."

"If you're determined to reminisce about the old days when you were dean of the Academy, Admiral, then I assume you'll remember that I took full responsibility for a subsequent altercation. The events of decades ago," and he fired an angry look at Detwiler, "are not in any way having an impact on my actions now. And may I further remind you that the chain of command exists for a reason: to distance decisions from the sorts of emotions that you're obviously displaying now and that you're accusing me of allowing to impact my judgment. My orders are specific, and so is General Order Twelve. They are not communicating with us and we have to assume them to be hostile. And I'm going to do my duty, and if there is anyone on this bridge," and he turned and glared at the whole of his command crew, "who wants to try and countermand that, then they can consider themselves relieved of duty! I do not get to question Starfleet officers, and neither does the Admiral, particularly when we're fulfilling a mission that comes from the highest levels!"

"Sir," said Hopkins, looking extremely uncomfortable, "permission to warn them that they're about to be fired upon."

Kemper turned and was ready to dismiss the notion out of hand. But then he saw the way that

Detwiler was looking at him, and what killed him most was the disappointment that he saw in her eyes.

"Open a channel," he said tersely. Hopkins immediately did so and Kemper strode toward the viewscreen as if that would enable the *Excalibur* to see him better. "*Excalibur,*" he said briskly. "This is Commodore Kemper of the *Dauntless*. You have been targeted and my orders are to destroy you on sight. You have sixty seconds from my mark to establish communications or we will carry out our orders. *Mark*." He turned and said defiantly to Jellico, "I've given them their window of opportunity. If they don't respond, or they so much as look funny in our direction, I'll blow them to hell."

U.S.S. Excalibur

Deaf and dumb although mercifully not blind, the *Excalibur* had no way of hearing Kemper's warning or knowing that they were on a deadline.

That didn't mean that they were unaware of their impending peril.

As the starship loomed on their screen, Tania Tobias said, "They're going to start shooting."

"How do you know?" said Burgoyne. "Other than that we're the *Excalibur,* which means that everybody starts shooting at us sooner or later."

"I know. I just . . . know," she said.

"Of course you do," and Burgoyne rolled hir eyes. "Because it wouldn't be right to have a conn officer who wasn't somehow strange."

"Word is out throughout the entirety of Starfleet," said Xy. "They're probably as eager to shoot at us as anyone else."

"I don't want to tell you how to run your ship," said Seven, "but you might want to consider a little less talking and a little more figuring out how to have them not start firing at us."

"Soleta," said the Doctor quickly. "Her vessel is fully operational. She could return to it and explain the situation—"

"Assuming she even has some sort of transportation recall device that would enable her to get back to her ship," said Burgoyne, "she's crawling around a Jeffries tube on deck fourteen."

"We're running out of time," and Tania's body was practically vibrating. "I know it . . . I know it . . ."

"Kebron! Do we have any communications capabilities at all!" asked Burgoyne.

"Nothing." Kebron looked ready to put his fist through his board. "Not a thing."

"We need some way to signal them," said Burgoyne.

Kebron said, "We could all climb out onto the saucer section and form the word 'help' with our bodies."

"You're not helping," Burgoyne said.

"True, but in my defense, I wasn't trying to."

And suddenly Robin, who was holding Cwansi close to her, said, "Wait . . . Tobias . . . you said you could turn the running lights on and off?"

Tania, in the throes of bracing herself for the phaser blasts that she just knew were going to be unleashed upon them at practically any time, looked up at Robin in confusion. "What? Yes . . . but what's—"

"Do it! Flash the lights at them! Flash three quickly—on, off, on, off, on, off—and then another three, holding them on for a second longer, and then three fast again! And keep doing it!"

"Why?"

"Because you're not the only one around here who knows about things! So just do it!"

"Do what she's telling you, Tobias," said Burgoyne. "She believes it, and that's good enough for me."

"Okay," said Tobias. "Three short, three long, three short?" When Robin nodded, she started flashing the lights as she'd been instructed, without the slightest idea why.

"Now what?" said Burgoyne as Tania continued as instructed.

"Now we pray that someone there knows about things, too," said Robin, clutching Cwansi even more tightly, as if in doing so she could protect him from the imminent destruction.

U.S.S. Dauntless

i.

Until the last moment, Jellico wasn't sure that he was just going to stand by and let Kemper open fire on the *Excalibur.*

The damning thing was that Kemper was absolutely in the right, and Jellico knew it. The orders had come from above Jellico and he had no authority to countermand them without some excuse, and at the moment he had none. It was the reason that Jellico was hesitating to take charge of the ship: because it would mean undercutting an officer who was doing nothing more than obeying the orders that had been handed down by Starfleet. The fact that Jellico believed they were wrongheaded was Jellico's problem and not anyone else's.

It would have been one thing if the captain was incapacitated or otherwise unavailable. Then Jellico, as the ranking officer, would have been able to take command of the ship. But Kemper, despite his negative history with Calhoun, was by all evidence operating with clear faculties and a full awareness of everything he was doing. Consequently, his direct authority as the ship's commanding officer would be the final arbiter, at least on all practical levels. It might be possible for Jellico to make a case at a subsequent disciplinary hearing that Kemper should have willingly ceded command to him, but none of that would solve the immediate problem.

Furthermore, there was no one in Starfleet who had a greater respect for the chain of command than Jellico. And he was loath to be the weak link in that chain. But was he really supposed to just stand by and allow Calhoun and his people to be blown to bits?

He needed a cause, a reason to intercede. He stared fixedly at the ship on the screen. *Give me something. Give me anything. Come on, you bastard, find a way to—*

Then he squinted. Was that—?

"Fifty eight . . . fifty nine . . . sixty seconds, Commodore," said Commander Williams, and there was a sense of real tragedy in his voice.

Kemper didn't share the sentiment. "Mr. Hopkins . . . fire pha—"

"Hold it!" said Jellico.

As if anticipating that Jellico was going to try and intercede, Kemper said, "Admiral Jellico, if I need to get security—"

"Magnify the image. I think I see something."

Kemper hesitated, as if suspecting that Jellico was up to some sort of trick. But then he nodded and said, "Increase by fifty percent."

The *Excalibur* grew in size. Jellico approached, staring at it for long seconds, and just at the point where Kemper was about to say that enough was enough, Jellico pointed and said, "Look! There!"

"What am I looking at?" Kemper said impatiently.

"The running lights. They're not flashing in normal sequence. They're flashing three short, three long, three short, repeatedly."

Kemper stared at him. "So?"

"It's SOS. Morse code."

"It's *what?*"

"Morse code. An ancient form of communication conveyed through a series of dots and dashes via a device called a telegraph."

"Sir, with all respect, are you making this up?"

Jellico almost laughed but caught himself, since this was hardly the type of situation where laughing would help anything. "SOS was the international signal for dire emergency. Some people claimed it stood for 'save our ship,' but it was just a handy way of remembering the key letters: three quick transmissions, then three slower ones, then three quick ones again."

Kemper regarded him suspiciously and then said, "Computer. Analyze image of vessel designated *Excalibur,* cross referencing for something called Morris co—"

"Morse."

"Morse code," he corrected. "Analyze and report conclusions." He then sat there with what was clearly an expectant look in anticipation of the computer informing him that it didn't know what the hell he was talking about.

And the computer reported crisply, *"Running lights*

*are signaling a pattern consistent with Morse code designation
SOS, indicating that vessel is in distress and requires assistance."*

There were impressed looks from around the
command crew. Even Kemper appeared stunned. "And
how do you know all about this code stuff?"

"I'm a history buff, Commodore. You ought to try
it some time, the entire concept of listening to history."

It was exactly the wrong thing to say. Kemper bristled and then said brusquely, "So what? This is exactly
the type of trap that Calhoun would set."

Jellico couldn't keep the incredulity from his voice.
"He would signal for help using an ancient means of
communication on the off chance that someone looking at it might see it? Seriously?"

"We're dealing with a madman. There's no predicting his actions or figuring out what makes sense
to him and what doesn't. The point is: This changes
nothing."

"Wrong, Commodore," said Jellico, his voice ringing with confidence. "This changes everything."

"How do you figure that?"

"Because the Starfleet Charter supersedes orders.
That's why the charter exists: to be a grounding for
right and wrong, something to measure orders against.
In this particular case, Starfleet Charter Article Fourteen, Section Thirty-one, clearly states that Starfleet
personnel can take extraordinary measures in times of
dire emergency. An SOS, by any definition, constitutes
probable belief that a dire emergency is present."

Kemper looked from the ship on the screen back to Jellico. "What are you saying, Commodore?"

"I am saying that if you do not stand down your weapons, I am authorized by the Starfleet Charter to take an extraordinary measure and assume command of your vessel immediately."

"That is a rather broad interpretation of Article Fourteen, Section Thirty-one."

"You can take it up with a review board if you wish. I emphasize that it is not my first choice, but I feel it is my only choice. It's up to you, Commodore."

Kemper took a long time to respond. That was fine with Jellico; the more time, the better.

"Mr. Hopkins," he said finally, "stand down the phasers. Secure from general quarters."

"Aye, sir," and Hopkins had never sounded so happy to obey an order as he did at that moment.

Jellico noticed out of the corner of his eye that Detwiler was smiling and nodding in approval, but he chose not to dwell upon it since it was none of his business.

"I'm going to prepare a security team to board her and see what's going on," said Kemper. "Admiral Jellico, I was wondering if you would like to head it up?"

It was a canny suggestion on Kemper's part. If he was right, and this turned out to be some sort of elaborate trap, then Jellico was going to be the one who found himself in the middle of it. But it was a chance that Jellico was willing to take, because he still firmly believed that Calhoun was innocent of the charges against him or that, at the very least, there was more to it than met the eye.

As it turned out, though, it wasn't going to be necessary.

ii.

The strange-looking vessel that dropped out of space moments before Jellico and the security team could be beamed aboard was completely unknown to anyone on the bridge. The *Dauntless* immediately went to yellow alert as Kemper prepared for a possible assault.

"There's every likelihood," said Jellico, who had been about to head down to the transporter room, "that their target is going to be the *Excalibur.* It may well be a member of the Protectorate that we're not familiar with."

"Well, then this will be a hell of a get-acquainted party," said Kemper.

"Sir," said Hopkins, "we're getting an incoming hail . . ." Then his voice trailed off for a moment before he looked up again with confusion and astonishment on his face. "I'll be damned."

"What's going on, Hopkins?" said Kemper, who wasn't thrilled with Hopkins's reaction.

"Commodore . . . it's Captain Calhoun."

"What is?"

"On the hailing frequency."

"So the *Excalibur* finally decided to talk to us?"

"No, sir. He's on the ship that just arrived."

Kemper couldn't believe it. "Say again?"

"He's not on the *Excalibur.* He's on the ship that just got here."

Not knowing what else to say, Kemper said, "Put him on."

Moments later the image of Mackenzie Calhoun appeared on the screen. The bridge crew made no attempt to hide their shock. Calhoun's hair was disheveled and he had a length of beard that had grown in. His clothing was torn, his skin was badly burned. He looked like he hadn't slept in weeks. All in all, it seemed impressive that he was still standing. Yet there was the customary determination in his eyes, as if he was resolved to ignore all the weaknesses to which a mere mortal's body was heir.

Slowly Kemper rose to his feet. "Calhoun . . . ?"

Calhoun squinted and then his mouth twitched into the semblance of a smile. "Well, if it isn't Glass Jaw Kemper."

There was a ripple of snickering from behind the commodore, which quickly ceased. Then Calhoun noticed that Jellico was there as well. "Admiral," he said, and there was definite exhaustion in his voice. "Wasn't expecting to see you here."

"Mac? What are you doing in that ship?" Jellico stared at him in confusion. "Why aren't you on the *Excalibur*?"

"It's an interesting story," said Calhoun with effort.

"I think we need to talk, about quite a few things. But first I have to get to my ship."

"Your ship appears nonresponsive," Jellico said. "Sensors indicate the normal crew complement, so she seems more or less intact. But we haven't been able to get a rise out of her."

"That's either a bad thing or a good thing. We'll have to find out."

"Bad or good. Not a lot of room in between."

"There rarely is," said Mackenzie Calhoun.

Starfleet Headquarters, San Francisco

i.

Admiral Nechayev strode across the pavilion in front of Starfleet Headquarters. It was a gorgeous morning, but she wasn't paying any attention to it. Instead her mind was literally light-years away.

She didn't understand why in the world she hadn't heard from any Starfleet vessels as to a confirmed kill of the *Excalibur.* Nor had she heard anything further from Morgan Primus, even though she had sent a pulse via a subspace channel in an effort to summon her, just as she had earlier. It had worked perfectly the first time, but this time: nothing.

Nor had any of her other "associates" been in touch with her. That was not necessarily unusual. They minimized contact with her as a matter of security. The less she knew, the less she would be able to tell someone else in the event that she was captured. Not that Nechayev considered that to be a genuine threat, but she supposed that one couldn't be too careful about these things.

Lost in thought, she almost collided with a man who was directly in her path. She stepped around him reflexively and then let out a startled cry as his hand clamped down upon her shoulder. She turned and reacted as if she had just been slapped hard across the face.

It was Mackenzie Calhoun, and there was quiet anger in his face, discernible by the way that his scar was shining a brighter red against his cheek. To his immediate right was Edward Jellico.

Neither of them seemed happy to see her.

"M-Mac . . ." she stammered out. "I . . . I don't—"

"It's over, Alynna," said Jellico flatly.

"What's . . . over?" She forced a smile. "Ed, what are you talking about?"

"I told you about Morgan," said Calhoun, "and about the D'myurj. Things that you wanted to keep quiet about."

"I keep quiet about a lot of things, Mac. That's my job. And I . . . I don't understand what you're doing here. Ed, what is he—?"

"He wasn't responsible for the slaughter on New Thallon. Neither was the *Excalibur* herself, as I'm sure you know," he said tightly. "Too many things came together from too many directions in order to make this happen. Too many disparate elements." Jellico watched her grimly, looking for any sign of a reaction that would indicate guilt. "Morgan, the ambassador, the Brethren, the kill order on the *Excal.* All of it. There had to be one person who was coordinating it all, and no matter how we look at it, it all keeps coming back to you."

She summoned massive amounts of indignation the way that someone else would summon courage. "That is an outrageous accusation, Edward, and I will see you busted down to ensign if you even dare to repeat such calumnies. And you, Calhoun," she continued. "You now say that you are innocent of all charges. What you say doesn't matter; you're still going to have to face the Federation Council—"

"Tusari Gyn admitted everything."

Calhoun said it so matter-of-factly that at first it didn't quite register to her. "I'm . . . sorry?"

"He put up quite a struggle," said Jellico, smiling at the recollection. "He was a tough nut to crack. He lasted a whole . . . what would you say, Mac? Twenty minutes?"

"Fourteen."

"Fourteen minutes before he gave you up."

Nechayev's eyes narrowed suspiciously. "You're bluffing, Ed. I can always tell. Calhoun is unreadable, but you have a lousy poker face. Furthermore, if you had any proof of these . . . these outrageous claims, then you wouldn't be here, the two of you. You'd be here with security guards, ready to take me in."

"We are." Jellico snapped his fingers and, pointing behind her, said, "Take her."

Nechayev spun, startled, expecting to see Starfleet security guards right behind her.

Should that have been the case, she would have killed them instantly. Her carefully designed, meticulously manufactured hybrid body had that capability for emergency situations, and this would certainly have qualified as such.

But she didn't see a guard. Instead, she found herself looking into the face of Soleta.

She hesitated, caught up in a moment of confusion.

The moment cost her.

ii.

Soleta's hand speared forward, clamping onto Nechayev's face as if she were about to tear it off.

Vulcans were forbidden from using the technique of the mindmeld in any manner that even vaguely resembled that of employing it as a weapon. Such a use would have been considered an abomination, a perversion of the sacred techniques that had developed the mindmeld in the first place.

During the time in her life when Soleta had thought she was pure Vulcan, she would have been as appalled as anyone else over the notion of utilizing the mindmeld as one would a spear or a club.

But Soleta knew her heritage, and had come to grips with it, accepting it and herself for all that she was.

Consequently, she was a good deal less delicate about it.

She slammed her mind into Nechayev's, having no idea what she was going to find. She was determined not to give Nechayev the slightest opportunity to fight back.

And a barrage of images comes at her, fast, relentless, so many, so much, that Soleta cannot discern or individualize any of it; she has never encountered anything like it, a mind so different from hers, so impossible to understand, that she cannot even conceptualize it, and she sees that Nechayev wants to attack her, she has some sort of neuralizing toxin built right into her DNA but she has to use an act of will and Soleta shoves that act of will back, back, back into the recesses of Nechayev's brain, or the thing that says it is Nechayev, and it may be her or may not be, whatever it is, wherever, it's overwhelming, and Soleta has no idea how long she has been inside Nechayev's mind, it must be hours, days, weeks, she is lost in there and will never find her way out, and she cannot let herself be taken down, there is too much riding on it, and Nechayev pushes back with her mind, and Soleta meets the challenge, and their consciousnesses collide, and Soleta is on the verge of destruction, just that quickly, just that easily, and Soleta focuses all her will, all her essence, her ego, her id, everything, into one great vicious destructive spear and she drives it forward with as much force as she can, and as she does this, as she commits this incredible act of determination, she wonders why she has done this, why she has, time and again, risked herself to serve, whenever possible, an organization that tossed her away, that treated her so very, very badly, and it is at that moment that she is struck with the thoroughly astounding realization that she is totally, madly, and completely in love with Mackenzie Calhoun, and she has just enough time to think, Well, of COURSE you are, how could it be anything else but that, you should have realized that ages ago, and that is when everything goes black . . .

iii.

Calhoun had not known what to expect when Soleta had agreed to force her mind into that of Nechayev so that they could discern just what it was they were dealing with. What ultimately happened transpired so quickly that it was hard for him to believe anything had occurred at all.

From the moment that Soleta clamped her hand onto Nechayev's face to the time that it all ended horribly, it was scarcely the blink of an eye. And then Nechayev screamed, and it was not a scream that sounded like anything remotely human or, for that matter, anything that Calhoun had ever heard before. It started low and then got louder and louder, escalating until it was earsplitting, like something that might be torn from the throat of a dying bat.

And Alynna Nechayev melted.

He had never seen anything like it. It was as if her body had simply lost cohesion, transforming into a gelatinous mass of protoplasm, suffused with a blue glow. Her head descended between her shoulders, her arms melted into her body, and her legs dissolved beneath her body, causing it to sink very rapidly as if she had just stepped into a pool of quicksand. She made the most appalling noise when she collapsed in on herself, like a sucking noise through a huge straw, and then her body utterly dissolved into a mass of flesh and liquid bones that mixed together into a disgusting, multicolored agglomeration.

Soleta pitched backward and Calhoun caught her. Her face, typically with a light green tint, was completely yellow. Were she human, she would have been diagnosed with kidney failure. He shouted her name but her yellow-tinted eyes rolled up into her head and she was nonresponsive.

Passersby stopped in their tracks, unable to process fully what they had witnessed. Instantly he hit his badge and shouted, "Calhoun to *Excalibur*! Emergency beam up, two to sickbay, now! *Now!*"

In a burst of color and molecules, Calhoun and Soleta vanished, leaving a stunned Admiral Jellico with a spreading puddle where an esteemed admiral had previously been standing, and a hell of a lot of explaining to do.

U.S.S. Excalibur

i.

The Doctor sat in Ten-Forward, looking around at the laughing couples. They were discussing the close scrapes that the ship had had, and the madness of Morgan Primus, and how terrific it was that everything was finally up and running again. He watched that Tobias woman from the bridge, the one who had somehow known that the *Dauntless* was about to fire upon them—which, as it had subsequently turned out, was a correct assumption. She was seated across the table from another young woman who had red skin and a haunted expression. Tobias was clearly trying to offer witticisms that would distract the young woman from her dour mood, but nothing seemed to be working. He hoped that whatever was bothering the young woman, it would all be sorted out in time.

"Is this seat taken?"

He looked up. Seven was standing there, with her hand resting on the chair opposite him.

"It is now," he said with what he imagined was a degree of suavity. At least it was as close as he was able to summon.

She pulled out the chair, sat, and folded her

hands on the table. "I just wanted to say that it was very brave, what you did. We didn't know for sure it was going to work. And if Morgan's capabilities had exceeded expectations, she might indeed have been able to detect the presence of the nano-virus within your mobile emitter. She could have turned it against you, caused you to—"

"I know what she could have done," he said. "I was there when we had the discussions. It had to be done and I did it. I . . . mourn her passing, as best I can. I acknowledge the part I played in it. And now I move on."

"I know you know it. I wanted you to know . . . that I knew it. You know?"

"I do. Or at least I do now. At least I think I do."

She watched him for a time, and then said, "And I wanted to thank you. And to tell you that what you said about me . . . about why you were doing it . . ."

He looked embarrassed. "Yes, I know, it was melo-dramatic claptrap, foolish words from—"

"I thought it was very sweet."

"Yes, I did, too."

She laughed softly and he was surprised at how gentle and unforced it was. Then she said with genuine interest, "So . . . if you don't mind my ask-ing . . . what are you doing here? I mean, you don't drink. You don't know anyone else. So why . . . ?"

"Sometimes . . . I just like to sit and watch people, and try to determine, just by watching them, what their individual situations are. How they eat, what their hobbies are, why they joined Starfleet. I find it a stimulating exercise."

"And are you correct in your surmises?"

"I don't know. I never thought to ask. It's the speculation that intrigues me. To wonder about what might be is always much more interesting than obsessing about what is."

Then he looked down. Seven was resting her hand atop one of his. Slowly, tentatively, he curled his fingers around hers.

"I couldn't agree more," said Seven.

ii.

"Come in," called Robin Lefler when she heard the chime at the door of her guest quarters.

The door slid open and Calhoun entered. Then he saw what Robin was in the middle of and immediately he averted his eyes. "I'm sorry, I can come back later."

Robin chuckled. "Are they *that* provincial back where you come from, Captain? This is why women have breasts, you know." Cwansi, uncaring about the adult conversation, continued to nurse with quiet enthusiasm.

"Yes, I know that . . . intellectually. But it's not something I dwell on."

"Sit. It's all right."

He did so, although it amused her to see that he was extremely focused on her eyes, diligently making sure that his gaze didn't drop below her neckline. But then the moment of amusement over his discomfort lapsed. "I was at sickbay to see Soleta about an hour ago. It breaks my heart. Do they have any idea when she's going to come out of it or . . ." She couldn't bear to add the word.

"Or if?"

She nodded.

Calhoun shook his head. "No. We're hoping, praying that it's soon." He looked grim. "Starfleet is anxious to know what's in her head."

"I would imagine," said Robin. "I mean, was Nechayev really an alien being in a body that was fashioned for her by the D'myurj? Was she an actual D'myurj wearing a . . . a meat suit? How long has she been that way? Always? Or was she switched out and there's a real Admiral Nechayev being held prisoner somewhere, or maybe even dead? And are there others like her, and if so, can we figure out who?"

"All excellent questions," said Calhoun, "and yet, oddly enough, the only one I give a damn about is whether she's going to be all right."

"I don't think that's odd at all."

"We've got the *Spectre* stowed down in the shuttlebay. I hope she's able to fly her again." He shook his head and thumped his fist on his thigh. "It was her suggestion, you know. To use the mindmeld to extract information from Nechayev while she was off guard. Jellico embraced it immediately, but I resisted it, and she talked me into it. I never should have let her."

"She's strong, Captain. She'll be back. Oh . . . I think someone's done."

Cwansi's head was slumping, and there was breast milk dribbling down his face.

"Speaking of someone being back," said Calhoun as Robin tended to cleaning up her son and adjusting her clothing, "my understanding is that you're going to be heading out with the *Trident.*"

"Yes, that's right. Captain Mueller has offered me—"

"I know what she's offered you. Don't take it. Come work for me instead."

"What?" Her face flushed with happy surprise. "Captain, I . . . that's very flattering. You have an opening in child care as well?"

"Child care is an important function, but that wasn't what I had in mind for you."

"What, then?"

"Well . . . and I'm hoping you won't reject the notion out of hand . . . but I was thinking about your old job at ops."

She looked astounded. "Ops? But—"

"I hope you won't think I'm being presumptuous when I say that I believe it's what your mother would have wanted."

"But . . . I resigned . . . and I'm not sure that I want to return to Starfleet. It may not be the life for me anymore."

"So don't. You didn't lose your knowledge or experience when you took off the uniform."

"Wouldn't your having a civilian at that post be against regulations?"

"When has that ever stopped me?"

She laughed delightedly at the notion. Then she said, "Can I think about it?"

"Of course. So what's your answer?"

"I meant . . ." Then she saw the look in his eyes, and it was the purest definition of not taking "no" for an answer that she had ever seen. "Sure," she said.

"Welcome aboard, Miss Lefler. Your mother would be proud."

"I like to think that she—"

"Bridge to captain," came Burgoyne's voice.

"This is Calhoun."

"Captain, I think you'd better get up here. We just received an emergency transmission."

"From where?"

"Xenex."

Calhoun felt a chill grip the base of his spine. "How bad?"

"Very."

"On my way," he said, and left her quarters at a dead run.

Xenex

i.

Calhoun stood on the streets of the city from which he had taken his last name. He had ordered the security troops and medtechs to spread out, see what they could find, see whom they could help. But the initial sensor sweeps had not been promising.

He had seen so much death in his life, and was the cause of a good deal of it, that he had thought he was inured to it. As it turned out, he was wrong.

The city had been leveled. There was rubble everywhere, the remains of buildings brought crashing to the ground, and gigantic craters blasted by vicious weapons. And the bodies, gods almighty, the bodies, they were everywhere, or at least what was left of them was everywhere. Men, women, children, it had made no difference to them.

There were no bodies of those who had committed the atrocities. But lying at Calhoun's feet was a single object that spoke volumes: a rounded helmet that could only have come from one of the Brethren. It was dented and carbon scored, and had obviously been left behind as a signature or calling card so that there would be no doubt who had been responsible for this atrocity.

It would have been bad enough had it been limited to the city in which he was standing.

But it wasn't. It was global. There were still some flickering lives that were fighting to survive around the world and the *Excalibur* had away teams everywhere they thought might be of help. And other rescue ships were on the way as well to provide whatever aid might still be possible.

Yet to all intents and purposes, Calhoun was standing at ground zero of the genocide of the Xenexian people.

The Brethren had returned in a manner that said: *You thought you were succeeding against us? You thought because you found a way to kill us that we were somehow just going to go away? This is how wrong you were. This is what we are capable of. We wiped out your people . . . in order to prove a point. Come and get us, you bastard, because we are more than ready for you.*

"This is my fault," Calhoun said tonelessly. "This is what he meant . . . that there would be consequences . . ."

He heard a footfall. He knew the exact location of all of his people, and this one was near him. He whirled, automatically reaching for his phaser, and then he stopped.

It was Xyon.

His son looked stunned, walking stiff-legged. "What . . . what happ—?"

Without a word Calhoun went to him and embraced him roughly. "You weren't here . . . oh, *grozit,* you weren't here. I . . . was afraid even to think about it . . ."

"I got a distress call . . . it was broadband, and it was from Xenex. I couldn't stay away, I had to . . . is . . . is there anyone—?"

"We're finding out now. We hope to know soon."

"But . . . what were you talking about, just now? That it was your fault? How is it . . . ?"

He told him. He told Xyon everything that had happened.

Xyon listened carefully, never speaking a word, taking it all in.

"So . . . so they sent the Brethren back in order to do this," Xyon said when Calhoun had concluded, "for no other reason than to punish you?"

It was the hardest single word Calhoun had ever spoken:

"Yes."

ii.

And at that moment, Xyon knew that it was entirely his fault. Not his father's. His.

Because he was the one who had told Calhoun about coming to Xenex in the first place. He was the one who had fed him the false information about the soldiers. Except he hadn't known it was false at the time. But he hadn't cared. He did it for the money. Someone whom he didn't know had hired him for a reason that he didn't understand. Now he realized that if he had simply refused to go along with it . . . if he hadn't been blinded by both his greed and his antipathy for his father . . . then perhaps none of this would have happened. Maybe it would have . . . but maybe it wouldn't.

"Xyon," said Calhoun with sudden urgency, his voice rough, "who gave you the information about the soldiers? You need to tell me."

"It was a Xenexian."

"Who?"

"I don't know his name. What does it matter? They're dead! They're all dead!"

"Xyon, listen to—"

And Xyon drew back a fist and hit his father as hard as he could. Or at least he tried to. Calhoun saw it coming, sidestepped, and slammed him to the ground. Instantly contrite, Calhoun said, "Xyon, I'm sorry . . . I—"

He reached for him and Xyon pushed his hand aside as he got to his feet.

"This is all your fault!" screamed Xyon. "I'll get you for this! I swear I will! You'll pay for it! You'll pay for what you did to all of them! Lyla, get me the hell out of here!"

And before Calhoun could stop him, his son's body was enveloped in transporter beams and whisked away to his orbiting ship.

Mackenzie Calhoun was alone.

ABOUT THE AUTHOR

PETER DAVID is the *New York Times* bestselling author of more than seventy books, including numerous *Star Trek* novels, such as *Imzadi*, *A Rock and a Hard Place*, *Before Dishonor*, and the incredibly popular *New Frontier* series. He is also the author of the bestselling movie novelizations for *Spider-Man*, *Spider-Man 2*, *Spider-Man 3*, *The Hulk*, *Fantastic Four*, and *Iron Man*, and has written dozens of other books, including his acclaimed original fantasy novels *Tigerheart*, *Sir Apropos of Nothing*, *The Woad to Wuin*, *Tong Lashing*, and *Darkness of the Light*.

David is also well-known for his comic book work, particularly his award-winning run on *The Hulk*, and has written for just about every famous comic-book superhero.

He lives in New York with his wife and daughters.